WEDDING BELLS *on* VICTORY STREET

BOOKS BY PAM HOWES

THE BRYANT SISTERS
The Girls of Victory Street

THE LARK LANE BOOKS
The Factory Girls of Lark Lane
The Shop Girls of Lark Lane
The Nurses of Lark Lane
The Midwives of Lark Lane

THE MERSEY TRILOGY
The Lost Daughter of Liverpool
The Forgotten Family of Liverpool
The Liverpool Girls

ROCK 'N' ROLL ROMANCE SERIES
Three Steps to Heaven
'Til I Kissed You
Always on My Mind
Not Fade Away
That'll be the Day

Fast Movin' Train
Hungry Eyes
It's Only Words

WEDDING
BELLS *on*
VICTORY STREET

PAM HOWES

bookouture

Published by Bookouture in 2020

An imprint of Storyfire Ltd.
Carmelite House
50 Victoria Embankment
London EC4Y 0DZ
www.bookouture.com

ISBN: 978-1-80019-221-8
eBook ISBN: 978-1-80019-220-1

Dedicated to the memory of our friend Glyn Geoffrey Ellis, AKA Wayne Fontana. October 1945–August 2020. Sadly missed. Thank you, dear Wayne, for the music, friendship and laughter. Hope you're enjoying fronting that big band in heaven, singing with the angels in your usual style.

Chapter One

Bella Rogers slid two photographs from the envelope she'd placed beneath her pillow, and in the dim morning light stole another look at them. She smiled, gazing at the bonny baby, who was laughing towards the camera, in Bella's mother's arms. Her beautiful Levi, the six-month-old son she'd had to leave behind to be looked after by her mam Mary, and Bella's younger sister Molly.

Both her mam and Molly had been evacuated from their family home in Wavertree, Liverpool, to the safety of a farm just outside Llandudno in North Wales. Mam enjoyed being at the farm and kept herself busy by helping the farmer's wife to look after the children also evacuated there from bombed-out inner cities. When she wasn't at school, Molly was enjoying learning all sorts of farming skills. Her sister's letter to Bella that had accompanied the enclosed photos told of milking cows and collecting eggs alongside the land girls also staying at the farm. It sounded like Molly was having fun, and that was good after being uprooted from all she was used to. Bella kissed her fingertips and traced them round Levi's face, wishing she was still with her family.

Levi was the result of a very brief affair she'd had with an American airman, bandleader Earl Franklin Junior, who was stationed at Burtonwood Barracks in Warrington. Three months after Levi's birth, Bella had resumed her position with the Bryant Sisters, a singing trio and part of the Entertainments National Service Association, who, along with other artistes, travelled the length and breadth of the country with the ENSA teams, entertaining the troops at their barracks, and the general public in theatres that still remained intact.

Many establishments in towns and cities up and down the country had suffered serious bomb damage due to Hitler's invasion into their lives in the Nazis' bid to win full control of Europe. For almost four years Britain had fought back relentlessly, resulting in the loss of thousands of lives, including many civilians as well as members of the armed forces. There wasn't a family in the country that hadn't been touched by war – in the world in fact. Even Bolivia had recently declared war on Germany, Japan and Italy according to recent newspaper headlines. Bella had no idea where Bolivia even was or why indeed they'd got involved. It wasn't just Europe now; the whole world seemed to be involved. What a dreadful waste of life.

Bella worried about her dad Harry, who was still away fighting in France as far as they knew. He could be anywhere. But just knowing that her mam and the children were at least safe and out of their ravaged home city of Liverpool meant that Bella could relax and enjoy her working life while earning a living in the best way she knew how. She'd always loved to sing, as did her best friends Fran and Edie, who made up the Bryant Sisters trio. They'd all sung in the local church and school choirs and had begun working together when they left school at Bryant & May's match factory as packers. Entertaining the staff and keeping up morale with their regular sing-songs in the works' canteen had led to a career they could only have dreamed of at one time.

Sighing, Bella turned over on her bunk bed as the clock on the bedside table started to ring. Edie, in the bunk above her, groaned but Fran, on the opposite side of the room, slumbered on. Bella's arm snaked out from beneath the covers and silenced the noisy alarm.

She sat up slowly, put her photographs back into the envelope and placed it next to the clock. Stretching her arms above her head, she yawned loudly. 'Fran, wake up,' she called. 'Remember, we're going home later for a couple of days. We need to get packed up and organised.'

Bella smiled as Fran grunted and burrowed further under the blankets, muttering, 'Just five more minutes.'

Edie swung her legs round and climbed down the ladder. She flopped onto Bella's bunk, rubbing the sleep from her blue eyes. 'Think that sherry we had after last night's show was double strength. I've got a right banging head and a mouth that feels like the bottom of a budgie's cage.'

Bella grinned. 'You'll be fine when you've had a shower and a nice hot cuppa. Come on, let's get cracking and we'll beat the crowds at breakfast.'

She and Edie grabbed their toiletry bags and towels and, shaking sleepy Fran by the shoulder, they hurried outside to the shower block. The queue was short and they were in and out within fifteen minutes, wet hair wrapped in towels, just as a bleary-eyed Fran arrived.

'That sherry…' she began wearily.

'We know,' Edie sympathised. 'Think they added something to it. My head feels like the drummer's doing a solo inside it.'

Bella laughed and linked her arm through Edie's. 'See you in the NAAFI, Fran. Be quick and we'll go bag a table.'

Bella and Edie hurried back to the Nissen hut that was reserved for visitors. They rubbed their hair as dry as they could get it, fastened each other's damp locks up on top of their heads with hairgrips and hurriedly dressed in black light wool slacks and white cotton blouses.

'By the time the bus gets us back home we'll have dried off and have nice waves and pin-curls to brush out,' Bella said with a laugh, patting her damp hair. 'At least we'll look half decent.' She fastened a red silk scarf around her head in a turban style.

Edie found a blue scarf in her case that matched the blue of her eyes and fastened it over her hair that was as blonde as Bella's was dark. They finished packing their belongings; their stage clothes, still hanging on the back of the door, could wait until later. They didn't get packed into the cases, where they'd be squashed; they would be handed over to the wardrobe mistress, who packed them carefully in roomy trunks. Linking arms, they dashed to the canteen, where the aroma of frying bacon and eggs met them.

'Oh yum, I'm starving,' Bella said, smacking her lips as they joined the queuing soldiers. 'A good breakfast will soak up any lingering alcohol,' she told Edie.

'That was a good show you put on last night,' a young lad with dark hair and twinkling blue eyes said to them as they waited to be served. 'Really cheered us all up. I hope you girls come here again, and soon.'

'Thank you.' Edie smiled. 'I'm sure we'll be back. We're having a couple of days' break at home in Liverpool and then we'll be off on our travels once more.'

Bella smiled as she drew level with the cook, who was holding two rashers of bacon over a plate. 'Oh, yes please,' she said, smiling gleefully as he laid a sausage and a scoop of scrambled eggs beside them on the plate.

'Help yourself to toast or fried bread,' he said and then looked in Edie's direction. 'Same as your mate, love?'

Edie nodded. 'Yes please.' She took the laden plate he held out. 'Thank you very much.'

'Always a pleasure to cook for our lovely entertainers,' he said. 'You did us proud last night. Come again soon.'

'We would love that,' Edie said and followed Bella to a table by the window.

'I'll go and get us a cuppa,' Edie said as she put her tray down and then walked across to another table, where a couple of young women in khaki uniform were pouring tea from two huge chrome teapots, and joined the short queue.

'Help yourself to sugar and milk,' one of the girls said, handing over two full mugs.

'Thank you,' Edie replied and put extra sugar into both mugs. Back at the table she sat down and took a mouthful of tea, sighing as it slipped down her parched throat. She wafted her hand in front of her mouth. 'Blimey, that's hot, even the milk's not cooled it, but I needed it and it's nice and sweet. It'll give me a bit of energy. And we might as well have sugar while we can because you can bet your life me mam will only have connie-onnie in and I hate the stuff in my tea, but I suppose it's better than no sugar and milk at all.' A jug of cold water and several glasses stood on the table. She picked up the jug and poured a drop into the mug. 'That'll help cool it down. Do you want some in yours?'

Bella nodded, her mouth stuffed with bacon. She grabbed the mug Edie pushed towards her and took a long swig of tea. 'Ah, that's better.'

Edie smiled. 'Are you looking forward to seeing Bobby again?'

Bella beamed. 'I can't wait. It's been ages. I wish I could stay at his place – but I haven't been invited. I'm really grateful that Fran's mam said she'll put me up though, as I'd hate being in my old home on my own.' Bella let her thoughts turn to her dear friend Bobby Harrison, the boy she loved with all her heart. Bobby had been her childhood sweetheart; they'd been friends since their early schooldays and had sung together in the Maia Choir until the war forced them apart. Bobby had joined the RAF and was training to be a pilot when the plane he'd been flying was shot down by enemy aircraft in a raid over London.

His father, Wing Commander Harrison, had also been on board and was killed outright, while Bobby, the only one of the crew to survive, had suffered horrific injuries that had left him with an amputated lower right leg and scars on his body from many serious burns. He was now back in Liverpool, living with his widowed mother and trying to pick up the pieces of his life. They wrote to one another regularly, but Bella couldn't wait to spend time with him again.

The arrival of Fran at the table broke her thoughts and she finished her breakfast while Fran sat down and got stuck into hers. She wolfed it down in no time, rolling her eyes with satisfaction. Fran's auburn hair curled naturally and she'd left it loose to dry in a halo of damp curls around her head, giving her an attractive, almost childlike appearance.

'Basil's just walked in,' Edie said, waving at the tall man who was smiling and waving in the girls' direction. 'He's got Freddie Cagney with him,' she added, lowering her voice.

Fran raised an eyebrow. 'Are they coming this way?' She had her back to the door.

''Fraid so,' Edie whispered. 'I don't mind our lovely Basil sitting with us of course, but—' She broke off as their leader Basil Jenkins, the talent scout who had signed the Bryant Sisters to ENSA, asked if he and Freddie could join them. 'Of course,' she said to Basil. 'We're almost done. The table's all yours.'

Fran finished her mug of tea and sat back with a contented sigh. She patted her full stomach. 'That was a wonderful breakfast. We'll be back to rations for a few days now. But still, it'll be good to see Mam again. I suppose I'd better go and finish packing and we'll wait for you by reception, Basil.' She got to her feet as Freddie Cagney leered at her cleavage. She glared at him and fastened the top two buttons on her white cotton blouse and he turned away and began to eat his breakfast.

None of the other artistes on this particular ENSA tour were that keen on him. He was fairly new to the circuit and worked as the Amazing Frederico – Master of Magic. They had to admit he was good at his job, and he certainly held the audience in thrall with his tricks, but the general consensus was that he was sly and creepy; none of the ladies in the troupe would chance being alone in a dressing room with him.

Basil looked at his watch. 'The bus will be here in an hour, so finish what you need to do, I'll get the trunk sent across for your stage clothes, and then we'll all be ready to go. The rest of the gang are coming in now.' He looked across towards the doors as several more people filed into the NAAFI canteen. 'You three ladies were quick off the mark this morning.'

Bella smiled. 'Me and Edie were, you mean.' She laughed as Fran groaned.

'I hate it when the alarm goes off,' Fran said. 'Especially this morning. Don't know what on earth they put in that sherry last night, but it was more powerful than anything I've ever drunk before.'

Edie nodded her agreement. 'Bella didn't have as much as us two so she wouldn't have noticed it, but after two small glasses I was seeing double, I tell you. Now that's never happened to me before.'

Basil frowned. 'Very odd. Did you notice anything amiss with the sherry last night, Freddie?'

'Can't say as I did,' Freddie replied, not meeting Basil's eye. 'But then, I only had a small glass and I stuck to whisky the rest of the night.'

'Yes, we know.' Bella raised an eyebrow. Freddie's neck had coloured a little, and why didn't he look at Basil when he answered the question? *Was he hiding something?* She gave Fran a little push away from the table and nodded for her to move towards the doors. 'See you later, Basil.'

On their way back to the Nissen hut Fran said, 'Is anyone thinking what I'm thinking?'

'I think I might be,' Bella replied. 'Freddie got all our drinks in last night. He carried the first tray of filled glasses to the table while we were talking to the dancing troupe in the dressing room. Don't you remember? He tapped on the door and announced that he'd get the drinks, and we just agreed to it or he'd have walked in, and us all in a state of undress.'

Edie clapped her hand to her mouth, eyes wide. 'Do you think he put something other than sherry in the glasses, you know, sort of mixed our drinks?'

'Possibly,' Bella said. 'It wouldn't surprise me. But we can't accuse him without any real proof. I suggest we keep a close eye on him from now on. Let him know that we've got his measure if we see him getting up to anything we don't like.'

'Should we warn Basil, do you think?' Edie said.

'Well, there's nothing really to tell him at the moment, is there? Nothing concrete anyway. Let's hang fire for now and not allow Freddie to get our drinks in again. We'll keep an eye out for the other girls as well, especially those two new dancers Tina's Tappers have recently taken on. They're only sixteen; they're just young kids really.'

'Oh, hark at Old Father Time,' Fran said, laughing. 'You're only nineteen yourself, Bella.'

Bella sighed. 'I know. But with all that's happened in the last couple of years I feel ancient at times. And I'm certainly wiser these days.'

'Yeah, course you are,' Fran teased, her green eyes twinkling.

Back in the hut, they packed away the last of their belongings and carefully loaded the stage outfits into the trunk that Basil had asked to be brought to the door. Then they stripped the bunk beds, leaving the bedding in a wicker laundry basket.

'That'll save someone a job later,' Edie said, nodding with satisfaction. She flopped down onto Bella's bare mattress and smiled. 'Can't wait to see me mam and granddad and give our Rebel a big cuddle. Bet he's missed me.' As an only child, Edie's little fox terrier had been her constant companion while she was growing up. 'He's getting on a bit now though, so I'm bracing myself for bad news in the not-too-distant future. Mam said he's not seeing as well as he should. Poor old boy.'

'Bless him,' Bella said, giving Edie a hug. She knew how fond of Rebel her friend was. 'I wish we had enough time off for me to go to Wales to see Mam, Molly and Levi. He's growing so quickly, he won't have a clue who I am when I next see him.' She swallowed hard and blinked a tear away. Levi had only been about three months old when she'd last seen him; now at six months she'd be a stranger and he'd probably think of her mam as his mother.

Edie rubbed her arm. 'When this war is over you'll all be back together at your house on Victory Street and you can start to be his mam properly.'

'That will be lovely for you when the time comes,' Fran said. 'But you still need to pluck up the courage soon to tell Bobby you've got a son, as well as tell your dad.'

'I know, I know.' Bella sighed. 'Mam said she'd write and tell Dad when she feels the time is right, and that's not while he's fighting in France. She doesn't want his mind being taken off him being careful out there by worrying about us back here. And I *will* tell Bobby, one day. I know I've got to, but I'm just not sure when. It all depends on what happens with us and if we develop our relationship to one that includes a future. I mean, we are really good friends and we do love one another dearly, but he might not want to know me when I tell him I have a son. I've got to be prepared for that eventuality, and I'm not quite ready for it yet.'

Fran nodded her agreement. 'Okay. Well you'll have to see how it all goes. Bit of a mess and a worry all round for you. But Edie and me will always be here to support you, you know that. And meantime, when we hit the road again, we've got troops to entertain, as well as keeping an eye on that bugger Freddie Cagney, and making sure he keeps his sweaty hands to himself.'

Chapter Two

Deep in thought, Bella wandered around her old home on Victory Street, checking for any problems in the old terraced house like she'd promised her mam she would do in her last letter to Wales. Wavertree had fared quite well in that damage to property in the area was minimal. Boarded-up windows were the worst damage Bella had seen so far in the nearby streets. She'd heard that the city itself was in a bad way with a lot of damage to shops, homes and schools. She thanked her lucky stars that her family home was a good way outside the city centre.

All appeared well in the downstairs rooms, and as she climbed the stairs to check the two bedrooms she recalled that the last time she'd been up them, she had been at the house with Earl, who had come dashing to her aid after her frantic screaming that she'd seen a mouse in her mam's bedroom.

By the time Earl dashed in the mouse had run up the chimney, and he and Bella had fallen onto the bed in fits of hysterical laughter. Levi had been conceived that afternoon, changing Bella's life for ever. Earl had told her he loved her and asked her to keep in touch with him while he helped to fight the war, but only a few weeks later, when she discovered she was pregnant and told Earl, he had

dropped the bombshell that he was already married and had a wife
and five-year-old daughter back home in New Orleans. Although
his marriage wasn't a happy one, he wasn't free to marry her after all.

Bella sat down on her mam's bed and smoothed the creases out
of the old green satin eiderdown with her hand. Her eyes filled with
sudden tears as she thought about the mess she'd accidentally created.
She didn't love Earl – she liked him and enjoyed singing with him,
but her heart firmly belonged to Bobby and hopefully his to her.

But Bobby too had made mistakes and was in the throes of
divorcing his young wife Alicia, who had tricked him into marriage.
She'd lied that she was expecting his baby, after she'd overheard
Bobby and Bella confessing their love for each other. Feeling hurt
and let down, Bella had turned briefly to Earl for attention, trying
to put her feelings for Bobby behind her.

Then Alicia had cruelly turned her back on Bobby after his
horrific air crash. But in a year or two Bobby would be free and
he and Bella could probably take up where they left off. However,
there was now Levi to consider and if Bobby wouldn't accept her
son as part of Bella's life, then she would have to think very carefully
about her and her child's future.

Bella wiped her eyes and went back downstairs. She closed all
the inner doors and locked the front door behind her. With the
rest of the afternoon stretching ahead before she made her way to
Bobby's home for tea, she set off to buy some flowers to take to
her little sister Betty's grave in the nearby churchyard. Betty had
died from diphtheria at the beginning of the war. She'd been just
five years old and a much-loved youngest child; her death had left
Bella's parents heartbroken.

Bella turned as someone called her name. Her mam's friend
Ethel Hardy was hurrying up the road behind her.

'Bella, hello, queen, it's good to see you. What a nice surprise.'

Bella smiled. 'Hello, Aunty Et,' she said, using the name they'd
all called Ethel when they'd been little girls. 'Where are you off to?'

'Just having a little walk, love. It's my day off work and I've been stuck in cleaning all morning. I just fancied some fresh air. What about you?'

'I'm going to get some flowers for our Bet's grave. Why don't you come with me? If the café is open on the park we could get a cuppa afterwards.'

'Why not,' Ethel replied. 'I could do with a bit of company. Both my lads are away fighting of course and I've nothing but the same four walls to go back to.' She linked her arm through Bella's as they set off up Grosvenor Road. 'You can tell me all about your exciting life, entertaining the troops. I bet you all have some fun. I've not been out properly at night for ages. The last time I went into the city centre it was in a right mess and it just doesn't feel safe. They're doing their best to clear it but as fast as they tidy one area the bloody German bombs wreck another.'

After they'd tidied Betty's grave and put the fresh flowers in a vase, Bella stood back and said a silent prayer. Ethel stroked her arm and sighed.

'I was working that night they rushed her into Olive Mount Hospital,' she said quietly. 'It was such a shock to see your mam and dad in the waiting room. I took them some tea in while they waited for news. Poor little Betty.' She wiped a tear from her eye. 'I don't know how your mam carried on after. And then this bloody war on top of all that. As if we didn't have enough to cope with. I dread every knock at the door, thinking it's the telegram boy.'

Bella took a deep breath. 'I'm sure you do. It must be such a worry when you don't know where your sons are and if they're okay.' She stopped as a sob caught in her throat. Tears ran down her cheeks and she rooted in her handbag for a hanky, thinking how lucky she was that she knew exactly where *her* son was and that he was being well looked after. She chewed her lip. Had Mam told Ethel about Levi? She hadn't said so in her letters from Wales. But she usually confided in her with them being so close. She took a deep breath as Ethel gave a half smile.

'Come on, gel, let's go to mine for a cuppa rather than the café. We can bawl our eyes out in private then. We'll get a couple of cakes from the bakery on the way back.'

'That sounds like a good idea,' Bella said.

In the little bakery on the corner of Victory Street, the smell of fresh bread made Bella's tummy rumble. Ethel asked for two vanilla cuts and the young assistant popped them into a white paper bag.

'Last two, that was lucky,' the girl said. She smiled at Bella and Bella smiled back, recognising her as the daughter of one of her mam's friends, but she couldn't for the life of her recall the girl's name. As Ethel thanked her and called her Beattie, she remembered her as Beatrice Reynolds, who had been a couple of classes below Bella and her friends at school.

'You still singing for the troops, Bella?' Beattie asked, wiping her hands down the front of her white cotton overall.

Bella nodded. 'I am. But I've got a couple of days off so I'm just doing a bit of running around for Mam. A few errands, like.'

'It was a right shame about your pal Bobby Harrison, wasn't it? Poor lad. Are you still in touch with him? I remember you used to be really good friends at school and sang together a lot.'

'Yes, I am still in touch with Bobby,' Bella said. 'In fact I'm going round to see him later. And yes, what happened was very sad. Especially losing his father like that.'

Beattie nodded and sighed. 'Well I hope he makes a good recovery from it all. At least he's at home and you know where he is now. My lad's over in France.' She held out her left hand. 'We got engaged before he went away. But some days I wonder if I'm ever gonna see him again. I wish he could write more often. I just live for his letters.' A big tear ran down her cheek and she swiped at it with the back of her hand. 'I try not to get too maudlin but it's hard at times.'

Ethel patted her hand. 'We know what you mean, chuck. Any time you need a shoulder to cry on, just pop round for a cuppa.' She looked at Bella. 'Shall we get off, gel, and then we've time for a brew before you have to get going to see your Bobby later. We'll see youse again, Beattie, and I meant what I said. We all need to support one another at times like this.'

They waved their goodbyes and set off to Plumer Street and Ethel's bay-windowed terraced house with its spotless white net curtains, gleaming brass letter box, and cream, donkey-stoned front step and windowsill. Ethel had been busy, Bella thought, and then felt sad as she realised there was no family coming home for their tea later; no one to appreciate her efforts or to make even a slight mess with their muddy boots and newspapers all over the floor. And so many homes in and around Liverpool and indeed the whole country were just the same. *When would it all end?*

'You make yourself comfortable,' Ethel said, pointing to the red velvet sofa in the back sitting room. 'I'll go and pop the kettle on.' She vanished into the small kitchen at the rear of the house. Bella took off her jacket, laid it over the arm of the sofa and sat down. She glanced around the spotless room, which smelled of lavender furniture polish, and her eyes alighted on two silver-framed photos on the well-polished sideboard. In one frame, Ethel and Bernie, her late West Indian husband, posed on their wedding day, broad smiles on both their faces. What a handsome man he had been. No wonder Ethel defied her family and married him. In the other frame were two good-looking young men, the image of their father, their dark hair thick and curly and their smiles a mile wide. Bella remembered that the family had always been happy and the boys fun to play with. Levi would probably have similar colouring to Ethel's boys and his hair had been springing up in fat curls even at three months old. On recent photos it looked really thick, and curlier than ever.

Ethel came in from the kitchen carrying a tray containing two floral-patterned china mugs of steaming tea and the vanilla cuts on matching dainty plates. 'Not often I get to use me best china,' she said, putting the tray on the coffee table. She sat down next to Bella. 'Admiring the rogues' gallery?' she asked with a smile, nodding towards the sideboard. 'It's too quiet in here without them. I miss my boys – and Bernie too, of course, but it's been a good few years since he died so I was just getting used to not having him around and this flaming war started and took my precious boys away.' Ethel's eyes filled with tears.

Bella remembered back to that awful day ten years ago when her mam had been so upset at the loss of her best friend's husband, killed while doing his job. Bernie had been employed on railway maintenance since arriving from the West Indies. He'd been working on tracks just outside of the city centre when he had been hit by a train that failed to stop due to a signalling problem. The little boys had only been eight and ten years old at the time.

'It can't be easy,' she sympathised. 'I know Mam worries about Dad if she doesn't get a letter for a couple of weeks. It's the not knowing.'

Ethel nodded. 'I'm glad I've got my job to keep me busy. At least I've got company while I'm in work. And apart from the few sick kiddies in isolation, we've a lot of wounded soldiers now the hospital has been given over to looking after them. Most kids are evacuated these days thank goodness. Apart from just doing my cleaning job, I've helped out some of them poor lads as much as I can, by writing letters they've dictated to me. Breaks my heart it does that half of them will never see to write a letter home again. But at least their mams know where they are now and that they're safe enough for the time being.'

Bella sighed and thought about Edie and Fran's boyfriends, Stevie and Frankie, both away with their regiments, and said a silent prayer of thanks that although Bobby was injured, he was at least safe at home.

'Anyway, let's talk about something a bit more cheerful,' Ethel said, reaching for a plate and taking a bite out of her vanilla cut. She savoured the moment before asking, 'Has Bobby managed to divorce the little madam that trapped him yet? I've seen Fenella at church but she's as tight as a duck's arse with news. She never lets on about anything.'

'Err, no, not yet. It takes a long time.' Bella half-smiled. 'But it's all in the hands of the solicitor, I believe.'

'And once he's free, will you and he tie the knot – well, when this war is over?'

Bella took a sip of tea while she considered her reply. 'Depends on a few things. Maybe we will. We'll have to see how it all works out.'

Ethel nodded and covered Bella's hand with her own. 'Your mam told me, you know. About your little lad, I mean. She needed someone to confide in and she wrote to me. I swore I'd never tell a soul. I'm not one for gossiping and she knows that.'

Bella's eyes filled with tears. 'I wondered if she'd told you. I'm glad, because that means you understand what I'm saying about me and Bobby and our future.'

'You still haven't told him?'

'No.' Bella shook her head. 'I have to, I know that, but to be honest I don't know where to start.'

'Pick your time,' Ethel advised. 'Do it when you know you've got a few days together. I know you haven't much time on this particular break, but maybe the next time in Liverpool will be the right one. If he loves you, he'll take the little one on board. He's a lovely little fellow. Your mam sends me the odd photo in her letters.'

Bella smiled proudly. 'He's the image of his father Earl. Did Mam tell you he was a married man?'

'She did, chuck. She said he's a black American pilot. You'll not be the only girl gets caught out by them Yanks, I tell you.

This war changes many things for us all. People are trying to grab a bit of love and happiness where they can, and while they can. You can't blame them. Just do your best for the little one, that's all that matters in the long run. He might get a bit of teasing at school about the colour of his skin, but my lads learned to stick up for themselves and made more friends than enemies. Just teach him to be proud of his background and he'll do okay. And if you and Bobby get wed eventually, Levi'll be a smashing big brother to any kids you may have. Not many lads can boast they've two pilots as their dads. He'll be the envy of his classmates. All little lads want to fly an aeroplane.'

Bella smiled at Ethel's enthusiasm. It made her feel a bit more hopeful for the future anyway. If her son took after his father *and* his mother, with a bit of luck he'd be a musician or singer. It was definitely safer than flying planes. 'Thanks, Ethel. It's been good to talk to you. I don't want to keep Levi secret, but you know what people are like round here for being a bit narrow-minded.'

Ethel nodded. 'Tell me about it. I've had my share. But you learn to grow a thick skin and ignore them. Me and my Bernie were happy as Larry and our lads were good as gold growing up. Okay, they got into a few scraps defending themselves against name-calling, but by and large they were never any bother and both did well at school. There's a few round here that can't say that about themselves and their families. So it's nowt to do with the colour of your skin, but how you bring them up to respect people and property that's important. And if Fenella Harrison has anything to do with it, your lad will grow up like Little Lord Fauntleroy.'

Bella laughed. 'Oh don't. Telling Bobby's one thing, but his mother, well I dread the thought!'

Ethel laughed with her. 'Well, if you and Bobby do get it together eventually, Fenella will have no choice in the matter. But you just watch, she'll be as doting a granny as your own mother is.'

'We can live in hope,' Bella said, and got to her feet to carry the tray back into the kitchen.

'Thanks for your company this afternoon, gel,' Ethel said as Bella came back into the room. 'It's done me the world of good to have someone to talk to.'

Bella smiled. 'And me. It's nice to be able to talk about Levi and to see that there's some hope for the future, no matter what I decide to do.'

Chapter Three

Bobby Harrison glanced up as his mother Fenella swept into the room. He was deep in thought, sitting in his wheelchair by the tall Georgian bay window overlooking The Mystery Park. He raised an eyebrow as she fussed around, plumping up the red velvet cushions on the sofa and tidying his *Daily Mirror* newspaper away out of sight. Bobby shook his head. His mother preferred *The Times* and had told him so on many occasions when she'd criticised his daily reading matter.

'Why have you done that?' he asked. 'I haven't finished with it yet. I was just reading about the actor Leslie Howard. He's been killed along with sixteen other passengers who were on a scheduled flight. The bloody Germans shot the plane down over the Bay of Biscay with the Luftwaffe aircraft. The same model that shot down Dad's plane over London—' He stopped and shook his head.

'I'm sorry to hear that,' his mother said. 'But we're expecting a visitor and it's so untidy in here. People will think our standards are slipping, having that paper lying around. It's as common as the *Echo*.'

Bobby rolled his eyes. 'There's nothing wrong with the *Echo or* the *Mirror*. They're the choice of the people today. You really are a snob at times, Mum. God knows why. We're in the middle of a war. Just let things slip now and again for goodness sake. And it's Bella that's coming round, not bloody royalty. She certainly won't be offended by a copy of the *Mirror* on the coffee table.

And anyway, I thought this room was all mine now, for sleeping as well as entertaining.'

He jerked his thumb towards the single bed positioned against the back wall, waiting to be hidden away by the decorative screen his mother insisted on placing round the bed when he wasn't sleeping. 'It would be quite in order for all my reading material to be on the coffee table.' His mother ignored him and he sighed. It was hard getting used to living with his mother again after being billeted away at Brize Norton air force camp in Oxfordshire. He'd got used to his freedom and enjoying the company of his fellow squadron members – until he'd married Alicia, that is.

But that was all behind him now and he was here, back home in Liverpool, his life tipped upside down by events that were out of his control, but hopefully, soon to be divorced; although his solicitor had told him it could take a few more weeks yet. One thing in his favour was that he hadn't consummated the marriage so it was possible to get it annulled. He'd slept with her once when they were engaged, and regretted it immediately. But when she told him she was pregnant he'd done the 'right thing' that had been expected of him by reluctantly marrying the girl, but he'd kept his distance on their wedding night as she'd complained that she didn't feel well, and within days she'd told him she was miscarrying.

A visiting doctor had confirmed what Bobby had suspected all along: that she wasn't even pregnant and had lied to trap him and prevent him from being with Bella, whom he'd loved all his life. And that had been that as far as Bobby was concerned. Alicia admitted to her deceit, but before Bobby had been able to do anything about ending the marriage, he'd had the accident that had killed his father and left him crippled for life himself. Alicia had soon turned her back on him, after just one visit to see him in the hospital.

And now he was almost free to ask Bella to marry him. He couldn't wait. They'd been writing regularly, and he'd joined the

ENSA team from time to time to sing with the Bryant Sisters. Once
he'd been fitted with his false leg he was determined to travel with
the troupe as often as he could. But for now he was stuck here in
Liverpool, in the house for most of the time, with his widowed
mother for company and very little else to do. He couldn't wait for
Bella to arrive and went back to waiting by the window.

'I'm off to my WI meeting soon, Robert,' his mother announced.
'Margaret has prepared tea for you and Bella and it's all laid out on
the dining table. She'll brew a pot of tea just before she goes, so
make sure you leave the cosy on the pot to keep it hot. She won't
be able to wait on you as she's got a doctor's appointment.'

Bobby nodded. 'I'm sure Bella and I can manage between us,'
he said, saying a silent prayer that the house would be empty and
he could enjoy Bella's visit in peace. 'I hope it's nothing serious
with Margaret.' People didn't see a doctor unless it was life or death
as each appointment cost more money than most could afford.

'I've booked her in to see my doctor,' his mother said, as though
she'd read his thoughts about the cost. 'She's having trouble with
her stomach. He'll look after her.'

'Right.' He nodded. Margaret had been the family maid all
of Bobby's life and she'd often looked after him when his parents
had to go out. He was very fond of her and she was like the aunty
he'd never had. Fingers crossed it was something and nothing. His
mother would never cope without Margaret's help.

'I'll see you later then. I may be back before Bella leaves but
please make my apologies to her if not. I need to be at the church
hall to supervise as we're packing boxes to send out to our soldiers
on the front line today. Much-needed socks and stationery so they
can keep their feet warm and write home to their dear mothers.
Goodbye.' She left the room and Bobby breathed a sigh of relief
as he heard the front door closing.

*

Bella had a stitch in her side as she hurried across The Mystery Park towards the grand and spacious Georgian townhouse where Bobby lived. Prince Alfred Road fronted the park, affording all the houses lovely views across the green area that had been bequeathed to the people of Wavertree by an unknown benefactor, thus earning it its unusual name.

The park used to be full of children playing football and cricket and running around enjoying the fresh air. Today it was quiet, with just the odd person out walking a dog or taking a leisurely stroll. Most of the local children had been evacuated and the majority of men from the area, apart from those in various trades that were needed to keep the country running, were abroad fighting the war. Wavertree was a bit like a ghost town, as the women were at work in the factories and hospitals or running what was left of the shops in the city.

Bella waved at Bobby, who she could see in the window. He smiled and waved back as she hurried up the steps of the house, noting the new ramp that had been erected at the side of them so that Bobby could get outside in his wheelchair. The door was opened at her knock by Margaret, who greeted Bella with a smile.

'He's in his room,' she said and knocked on the first door in the hallway.

'Come in,' Bobby called and Margaret opened the door and stepped back to allow Bella entry into the room.

'I'm just going to make a pot of tea and then I'm getting off, Robert,' Margaret said. 'I'll put the pot on the dining table and then I'm sure you and Bella will manage between you. Everything's laid out in there. You'll just need to remove the cloths I've covered things with.'

'Yes, thank you, Margaret. And, err, good luck at the doc's,' Bobby said, a little awkwardly, not wishing to embarrass her. 'We'll see you tomorrow.'

Bella smiled. 'Thank you, Margaret.' She turned to Bobby as the door closed. 'Is she not well?'

He shook his head and his blue eyes clouded. 'Apparently not. Mother has booked her in with her own doctor.'

'Sorry to hear that. Hope it's nothing serious.' Bella took off her jacket and threw it and her shoulder bag down on the coffee table and went across to stand by his chair. She reached for his hand and he pulled her close.

'Kiss me, Bella, I've waited long enough.'

She dropped to her knees beside him and he enfolded her into his arms. Bobby bent his head and their lips met for the first time in weeks. Bella felt that the kiss would go on all afternoon unless one of them came up for air. Eventually Bobby did.

'Wow,' he said, taking a deep breath. 'That was worth waiting for. God I've missed you so very much. You've no idea.'

'I have,' she said. 'Because it's been the same for me too. I wish you could come away with us.'

'So do I. When I've got the new leg fitted it may be possible. As long as I can do up and down stairs and steps I should manage okay. There's usually only three steps up on most of the touring buses, so all being well if I can do those I can come with you every time.'

'I can't wait,' Bella said, her brown eyes filling with tears. They belonged together, she and Bobby; there was no doubt about it. They'd have been married by now – or at least engaged – if it hadn't been for bloody Alicia. All Bella wanted was to spend the rest of her life with him. There had to be a way.

'I've got a surprise for you,' Bobby said. 'Let's go and have our tea and then I'll show you what I've been doing to keep myself busy. Would you like to push me into the dining room?'

Bella nodded and got behind his chair. A rush of emotion filled her heart as she pushed the boy she loved out of the room and down the long hallway to the dining room. 'Maybe tomorrow we could go for a walk around the park,' she said.

Bobby looked up at her and smiled. 'I was hoping you'd suggest that,' he said. 'I'm not too heavy for you, am I? I think the chair weighs more than I do.'

'Not at all, Bobby. It will be my pleasure. You do realise that as soon as I tell Fran and Edie though, they will want to come and join us. They're dying to see you again.'

'And me them,' he said. 'That will be lovely. We could have a picnic. The four of us together just like old times.'

As Bella cleared the table after they'd consumed everything Margaret had left out for them, Bobby asked her to help him to get his wheelchair to the cloakroom in the hallway. She hesitated momentarily and then took the handles and manoeuvred him into the cloakroom. It was ages since she'd last been in here and she was surprised to see that the old sink and toilet had been removed and the room had been completely transformed into a washroom with a shower stall where Bobby could be transferred to a seat that was placed in the centre under a shower head, a toilet with a grab rail fastened on the wall beside it, and a small washbasin.

'This is perfect for you,' she said. 'I wondered how you'd manage to get to the bathroom upstairs.'

'Not a chance of it,' he said with a smile. 'Mum had all this done while I was convalescing in that home on the Wirral. The RAF helped with some of the cost so that I could rehabilitate at home.'

'How do you manage to get from the chair to that seat?'

'Mum pays for a private nurse to come and give me a shower each morning. It was a bit embarrassing at first but it's her job, what she's trained for and we've got used to each other now. We have a routine where I sit clothed on that chair and then whip my pyjama jacket and pants off while her back is turned. I do the bits I can reach and she does the rest, and the same with getting dry.

I'm trying to learn to balance on one leg against the wall but it's not easy. Especially when the floor is wet and slippery.'

'I expect that will come with practice and time,' Bella said. 'And erm, well, what about when you need to use the lavvy, how do you stand up and…'

'Aim and fire?' He laughed. 'That's exactly what I do. That handle on the wall there means I can hold on with one hand and with the other, well, you know.'

'Aim and fire.' Bella giggled. 'Oh, Bobby, I never even gave a thought to how you'd manage all your personal stuff. I mean when you've come along and sang with us; well, who's helped you then?'

'Basil, of course.' He grinned. 'He's a good man. He was determined nothing would hold me back if he could help it. So, do you think you'll be able to cope with a cripple for a husband, if and when we get married?'

His face was serious now and Bella realised that this was something they needed to talk about. She was determined not to show him she felt a bit nervous. She'd get over it. 'Of course,' she replied. 'And we won't need the nurse if I'm your wife, will we?'

He smiled and she could see the relief in his eyes. Alicia had shown repulsion towards his injuries. Bella would never do that.

'No,' he replied. 'We won't.'

'Right, tell me what to do and I'll help you to use the toilet,' Bella said in a voice that meant business. 'Come on, we need to make a start.' She followed Bobby's instructions and helped him upright to a position that meant he could steady himself by holding the handrail.

'Can you undo my zip please?' he said, a hint of amusement in his blue eyes. 'You can turn your back while I…'

'Aim and fire,' she finished for him.

'Precisely, Miss Rogers,' he said.

Bella turned her back discreetly while Bobby had a pee, and then she helped him back into his chair and over to the sink to wash his hands.

'Thank you,' he said. 'That wasn't too embarrassing, was it?'

'Not at all,' she replied. And she meant it. If she and Bobby were to be together eventually, she would be proud to do all that she could to make life as normal as possible for him.

'Right, back to the dining room, driver, and I'll show you my surprise,' he ordered.

'You mean that wasn't it?' she asked, laughing as he raised an eyebrow and laughed with her.

'Not quite. Push me over to the piano and then can you help me sit on the stool. This chair is too low to play and the wheels at the front get in the way of the pedals.'

Bella slipped her arms round him and with her support he pushed himself upright on his good leg and she helped him into position on the piano stool and then rolled the wheelchair out of the way.

He sifted through some sheet music that lay on top of the piano and selected a few. He handed them over and her eyes opened wide as she looked through them.

'You've learned to play all of these? Really? Gosh, you've been busy.'

'There's not much else I can do right now,' Bobby said. 'Learning new songs makes me feel closer to you. Knowing one day we'll get to sing them together.'

She smiled and handed him 'That Old Black Magic'. He played the opening bars and the pair began to sing, their voices blending in perfect harmony. Next was 'As Time Goes By'. They did a couple of their favourite Andrews Sisters songs, 'Don't Sit Under the Apple Tree' and 'Boogie Woogie Bugle Boy', and finally Bobby picked up 'For Me and My Gal'.

They made eyes at one another just like they'd seen Judy Garland and Gene Kelly do in the film of the same name on a rare night out the last time Bella was in Wavertree, when the kind usherette at the Abbey Picture House had helped Bobby's mother's driver to park his wheelchair in the middle aisle next to Bella's end-of-row seat. So engrossed were they now that they hadn't heard Fenella Harrison coming in at the front door and standing in the open dining room doorway, where she smiled and clapped as they finished.

'Bravo,' she said, her eyes filling with tears. 'That was wonderful. You two really are something special, you know. Your voices were meant to sing together. I'm so proud of you both.'

'Thank you, Mum,' Bobby said.

'Thank you, Mrs Harrison,' Bella said shyly. Bobby's mum always looked at her as though she wasn't quite sure she was right for her son, but today her face was alight with joy.

'I haven't seen Robert look so happy for a long time, Bella, you've no idea how much that fills me with gratitude. Thank you for coming round and keeping him company while I was out.'

'It was my pleasure,' Bella said. 'And thank you for the lovely tea. I'm afraid we ate it all, it was so good.'

'It was meant to be eaten,' Fenella said with a smile. 'I hope you'll manage to come and visit us again next time you're in Liverpool. How is your dear mother coping in Wales, and your sister?'

'Very well,' Bella said. 'Mam loves helping with the evacuated children and looking after my, err, my sister.' Bella took a deep breath. She'd nearly said my son. That's what comes of being so relaxed and not thinking straight. Her time with Bobby today had almost made her forget her problems, but they were still there and one day she'd have to come clean and tell him the truth.

'Can you let me have your mother's address before you leave?' Mrs Harrison said. 'I have an idea to put to her that I think she may like to participate in. It's something she can do while she's at the farm.'

'Yes, of course,' Bella said, wondering what on earth Mrs Harrison was going to suggest to her mam.

'I'll just get a pad and pen.' Fenella left the room and Bobby grabbed Bella by the hand. 'Kiss me quick before she comes back,' he whispered and pulled her into his arms, raining kisses on her face. 'I love you so much, Bella.'

'And I love you,' she whispered back, holding him tightly, until his mother coughed loudly as she came back into the room.

Bella wrote down her mother's temporary address. 'I'd better get my jacket and handbag,' she said. 'They're in Bobby's room.'

'I'll come with you, Bella,' Bobby announced, 'Just help me back into the chair.'

'You be careful you don't hurt your back, Bella,' Mrs Harrison said, but Bella had Bobby in the chair as quick as a flash.

'See, Mum, we're a good team,' Bobby said as Bella pushed him into the hallway.

'So it would seem,' Mrs Harrison agreed.

'Oh, by the way,' he called. 'We're going out tomorrow. It's Bella's last day so we're going to have a picnic with her friends on The Mystery. Can Margaret do us some food?'

'I'm sure that can be arranged,' Mrs Harrison said. 'I'll see you tomorrow then, Bella. I'm just going upstairs and then I'll come and help you into bed, Robert.'

In Bobby's room Bella closed the door and pulled the curtains together. They should have been closed ages ago due to the black-out, but at least fortunately there had been no lights on. It wasn't quite dark yet and the moon was bright enough for Bella to see her way back to Fran's house safely. It's what her mother would call a bomber's moon, bright enough for the Germans to see the streets below. Bella hoped there wouldn't be an air raid tonight, or certainly not until later, when she was in the house.

'One more kiss,' Bobby said. 'And then you'd better get back to Fran's while it's safe. I wish you could stay here with me. I just want to be in your arms all night. It's what I want more than anything.'

'Me too. And one day we will. Maybe when we're on the road and we need to stay in a hotel rather than a camp we can persuade Basil that you need me with you to help you.'

Bobby's face lit up. 'Now that's a good idea. We'll keep our fingers crossed that the opportunity arises in the not-too-distant future. Thank you for a lovely time today. I'll see you tomorrow.'

Chapter Four

Conwy, North Wales, July 1943

Mary huffed and puffed as she pushed the old, coach-built pram up the hilly track. In spite of being bounced around as the wheels hit the rocky bits and potholes, her grandson Levi still slept soundly. They'd had a bit of a sleepless night with him. He was cutting teeth and didn't they all know it. Poor little mite. She'd offered to walk down to the village and pick up a few groceries and the post in the hope he'd go off to sleep for at least a couple of hours. So far so good.

The first week of July already and the day was warm and dry and the sky cloudless and blue over the nearby mountains. The war felt a million miles away here, Mary thought. Although a village inland near Wrexham had suffered during the 1940 blitz on nearby Liverpool, when the Luftwaffe had launched a series of raids on the city. As the planes flew over towards their target a bomb had been dropped, killing several villagers and injuring more. But by and large Mary felt much safer out here than she'd done at home.

There were quite a few letters for the farm in the bag at the foot of the pram. One for her and Molly from Bella for starters, and another for Mary in a hand she didn't recognise; the envelope, with a Liverpool postmark, looked a bit on the posh side – fancy blue vellum, and the handwriting was elegant. She frowned, wondering who could be writing to her in Wales. No one, apart from Bella, Ethel, and Fran and Edie's mams, knew she was here and they used plain brown or white envelopes. Ah well, she'd soon find out.

They were nearly home and she was gasping for a cuppa as she reached the old wooden gate of the large Welsh stone farmhouse that was her very nice and comfortable current home. The sleeping Levi could stay outside under the apple tree in the garden while Mary and Ruth Jones, the farmer's wife, got on with their chores. It would soon be dinnertime and the land girls working on the farm would be starving, as usual.

Her daughter Molly waved from across the garden as Mary parked the pram and lifted out the shopping bag. She put her finger to her lips to indicate Molly should be quiet, and walked across the garden to where the three little evacuee brothers were sitting on the grass with Molly reading them a story.

'Hiya, Mam,' Molly greeted her. 'He's gone off then,' she added, nodding towards the pram.

'He has, thank God.' Mary rolled her eyes. 'I got him some Fennings powders from the chemist. They used to help you girls when you were cutting teeth. I'll add one to his next bottle feed.'

'Molly's reading us a story, Aunty Mary,' little red-haired Georgie announced, his big green eyes wide. 'It's dead good and there's a wolf and he gobbles Grandma all up.'

'Does he now? Oh dearie me. That's not very nice, is it, boys?'

Blond-haired twins Eric and Tony shook their heads. Eric's lips trembled and his blue eyes filled with tears.

'Read them the end, quick,' Mary said. 'Before they start bawling and wake Levi up. It's okay, boys,' she reassured them. 'Everyone is safe and happy again soon, including Grandma. Right, I'm off inside to help get the grub ready. See you all in a while. Give me a shout if his lordship wakes up,' she directed at Molly.

'Will do,' Molly called quietly after her.

In the large kitchen Mary sniffed appreciatively as Ruth stirred a big pan on the gas stove. 'Smells good, Ruth. Mmm.'

'It's just vegetable soup with a bit of chicken off the carcass thrown in. It does smell tasty though. There's a fresh loaf cooling on the side for dunking. And all those apples the girls collected the other day to donate to the WI for their pie-making session; well I've pinched a few back and made us an apple crumble for afters with custard.'

'Sounds smashing,' Mary said, her stomach growling in anticipation. 'I bet we eat better than Buckingham Palace here.'

Ruth laughed. 'We're very lucky really. Almost everything we eat is home-grown, including any pork or lamb. There's always a good supply left for us even after we've filled the ministries' quota of food for public use.'

Mary nodded. She'd miss this lifestyle when the time came for them to return to Liverpool. And that was something she wasn't looking forward to. They had yet to come up with a plan for what to tell the neighbours about Levi and where he'd come from. It was easy enough keeping her daughter's secret out here, but that couldn't go on for ever.

'We've quite a lot of letters today,' she said, pushing her problems to the back of her mind for now. No point in worrying about things until she really needed to. 'There's some for the land girls.' She put the envelopes on the sideboard. 'And a couple for me and there's an official-looking brown envelope for you and Mr Jones.' She handed the letter over and watched as Ruth frowned.

'I'll wait for Bertie to come in for his dinner and then we can look at it together,' Ruth said, turning the envelope over and over. 'I wonder if it's from the children's department about the boys at long last. Some news about their family, maybe.'

Mary chewed her lip. 'I hope it's not bad news,' she said. 'Although I think they'd have paid you a visit if it was rather than put it in a letter.'

Ruth nodded. 'Or even phoned me. Ah well. We'll eat first and then read it later.'

'I'll just pop upstairs and wash me face,' Mary said. 'I'll have a look at our Bella's letter when we've eaten as well. And *I've* also got a mystery one. No idea who it's from but it's a got a posh air about it.' She put both her letters in the pocket of her skirt and ran up the stairs to the bathroom.

Dinnertime, which was done in two sittings due to lack of table space, was a noisy affair, with little Georgie pretending to be the wolf that had eaten Grandma and making his twin brothers shriek and hide behind their hands by growling at them. Molly laughed, which only encouraged him more.

'Boys,' Ruth scolded. 'Stop it now or you'll frighten the chickens outside and then they'll stop laying and you know what that means don't you?'

'No more chucky eggs and soldiers,' Georgie said.

'That's right. So just calm down a bit. Here's Uncle Bertie now so off you go back into the garden and have a play, but don't wake Levi up just yet or Aunty Mary will have your guts for garters.' She smiled at her husband, who took his cap off and went to wash his hands at the sink. 'Sit down when you're ready, Bert, and I'll dish yours up. Ah, here are the girls,' she said as her three land girls came into the kitchen. They all dashed to wash their hands and took seats at the now vacated table.

'Me and Molly will just pop up to our room and read our letters,' Mary announced. 'That was a lovely dinner, Ruth. Thank you so much.'

'You're very welcome,' Ruth said. 'It's a pleasure to see everyone tucking in and enjoying their food. I've put a bit of soup in a dish for Levi and mashed some potato into it. It's keeping warm in the oven. It's time he was trying a bit of mixed feeding. I remember my boys loved mashed potato with gravy or soup to thin it out.'

'So did my girls,' Mary said. 'Thank you. He'll enjoy it I'm sure.'

Upstairs in the bedroom they shared, Mary and Molly settled down to read the letter from Bella. Enclosed with it was a photograph of the Bryant Sisters in army uniform standing onstage singing with a band. Mary smiled with pride. They looked the part. Proper professionals just like the Andrews Sisters. Bella wrote that she'd checked over their house and all was well, that she'd put flowers on Betty's grave, which brought tears to Mary and Molly's eyes, and that she'd spent a couple of hours with Ethel and they'd enjoyed each other's company.

She also said that she now knew Ethel had been told about Levi and that it had been nice to be able to talk about her son to someone who understood what it was like to bring up children of mixed nationalities. Mary nodded her head. Bella then went on to tell them about the couple of days she'd spent with Bobby, singing together at his home, and a picnic they'd had on The Mystery Park with Fran and Edie. She also said that Bobby's mother had asked for her address; so that was who the mystery letter was from then – Fenella Harrison. Mary couldn't imagine why Fenella would want to write to her and was curious now to read the letter.

'Right, Mam,' Molly said, breaking Mary's train of thought. 'I'm going back outside with the kiddies. I'll see you later.'

'All right, chuck. I'll read this then.' She picked up the blue envelope. 'See what Fenella Harrison wants.'

Mary scanned the couple of pages written in Fenella's neat hand. Then she reread it, as she wasn't quite sure what it all meant. After enquiring after her and Molly's health and hoping they were settled in Wales, Fenella wanted to know if Mary had heard of a project called Mass Observation. She went on to give details and an address to apply to, to become part of the project.

Fenella herself, and a few of her WI ladies, had volunteered to keep daily diaries that they submitted to the social research team at this address. Apparently it was thought to be a good idea to see how various members of the nation were coping with what had now become their normal daily lives. Fenella said she found it a very cathartic thing to do and writing about it helped her to come to terms with all that had happened since her husband's death and her son's injuries. She thought it might help Mary to share her experiences of being evacuated and spending time with the children in her care. How they all coped and the pattern their new lives had taken on.

Mary nodded thoughtfully and chewed her lip. It sounded like a good idea and would be something nice to do at night when everyone had gone to bed. She could sit quietly and recap her day. She'd have a good think about it later. She had plenty she could share. And the beauty of it all was that everything was private and she could remain anonymous. She'd be given a number, according to Fenella, and that's what she would sign her daily jottings with.

So she could even share her secrets about Levi and no one would have a clue whose child he was. When the kitchen was quiet tonight and she and Ruth were having their cocoa before going to bed she'd see what Ruth's thoughts were on the project. Pushing the letter back into the envelope, she put it in her bedside drawer and went back downstairs.

Ruth and Bertie were sitting alone in the kitchen, both wearing worried expressions. The brown envelope and a letter were discarded on the table. The land girls had gone back to their chores and Molly and the little ones were outside. Mary could hear them squealing through the open door. Levi would soon be awake, no doubt.

Bertie got to his feet and put his cap on. 'I'll leave you to tell Mary, love. I'll be back in later for my break. Try not to worry.'

He patted Ruth's shoulder, nodded solemnly at Mary and went outside, closing the door behind him.

'Sit down, Mary.' Ruth poured her a cuppa from the old brown earthenware teapot and pushed it towards her along with the letter. 'Help yourself to milk and sugar and read that.'

Mary read the typewritten single-sheet letter and shook her head. Tears sprang to her eyes and she looked at Ruth, who was crying too. Written by the child welfare officer, it was to inform them that the mother and grandparents of the three little boys had now all been confirmed as deceased following an air raid attack on their dockside tenement home in Liverpool. It had taken months to identify everyone involved, which was why there had been no information for quite some time. Also, the children's father had been reported as missing in action and believed dead. 'Oh Ruth, I don't know what to say,' Mary said, her voice breaking.

'Have you read the bit near the end where it says they are coming to visit us next week to make arrangements for the boys to go into permanent foster care?'

Mary nodded. 'I don't see why they can't stay here with you and Bertie. What's the point in uprooting them now after all this time?'

'Bertie and I would like to adopt them,' Ruth said. 'We've both said all along that if anything ever happened to their family we'd bring them up as our own. The twins call me Mammy and even Georgie has called me Mam occasionally. He's due to start school in September and we've got him a place. I don't want to lose them. What if they split them up? Or they could even end up in an orphanage or sent abroad to America or Australia like so many kiddies have been during Winston Churchill's Operation Pied Piper. I mean, I know it was meant for the best, but just look what happened to all them little souls when the SS *City of Benares* was torpedoed at sea. Those poor little devils never got to Canada,' she sobbed.

'I remember that ship,' Mary said and took a deep breath. 'It went from our dockside in Liverpool. A very sad day.' *There but for the grace of God*, she thought. That was one of the reasons she hadn't wanted her younger two going off on their own in the first years of the war. Sadly her little Betty had passed away before any decisions had been made. But now Mary was able to be with Molly it made life a bit easier and less of a worry. In spite of her own loss she knew she was one of the luckier of all the mothers doing their best for their children at this trying time. Her thoughts were broken as Molly carried a whimpering Levi into the kitchen.

'He's awake and he's very smelly. Shall I change him or do you want to do it, Mam?' She held her wriggling nephew at arm's-length and wrinkled her freckled nose.

Mary took her grandson from Molly and held him close. 'I'll change him and give him his dinner. You see to the little ones, love. Take them for a walk up the lane.'

'Are you all right, Mam?' Molly asked, frowning. 'Only you and me Aunty Ruth look a bit upset.'

'We're fine love,' Mary reassured her daughter. 'Take a couple of carrots out with you and then the boys can feed the donkeys in the next field. They'll enjoy that.'

Molly smiled. 'Okay, if you're sure. We'll see you in a bit,' she finished, accepting the three carrots Ruth handed her.

'Better have one each and then they won't be arguing,' Ruth said.

Mary sighed as the door closed behind Molly. 'No point telling her what's happened and upsetting her as well. She's really close to those boys now. They're like little brothers to her. She's really missed our Betty and they've helped her come to terms with losing her, sort of filled that gap. She'll be heartbroken if they're not allowed to stay.'

*

Mr Jarvis, the children's officer from the welfare department, finished his cup of tea and slice of Victoria sponge cake, cleared his throat and shuffled the sheaf of papers on his knee. He'd been at the farmhouse for over an hour now and Ruth and Bertie had shown him everything he'd asked to see. The children had been on their best behaviour and were currently outside in the garden playing with Molly and Bess, one of the sheepdogs. Mary had taken Levi out in his pram for the afternoon to give the couple some privacy.

'I can see the boys are very attached to you, Mr and Mrs Jones, and they seem to be settled well in your home. And as you say, the eldest is due to start school in September. It is rather unusual for a couple your age to adopt, I mean with you having adult children of your own; however, if that is something you want to consider seriously then I will certainly make the necessary application for you and this will go in front of a board of governors who will decide what is in the best interests of the children.'

Ruth frowned. 'We're not that old you know. People our age are still having children of their own. We married young and I'd had both our boys by the time I was twenty years old. In fact, I think you'll find I'm a fair bit younger than you and so is Bertie.'

Bertie patted her hand. 'Our lads are eighteen and nineteen respectively and we're not even forty yet. I know we'll manage fine. Those little ones love it here. They have the life of Riley. We'll give them the best of everything. They get plenty of good fresh food and they're fit and healthy. If you took them away and put them in an orphanage, like as not they'd starve to death from what I've heard about them places.'

Mr Jarvis smiled reassuringly. 'Our Barnardo's homes are not like the orphanages of yore,' he said. 'But I can assure you, I will do all that I possibly can to assist in your application to adopt the children. I have no intention of removing them at this stage as I can see they are happy, very well cared for and loved. That is what all children deserve, especially in times like we are experiencing now. Security and feeling they belong is important. Now how will you deal with telling them about their family? Would you like me to do it? The twins may not understand but the older boy probably will.'

Ruth shook her head. 'Leave it with us. We'll pick a moment when we think we can broach the subject and we'll do it gently and respectfully.'

Bertie nodded his agreement. 'I grew up on this farm and when my mother died I was only six years old. But see that rambling rose down there growing up the barn?' He pointed towards a bright pink rose bush in full glorious bloom. 'My late dad planted that in her memory and each year on her birthday in August we fill a vase with them and place it in front of that framed photo of her on the mantelpiece. We can do something along them lines for the kiddies. Plant something nice and then they will always have a memory like I do. We need a photo of their mam though if possible.'

Mr Jarvis looked like he might burst into tears as he said, 'What a lovely idea. A suitcase and box of belongings were salvaged from the flat when the body of the children's mother was discovered. I will make certain that they are delivered here to you and hopefully you may find photos among them. Now I'll leave you in peace and get on my way back to Liverpool. I'll be in touch as soon as I have anything to report. Thank you for the tea and cake. Someone is a good baker round here.'

'Ah, that was made by Molly, who is also one of our evacuees. She's a good little cook,' Ruth said, getting to her feet. 'Thank you for your time and we look forward to hearing from you.'

As she saw Mr Jarvis out Bertie let out a loud sigh. 'I think we did our best, love. All we can do now is keep our fingers crossed.'

Chapter Five

Bobby looked down at the artificial leg he'd been fitted with below the right knee and grimaced. It wasn't a pretty sight and he knew he'd never win any dancing competitions with it, but if it got him from A to B it was a start. The limb was fitted to his stump by leather straps and the foot was supported on a metal sort-of joint that was supposed to resemble an ankle.

The limb specialist who'd overseen the fitting helped him to stand and padded crutches were placed under each arm. Bobby stood frozen to the spot as Mr French nodded his encouragement to try to get him to move. The leg felt heavy and ungainly, but he had to try. At the end of next month, if he could manage it, he was meeting up with the ENSA troupe at RAF Burtonwood base camp and he was determined to join the Bryant Sisters onstage and on his feet, not in his wheelchair.

He wanted to surprise Bella by standing beside her. That thought was keeping him going. He'd got several weeks to crack this and he was determined to try his best. He thrust his right hip forward and the leg came with him, then he let it bear his weight while he brought his left leg in line. He smiled and tried the move again.

Mr French stuck up his thumb and a young nurse who had just come into the room gave a cheer and clapped.

He smiled again and slowly managed the length of the room. Realising he'd been holding his breath, he exhaled and spluttered.

'Well done, Robert,' Mr French said. 'Take a short break and then we'll have another go. Rome wasn't built in a day, but I can see the determination in your eyes and that's a good sign.'

'Would you like a cup of tea, Robert, while you get your breath back?' the young nurse asked him. 'I can probably get you a ginger snap to dunk as well.'

'Oh go on then,' Bobby said with a grin.

'One for me too please, nurse,' Mr French said. Turning to Bobby as she left the room, he asked, 'How do you feel about your progress now? You did well there.'

Bobby nodded. 'I feel good, really good. Being upright again and not wobbling to one side felt almost normal.'

'We'll book you in to have regular physiotherapy sessions and try to build up the muscles in both your thighs. With spending so much time in bed and sitting around, you have a lot of wastage. Once we get those muscles rebuilt your legs will be stronger and will support your body better.'

'I'll be running before you know it,' Bobby said as the nurse came back with a tray of tea and biscuits.

'Enjoy those, and good luck,' she said, handing them a cup and saucer each.

'Thank you, nurse,' Mr French said. 'Will you book Robert in for his first physiotherapy appointment for Friday afternoon please?'

'Of course,' she replied. 'Back in a moment.'

Bobby took a sip of tea and sighed. 'Can't believe we're actually getting this done now after all the time we've been waiting for me to heal properly. Feels like a lifetime since the accident.'

Mr French nodded. 'We have to make sure the site is healthy enough or we'll get breakdown of skin and soreness and the chance of a bad infection. You will need to keep a careful eye on the bottom of your stump. Make sure there are no sore areas. If there are then you will need to leave the limb off and keep the area dry and clean until you heal again. The last thing we would want at this stage is septicaemia setting in.'

'I will do my very best to follow instructions,' Bobby said. 'It's really important to me to get this right. I've got something very special I'd like to do soon and this leg needs to fully support me for that.' He smiled. One day he would get down on his good knee and ask Bella to marry him, hopefully after the next show in September. Even if he had to be helped down and then back up again, he would do it.

By the time his mother's driver Martin had come to collect him and they'd arrived home Bobby felt a bit weary and uncomfortable, but he was determined to master walking if it was the last thing he did. He'd refused the wheelchair even though it was in the car boot, but now, as he stood and looked at the four stone steps leading up to the front door, he had to admit defeat.

Martin, seeming to read his mind, patted his shoulder and went to get the chair. Bobby flopped down gratefully onto the seat and Martin whizzed him up the ramp and rang the doorbell. Mastering step-climbing would have to wait. His mother opened the door and invited Martin in for refreshments. This wasn't his only trip to assist with a hospital visit today, as he was collecting Margaret at two o'clock from her appointment with a specialist.

'Do take a seat, Martin,' Fenella said. 'I've made a bit of lunch, only sandwiches I'm afraid but it's better than nothing. And there are scones that were baked yesterday.'

'Sounds fine to me, Mrs Harrison.' Martin removed his cap and took a seat at the dining table, after manoeuvring Bobby into position. It felt nice to be made welcome and treated like a friend,

Martin thought. Funny how the war had changed people. Mrs Harrison would never have thought to invite him in for a cuppa a few years ago.

Fenella poured tea for them and told them to help themselves. 'How did you get on, Robert? Is it uncomfortable?' She indicated his leg with her hand.

'A little, Mum, but I think I did quite well and I managed the full length of the consulting room twice. Mr French was very happy with my progress. I'm to go back on Friday afternoon for a physiotherapy session to help strengthen my thigh muscles.'

'Well that's good news. I'm proud of you, son.'

'I'll get there, Mum.' Bobby smiled confidently.

'I know you will. How are things down in the city, Martin? Have they managed to make much headway with clearing some of the damaged buildings? I believe it was a dreadful mess when the blitz happened but of course we were down in Oxfordshire at that time and I've seen little since we came home. Apart from our own local area of course. I feel most of Wavertree fared quite well, considering.'

Martin shook his head. 'They're doing the best they can. But I heard they are still finding bodies buried under houses and blocks of flats that collapsed like packs of cards. Very hard to identify folk after all this time. There'd be nothing left of them. Must be dreadful. I wouldn't want that job for a gold clock.'

Fenella gasped. 'No, indeed. Doesn't bear thinking about.'

Martin finished drinking his tea and set the cup back on the saucer. 'I'd better get off now and make my way to pick up Margaret from the hospital. Have I to bring her back here or take her home?'

'Whatever she wants to do. Give her the choice.'

Fenella helped Bobby back to his room and watched as he removed his false limb. She'd walked behind him in the hallway, bringing his wheelchair with her, while he'd managed to walk with the help of his crutches. He was doing quite well and although she could see it was going to be a challenge, she was proud of his progress so far. He swung into the front room and heaved a sigh of relief as he settled into his wheelchair.

'Let me help you onto your bed, Robert, and then you can have a little rest before dinner,' Fenella suggested. 'I've just got some paperwork to do while I wait to see if Margaret comes back here with Martin.'

'I think I will, Mum, thank you. Today has tired me out more than I thought it would,' Bobby said.

'Come on then, let's get you comfortable.' She removed the shoe from his foot and helped him to shuffle from the chair across to the bed, then popped a couple of extra pillows behind his head. 'That okay?' She smoothed his floppy blond fringe from out of his blue eyes and her heart swelled with pride. Her son was such a handsome young man and she hoped that one day he would achieve his dream of walking again, the best that he could. She knew he lived for the day he could stand onstage alongside Bella and sing with her once more.

'Actually, Mum, will you pass me my writing things please? They're on the top of the chest of drawers. I want to write to Bella and tell her I've got my, err, leg.' He raised an eyebrow and laughed. 'Well, you know what I mean.'

Fenella smiled and passed him the pen and pad. 'I'll post it for you later. I've something to take to the post office myself. I'll give you a shout when I'm ready to go.' She stopped as the doorbell rang. 'That'll be Margaret. I'll see you later.' She dashed to open the door to Martin, who was supporting a distressed-looking Margaret.

'Shall I take her through to the dining room?' he said, shaking his head slightly. 'Not good news,' he mouthed over Margaret's head.

Fenella nodded, her hand flying to her mouth. Margaret was pale and tearful and struggling to take a breath after each gulping sob. 'Of course.' She led the way.

'I'll get you a nice cup of tea, Margaret,' Fenella said as Martin helped Margaret off with her coat and sat her down on a dining chair. Fenella frowned, really seeing for the first time how very thin and gaunt her maid had become lately. 'I think she'd be more comfortable on the sofa by the window, Martin.'

Fenella went into the kitchen and poured tea into a china cup, and spooned extra sugar in. Margaret looked like she'd had a shock and the sugar would do her good. Martin appeared in the doorway, a concerned expression on his face.

'Mrs Harrison, she wants me to tell you because she can't stop crying and her words are all muddled up, she says.'

Fenella indicated for him to sit down on a kitchen chair. 'Let me just take this cuppa through to her then.'

Back in the kitchen, she sat opposite Martin and chewed her lip. 'I gather it's serious,' she began.

He nodded. 'Cancer, and it's spread right through her. Nothing they can do but help her manage the pain when she's towards the end.' He took a deep breath. 'Which, between you and me, won't be very long now.'

Fenella felt tears rolling down her cheeks. 'Oh no, how dreadful. Have they said where she's to go, hospital or home?'

'They're going to let her know as soon as they have a bed for her. With this war and all the injured people there's a shortage, of course.'

'Then she must stay here with us. She has a room she uses here for when she stays over if she's worked late for me. I can't let her go back to the rooming house she lodges in. Not when she's so poorly. She's practically family and I will look after her. I wish we'd found out sooner and then we could have been more supportive.'

'Can you manage that, Mrs Harrison? I mean, you've young Robert to see to and your work with the WI and what have you as well. What about if you need to go out?' Fenella shook her head. 'Margaret is more important than the WI right now and I've someone I can put in charge of things for a while. And if you wouldn't mind helping me with Robert from time to time, we'll manage. You already take him to his appointments and run him about. Maybe the pair of you could do the shopping between you? I've got Josie the cook part-time – maybe she will do a few more hours. We should manage between us, I'm sure.'

Martin nodded. 'Whatever it takes. I've got to also fit in my ARP duties at night of course, but we'll cope. You just let me know when you need anything.'

Fenella got to her feet. 'But like you say, we'll cope. Let's go and tell Margaret what we'd like to do to help look after her.'

Margaret looked up as Fenella and Martin walked into the room. Fenella outlined her suggestions and was happy to see the look of relief on her maid's face. She held Margaret's hand as she spoke. 'Now, if you want to go with Martin and collect all your things from your lodgings, I'll get some fresh linen on your bed and have your room ready for when he brings you back. Tell the landlord you won't need the room any more. No matter what happens, Margaret, I'd rather you lived here with us now anyway. I will get my doctor to come here to visit you. We'll look after you properly. After all, you're like family to us.'

'I don't know what to say. Mrs Harrison,' Margaret said, a sob catching in her throat. 'I'm so very grateful. I was dreading going back to my room and dying all alone if they don't find me a bed at the hospital in time. It won't be for long, you know. A matter of weeks at most, they told me when I asked.'

Fenella took a deep breath. 'Then we're doing the right thing,' she assured her. 'I just want whatever time you have left to be as happy and comfortable as it can be, my dear. We'll take care of you as well as you've done for us.'

She saw Martin and Margaret out and popped her head round Bobby's door. He was sleeping but she spotted his letter addressed to Bella lying on the bed. If she hurried she could get it in the postbox for him before the last collection. Her own letters would have to wait as she hadn't had time to write them. Tonight when the household was settled; she'd do it then.

Chapter Six

Isle of Anglesey, Wales, August 1943

As Bella and her friends waited in the backstage corridor for the cue to go on from Basil, they stood talking to the dancing troupe who were next on to do a quick routine before the Bryant Sisters closed the first half of the show. They were currently based at RAF Valley on the Isle of Anglesey in North Wales, and Bella couldn't believe her luck that she was so close to her mam and family.

In two days' time they were performing at the Arcadia Theatre on Llandudno Promenade. It was a rare show especially for civilians for a change and Basil had told her to invite her family along. Bella had spoken to her mam yesterday and she'd promised to be there with Molly and Ruth Jones and hopefully the land girls. Mr Jones had been commandeered to babysit the evacuee children and Levi. Her mam had sounded really excited and told her she was looking forward to seeing them all perform. They were meeting up in the early evening to have a catch-up before Bella had to get ready to work. She was hoping that the following day she would be able to pay a quick visit to the farmhouse to see her son. Mam told her he'd cut a lot of teeth and his hair was an abundance of curls. He loved his food, smiled a lot and babbled to himself most of the day. Bella couldn't wait to see him and cuddle him again. It had been a long time.

As a mild ripple of applause and a few shouts of 'BOO – get him off!' broke her thoughts, Freddie Cagney, billed as usual as the Amazing Frederico – Master of Magic, came offstage and pushed his way past Tina's Tappers, deliberately manhandling the younger girls. As he drew nearer to the Bryant Sisters Fran blocked his way by neatly sidestepping, so he had no choice but to stop.

'Get out of my way,' he growled, his face flushed and angry.

'Sorry, did you say something?' Fran asked, glaring at him. 'Don't think I heard a please, or an excuse me in there. You need to learn some manners and to keep your sweaty hands to yourself.'

'And you need to mind your own bloody business.' Freddie shoved Fran hard, knocking her back into Bella and Edie.

'Hey, you just watch who you're shoving around,' Fran yelled.

'Well get out of my way then, you tart,' he shouted in her face, spittle flying.

Fran turned her head away.

The stale smell of booze on his breath was enough to turn anyone's stomach, Bella thought, as the stench came wafting her way. She almost gagged but took a deep breath instead. Basil appeared from behind the stage curtains and looked down the corridor. He shook his head angrily. 'Freddie, pack it in. Don't take your failures out on the girls. I suggest you go and sober up and I'll talk to you later.'

Freddie stormed off, muttering under his breath, his top hat drooping to one side. The girls in the dancing troupe turned to thank Fran.

'He does that every night,' the leader Tina Smyth said. 'Pushes into us and touches the younger two inappropriately. It's horrible. And it's not all he does either. He's disgusting, some of the things he says to us.'

'You should have said something to me before,' Basil told her.

'We didn't want to lose our jobs,' one of the younger girls spoke up, her cheeks flushing bright pink with embarrassment. 'I told Freddie not to touch me ages ago and he said it's part of the job and if I didn't do as I'm told I'd be sacked from the show. He said he was one of the ENSA bosses.' Her lips trembled and she blinked away tears.

Basil shook his head. 'He's not, love. Don't you worry. I'll get this sorted out. Let's get on with the show for now; I'll deal with him later. Off you go and give the lads your best shot.'

The dancers ran onstage to cheers and whistles as the opening chords to the cancan dance rang out. Basil turned to Fran. 'I've had my suspicions for a while about Freddie. But the drinking is getting out of hand now. He's just fluffed every trick onstage tonight. Even the white dove he takes out of his hat flew off to the rafters as though it's had enough.' He rolled his eyes. 'I'm going to have to let him go. His act is rubbish now and I can't have the sort of behaviour he's displaying around the young women I'm supposed to be looking after. It's just not on. I've never had this problem before, and I've been doing this job since war broke out.'

'We've been keeping a close eye on him,' Bella said. 'We're pretty sure now that he did do something to our drinks the other week, trying to knock us out or something. We've been getting our own drinks in since that night and we've all been fine. We just don't trust him at all. If he gave one of the younger girls alcohol in the guise of squash heavens knows what he might get up to. They wouldn't have the strength to fight him off; he's a big bloke.'

Basil sighed and shook his head. 'I agree. And I don't blame you girls for not trusting him. But I'll need someone to replace him and there are so few good magic acts around right now. It's a pity Marvo the Magician from our earlier shows retired. He'd been with me years but he and his wife were getting too old to cope with all the travelling, so I guess they did what's best for the pair of them. I'll speak to someone in HQ tomorrow and see what they can do to get a replacement act lined up. Meantime, perhaps you girls can do a bit longer onstage to fill in the gaps for me.'

The threesome nodded. 'If it gets rid of him then we'll do whatever it takes to help,' Bella said.

*

Mary, Molly, Audrey and Moira, two of the Geordie land girls, and Ruth, all piled into the smart Humber Snipe car that had been sent by Basil to collect them for their trip to the Arcadia Theatre. It was a bit of a squeeze but the three younger girls in the back were slim-hipped and wriggled into position so that Mary could squash in beside them. Ruth, who was the plumpest of the five, sat in the front passenger seat. Their driver was a pleasant young man who introduced himself as Danny West and told them he helped with stage props and looking after the equipment, but he also ran about for Basil when required.

'I'm that excited,' Mary announced. 'I haven't seen my Bella sing on a proper stage in a show yet. She's done a lot of travelling since she started, and I've been out here at the farm, so there's not been the opportunity.'

'It's such a treat for us to have a night out,' Ruth said. 'I can't remember the last time I left the farm other than to pop to the village shops, or even when I last wore lippy.'

Moira and Audrey laughed. 'Neither can we,' Audrey said. 'We had to do "Ip dip, my blue ship" to choose who would be left behind tonight out of the three of us, and poor old Mavis lost out.'

'We could have tied her to the roof,' Molly said with a giggle.

'She'll be able to help Uncle Bertie with the boys' bedtime and she loves looking after Levi as well,' said Audrey.

'She'll be fine,' Moira said. 'We promised to try and get her some chocolate if possible. That'll make up for it a bit.'

Mary looked out of the window as the car wound its way carefully down the narrow lane and out onto the main road in the village. Danny took the turning for Llandudno and as the girls chatted among themselves, Mary planned in her head the next few pages of writing for her war diary project. She'd taken up the challenge from Fenella and so far had enjoyed doing her daily jottings. It was a very cathartic and also comforting experience to be able to get things off her chest without actually having to talk to anyone about her life and worries and her fears for the family's future.

She'd poured her heart out about the tragedy of losing her youngest child, her coming to terms with evacuating Molly, but her joy at being able to eventually join her at the farm. The worry of having a husband on the front line, and her concerns about her eldest daughter when she was travelling the length and breadth of a war-torn country, and hoping and praying she was safe from air raids and accidents. She struggled with constant worries that their house in Wavertree would be flattened by a German bomber and they'd have no home to go back to.

It all seemed never-ending at times, but it was good to get it down on paper rather than it clogging her mind while she was trying to sleep. The one thing she hadn't been able to write about was Levi and she knew that once she started, her emotions would overrule anything sensible in her head. She loved that little boy like he was her own and the thought of having to hand him back to her daughter at some point filled her with despair.

He didn't even know Bella; she was a stranger to him. But tomorrow she was coming to visit him at the farm for an hour before the troupe moved on. Basil was going to bring her over in this car. Mary let out a loud sigh and concentrated on what Molly was saying about how nice it was to see the sea as they drove along Llandudno promenade.

'I've been told to take you to the hotel where the ENSA troupe is staying. Refreshments are being laid on for you,' Danny the driver said as he pulled up outside the Imperial, a large Victorian hotel on the seafront. He jumped out of the car and helped them all onto the pavement. 'Enjoy yourselves, ladies,' he said. 'I'll see you later for your return journey. There's Basil on the doorstep. I'll just go and park the car round the back.'

Basil greeted them all and invited them inside. 'We have a table booked for you if you'd like to follow me, ladies. Bella and the girls will be down shortly.' He led them into a spacious dining room and over to a large table, near a window with a view of the sea and promenade. The table was set with a pretty hand-embroidered cloth and matching napkins, dainty, floral-patterned china and sparkling silver cutlery.

'It's very posh,' Ruth whispered to Mary. 'Very nice indeed.'

'It all looks lovely,' Mary said. 'I wasn't expecting this.'

'Bella and the girls thought a nice treat was in order,' Basil said. 'This was their idea. Take a seat and the waitresses will be on hand with the food shortly.'

Mary took off her jacket and hung it on the back of a chair and Ruth did likewise. They sat down and looked at one another. Ruth raised her eyebrows and Mary started to laugh. 'It's not often we get waited on, is it?' she said.

'I'd say never,' Ruth agreed. 'What a treat this is. I feel like royalty. I knew I should have worn my tiara today.'

'Here's our Bella,' Molly announced, running towards her sister and throwing her arms round her. 'Oh it's so good to see you.'

'And you,' Bella said. 'And Mam, come here, let me give you a hug.'

After they'd all done hugging and Audrey and Moira had been introduced to Fran and Edie, they all took seats at the table and two young waitresses brought laden tea trolleys over.

'Oh my goodness, there's enough to feed an army,' Mary exclaimed as plates of daintily cut sandwiches and sausage rolls were lifted onto the table alongside scones and a Victoria sandwich filled with fresh cream and jam. Two large china teapots, jugs of milk and bowls of sugar were placed on the table and the waitresses left them to enjoy their afternoon tea.

'You'd never believe there was a war on looking at this lot,' Mary said, admiring the feast. 'You can tell it's all home-made and fresh and these sausage rolls are beautiful. The pastry just melts in your mouth. What a wonderful treat. Thank you so much, girls,' she directed at Bella, Fran and Edie. 'It's so lovely to see you and you are all looking really well. So very glamorous.'

'That's because we've got our stage make-up on and had our hair set earlier to save time after we've eaten,' Fran said, laughing. 'All we'll need to do is touch up our lippy. We don't normally look like this until show time.'

'We can't wait for the show,' Moira said excitedly. 'What other acts are on besides you three?'

'We have a full swing band, a dancing troupe called Tina's Tappers, a couple of acrobats with dogs – they're a new act to us and the dogs are so sweet – and a male solo singer,' Fran told them. 'We used to have a magician, but he's just been sacked for misbehaving.'

'Oh, really?' Moira said. 'What did he get up to then?'

'Drinking too much and always touching the dancers when they were waiting to go onstage,' Bella said.

'Sounds a bit iffy,' Audrey said. 'Shame though as I love a good magic act.'

'So do we,' Edie said. 'Basil is trying to get him replaced but it won't be easy with most of the menfolk away.'

'When's Bobby joining you again, Bella?' Mary asked, helping herself to a scone and spreading it thickly with butter and jam.

'Next month, as far as I know, Mam. We're up in Burtonwood again and he's able to get to us easily as his mum's driver will bring him over.'

'You should hear my girl and Bobby singing together,' Mary said, a hint of pride in her voice.

Bella smiled. 'Us three will do you proud tonight. We'll make sure we give our best.'

'Do you sing any Vera Lynn songs?' Moira asked.

'Bella sings "White Cliffs of Dover" as a solo,' Edie said, 'and then we will probably finish with the whole cast singing "We'll Meet Again". But you'll have to wait and see what's on the set list that the band gives us once we're onstage. They sometimes change things around for a bit of variety.'

Molly smiled and clapped her hands together. 'I'm really excited. I can't wait.'

'Me neither,' Ruth said. 'It's all so *very* exciting, especially for me who hardly ever leaves the farm. I've never been to the theatre in my life, or had tea in a hotel. I could get used to this. Bertie had better watch out.'

Chapter Seven

Tina's Tappers took a final bow and, to tumultuous applause and cheers, danced in formation off the stage. The red velvet curtains with gold tassels swung closed across the stage and Molly tugged on Mary's sleeve as the house lights came on.

'Mam, Mam, that's what I want to do. Be in that dance troupe, or one like it. Bet our Bella could get me a job if I asked her. I've always loved dancing.'

Mary sighed as she looked at Molly's glowing face. 'You're too young,' she said, shaking her head. 'And we need your help at the farm with the boys.'

'Mam, I'm sixteen. Seventeen in December, and if we were in Liverpool right now, I'd be working full-time in a factory or something. Our Bella's been doing this since she was sixteen. If it wasn't for Levi we would be home now. I don't need to be evacuated any more. I'm not a kid.' Molly folded her arms, a mutinous expression on her face.

Mary chewed her lip. What Molly said was right, in that they would be back in Wavertree by now had they not taken on the responsibility of looking after Levi and Molly would have been working full-time for over a year now. But it wouldn't be safe to take Levi home, although Ethel's last letter had told her things weren't too bad except for the almost nightly trips to the cellar when the air raid warning sirens went off. Ethel had written that

most of the nightly bombings were in the city centre and down
near the docks, but even so…

'I enjoy living in Wales, Mam, but I do get a bit fed up of
looking after kids at times you know,' Molly went on. 'I miss not
having anyone my own age to knock about with as well. When I
finished school I thought I'd be getting a job but there's nothing
round where we are, just farm work and I do a lot of that anyway
with the land girls.'

Mary smiled. 'I'm glad you're having a good time, chuck.
We'll talk about this when we get home.' She looked across as
two uniformed theatre usherettes made their way to the front of
the stage with laden trays of refreshments round their necks. 'This
isn't really the place. Here, go and get us some tubs of ice cream.'
She handed Molly two half-crowns. 'Not sure how much they are
these days but that should more than cover it. Tubs all right for
you girls and Ruth?' she asked. Everyone nodded and Molly got
up to join the nearest queue.

'Is she okay?' Ruth asked. 'I heard her saying she's a bit fed up
at the farm. I can't say as I blame her. It's not the most exciting
place for a girl her age, especially when she sees her sister having
this sort of lifestyle.'

Mary raised an eyebrow. 'I don't want our Molly going off
mixing with soldiers and what have you, and getting involved with
anyone unsuitable like our Bella did. Look what happened there.'

Ruth smiled. 'Oh, I think your Molly has her head screwed on
right. I'm sure she would be sensible.'

Mary blew out her cheeks. 'Well I thought that about Bella.
Anyway, we can't go home yet. You need our help at the farm.'

Ruth nodded. 'We do, but if being there is making Molly
unhappy then we'll manage if you have to make a choice and go
back to Liverpool.'

'It's the first I've heard of her being fed up,' Mary said. 'I thought
she was happy. It's seeing those dancing girls up there that's turned

her head.' She nodded towards the stage. 'It must seem an exciting life to Molly. I'll talk to her tomorrow. Here she is now with the ice creams.'

Molly slid back into her seat and handed out the five tubs.

It wasn't long before the lights dimmed again and the curtains swung back. The band played a couple of Glenn Miller tunes, the audience swaying and clapping along to 'In the Mood', and then Basil, in his role of compère, announced the next act as Tommy, Tuppence and the Tumbling Terriers. A couple, both aged about forty, danced onto the stage with two little Jack Russell dogs walking in between them, both on their hind legs, tongues hanging out and tails wagging. The dogs performed tricks and the couple danced and did handstands and tumbles with the dogs joining in.

'See if you can teach our two collies some tricks tomorrow, Molly,' Ruth said as the act came to a close. 'All you need is a handful of treats and they'll be your slaves for life.'

Molly laughed. 'I've already taught them to sit and wait and to give me a paw to say thank you. Ben's smarter than Bess though. He gets more treats. She just wants to mess about.'

'He's a good dog, is Ben. Always been great with the sheep. Oh listen, Basil's announcing the next act.'

'And now, ladies and gentlemen, boys and girls, it's my great pleasure to bring you three young ladies who are taking this country by storm. They are Britain's answer to the Andrews Sisters. Please put your hands together and welcome onstage Liverpool's own... the Bryant Sisters.'

Mary held her breath as her eldest daughter, accompanied by Fran and Edie, all dressed in smart khaki military uniforms, caps perched at a jaunty angle, took to the stage and, as the band struck up with the opening chords, launched right into 'Oh Johnny Oh', followed by 'Rum and Coca Cola'. Bella thanked the audience and announced that they would sing two more Andrews Sisters songs and then take a short break to get changed for the finale. 'Don't

Sit Under the Apple Tree' was followed by 'Boogie Woogie Bugle Boy' and the audience went wild at the bugle solo. As they left the stage, waving, Tina's Tappers filed on and went straight into the cancan routine, kicking their legs high, waving their frilled dress hems and wiggling their frill-clad backsides at the audience.

Mary watched as Molly sat forward holding her breath, her head nodding in time to the frantic beat. As the dance finished, and they all dropped to the stage in the splits, cheers rang out and shouts of 'More!' echoed around the theatre. Mary marvelled how none of them fell and broke their necks in those high-heeled shoes. The dancers all jumped to their feet and waved as they filed offstage.

Basil clapped and smiled as the last girl turned and blew him a kiss. He addressed the audience. 'Okay, when you've all got your breath back, we've got the final leg of the show coming up. The Bryant Sisters will open with a couple of songs and then Bella Rogers will perform a solo spot. And then we'll have everyone back onstage for our finale. It's been a wonderful night and my ENSA members have been happy to entertain such a marvellous and appreciative audience. Now if you'll put your hands together and welcome them back onstage – I give you, the Bryant Sisters.'

Mary smiled as the girls ran back onstage, took a few bows and blew kisses as the audience gasped. She had to admit they all looked beautiful in their change of outfits. Their dresses, in shiny satin, were all in the same style, a full skirt and fitted bodice, with a sweetheart neckline and long lacy sleeves. Bella's was a deep rose pink that set off her rich dark hair and big brown eyes, blonde Edie's was periwinkle blue to match *her* eyes, and auburn-haired Fran's was a rich jade green that was a perfect match for her eyes too. *Good choices*, Mary thought. Their wardrobe mistress and dressmaker knew what they were doing. They had it all just spot on.

'Our Bella looks right posh, Mam,' Molly whispered.

'She does that,' Mary whispered back. 'Oh I do wish your dad could see her now. He'd be so very proud of her.'

When it was time for Bella to sing solo, she spoke into the microphone, asking her sister and mam to wave as the lights were blinding her and she couldn't see them.

Mary waved her hand in the air and Molly leapt to her feet and yelled, 'We're down here, our Bella, three rows from the front.' She waved frantically as Bella shaded her eyes and smiled.

'I see you now,' Bella said waving back. 'Okay, well this is for you two and also for Ruth and her land girls, Moira and Audrey. And for everyone else that's come here tonight to see our show. Thank you all so much.'

Mary felt tears running down her cheeks as her daughter's beautiful clear voice filled the theatre. Vera Lynn's 'White Cliffs of Dover' was one of her favourite songs and Bella was certainly doing it justice tonight. You could have heard a pin drop as everyone stayed quiet and simply listened.

Bella took a bow as the song finished and the audience got to its feet and clapped and cheered.

Basil brought all the other artistes back onstage ready for the finale, which he asked that the audience join in with. 'We'll Meet Again' was a perfect song to finish the show with and everyone stayed on their feet, singing along.

As an emotional and proud Mary and the others made their way to the side of the stage, where they'd been instructed to wait until Basil's driver finished helping to dismantle the equipment, Bella popped her head round the curtains.

'Mam, I'll see you tomorrow about one o'clock. Basil or Danny will bring me up to the farm. I won't be able to stay too long as we've got to drive to Chester late tomorrow afternoon. Will that time be okay?'

'Yes, chuck. We'll see you tomorrow. Thank you for a wonderful night. Thank Fran and Edie for us. Are they coming with you tomorrow?'

'No, they said they'd give us a bit of time on our own, so they're having a stroll up the prom and maybe sit on the beach for a while until I get back.'

'Okay then, love. See you tomorrow.'

*

Bella held her breath as her mam brought Levi down from upstairs, where she'd put him down for a little nap in the hopes he'd be in a happy mood to see his mother for the first time since March. He'd been a bit grumpy, Mam had said, as he was cutting more teeth. He turned sleepy dark eyes in her direction and frowned. Mam handed him to Bella but he wriggled and cried and held his arms out to his grandmother, his lip pouting.

Bella sighed and looked at her mam. 'He doesn't know me, does he? Not surprising he's crying really. I'm a complete stranger. You take him, Mam and sit beside me with him while he gets used to me.'

Mary took her grandson back and she and Bella sat side by side on the sofa in the large kitchen. Everyone was outside in the garden having a picnic lunch to give them some privacy, and Ruth had invited Basil to join them. Levi plugged his thumb into his mouth and stared accusingly at Bella with Earl's eyes. Bella smiled at him and held her hand out to his. He grabbed her thumb and tried to ram it in his mouth as well as his own.

'Them peggys are giving you some gyp, little one, aren't they?' Mary said sympathetically. 'He's cutting one after another, there's no respite,' she told Bella. 'He's had a Fennings powder in his bottle earlier to try and help and he's got a teething ring to chomp on, but nothing seems to soothe him.'

Bella nodded. What she knew about teething babies could be written on the back of a postage stamp. But she could see how tired her mam looked and felt guilty that she wasn't around to be of more help. She held her arms out to Levi, who stared at her curiously. She tickled him under his dribbly chin and he half-smiled, and then chuckled as she gently tickled his ribs. 'Come on then,' she said and held her arms out again. He responded and Mary handed him over. Bella held her breath and sat him on her knee. He was chunky and rounded and his hair was a mass of curls, his eyes huge and his lips generous, just like Earl's.

She'd got Basil's box brownie camera in her handbag. She would need to take some photographs so that she could give some to Earl when they played RAF Burtonwood next month. It was only fair to keep him up to date with their son's progress, even though he couldn't be in his life for the foreseeable future. Life was so unpredictable at the moment and if anything happened to Earl while he was out flying, she wouldn't be able to forgive herself that she hadn't sent him the occasional photograph of their son.

'See, he just needs time,' Mary said as Levi snuggled close to Bella. 'I got a letter from your Bobby's mam this morning. I've been corresponding off and on with her. She suggested I do this secret diary project thing called Mass Observation where I write down all me thoughts about the war and how we are coping and surviving and send it in to an address she gave me. I have a number and I just sign it with that number and no other identification. It's so the powers that be can see how we are all managing, I think.'

'That sounds great Mam, good for you.'

'Thanks, queen. Anyway, it's an interesting thing to do when I'm relaxing at night and I enjoy it. Bobby's mam is doing it too, so we've kept in touch. Her maid Margaret, who we met that Christmas we were invited round there after our Betty died, is very poorly. Fenella has got her staying with them and is looking after her as well as seeing to Bobby's needs. The doctor's not given her much longer to live. Cancer, Fenella said, and it's gone right through her.'

'Oh no, Bobby did tell me she wasn't very well in his last letter and that she was staying with him and his mother for now, but he didn't say what was wrong. That's very sad. Margaret's a nice lady.'

Mary nodded. 'She is. I bet Fenella is struggling. She's not used to doing her own housework and what have you.'

Bella raised an eyebrow. 'True, but she'll no doubt have got another maid or housekeeper lined up.'

Mary smiled. 'Maybe. I'll write back to her tonight to ask how she's managing.' She nodded towards Levi, who was smiling and twiddling a length of Bella's hair round his fingers. 'Why don't you carry him outside and see our Molly for a few minutes. Grab a sarnie as well if the kids have left any for you. I'm just popping up to the bathroom.'

Bella got to her feet and slid Levi round on to her hip, where he jiggled up and down and still held on to her hair. 'There's a good boy. Let's go and see Aunty Molly and Uncle Basil, shall we?'

'Bella,' Molly called as she made her way up to the top of the garden. 'Basil said I might be able to join the dance troupe if Mam says it's all right.' Molly's eyes were bright with excitement and Bella smiled. 'He said Tina would train me, but I've always enjoyed dancing, haven't I?'

Bella nodded.' Yes, you have. But aren't you needed here to help with the children and farm work?'

'Ruth said she can manage without me,' Molly said. 'Didn't you, Ruth?'

Ruth nodded. 'We can, but it's not up to me really, Molly. You need to talk to your mam properly about this and see what she says. Basil said you can wait until next year maybe.'

Molly chewed her lip. 'I'd rather do it sooner.'

'Well look, why don't you have a good chat with your mother and then we can talk about it when we are near here again,' Basil suggested diplomatically. 'We are leaving the area later, so we can't get anything organised and signed up today. Stay a bit longer here,

Molly, and we'll get together in a while to discuss things in more detail. Let your mother get used to the idea for a while. How does that sound?'

Bella nodded. 'That sounds good to me. Molly, it will give you something to look forward to as well. But you really do need to talk things over with Mam first – and no sulking or making her feel bad if she says no. She might come round if you are nice and grown up about it. It's hard work and not all fun, you know. You have to be prepared to put hours into rehearsing each day and we do a lot of travelling. So bear all that in mind.'

Molly smiled. 'I will. But it's something I really want to do.'

Bella sat down on the grass next to Basil and sat Levi next to the little evacuee boys. 'Molly, nip inside and get my handbag please. It's got the camera in and I want to take some photographs.'

Basil shook his head as Molly got to her feet and ran off down the garden. 'Sorry about all that. She had obviously planned and plotted all she wanted to say to me. She took me by surprise.'

Ruth nodded her agreement. 'She did. You didn't stand a chance. She was in there as soon as you sat down. Last night at the theatre she announced that she wanted to be a dancer.'

Bella rolled her eyes. 'Well, there are worse things to aspire to I suppose.'

*

Mary's head felt like it was spinning as she walked back to the farm with the pram and the post. It was a week since Bella and Basil had paid them her visit. Molly had done nothing but go on and on about joining ENSA as a dancer and how it wasn't fair that she should be stuck on the farm when she'd rather be working and earning a living. Ruth was still awaiting a letter from the children's department and there was an official-looking letter among the pile Mary had collected today. There was also one for Mary from Fenella Harrison in the usual blue vellum envelope.

Molly and the boys were in their spot in the garden, where Molly was teaching them the alphabet and colours. She'd make a good infant school teacher, never mind a dancer, Mary thought watching the faces of the boys as they listened to what Molly was saying. She had them totally captured and interested. Georgie would have a head start once he began school in September, thanks to her daughter's patience.

'Anything for us, Mam?' Molly yelled.

'Not today, chuck, just one for me from Bobby's mam.' Mary parked the sleeping Levi beneath the apple tree, retrieved the post from the bottom of the pram and went indoors to where Ruth was just filling the teapot with boiling water.

'You timed that well,' Ruth said. 'Anything for us?'

Mary handed her the farm's post with the official brown envelope on the top. Ruth's hand flew to her mouth and her hands shook.

'Shall I go and get Bertie for you?' Mary offered. 'He's just out by the barns.'

Ruth nodded, her eyes shining with unshed tears. 'Please.'

Mary dashed outside just as Bertie looked her way. He saluted her as she beckoned him over. 'It's come,' she said as he reached her side. 'You go in to Ruth. I'll wait outside until you call me in.' She watched as he hurried into the kitchen. Mary stayed where she was and crossed all her fingers and tried to cross her toes as well.

She needed the carsey, so she also crossed her legs, shut her eyes and did a little jig, willing it to be the news they'd all been waiting for. A loud scream followed by excited laughter brought her back to her urgent needs and she dashed indoors to see Ruth and Bertie in one another's arms. 'Don't mind me,' she called as she dashed past them and ran upstairs to relieve herself. Then she dashed back down again.

'They're ours, Mary,' Ruth told her excitedly. 'They've approved the adoption. I can't believe it. Oh, but we are so relieved.'

'Oh thank the Lord for that,' Mary said, giving them both a hug. 'That's just wonderful to hear. I'm so happy for you both and for them lovely little boys.'

In bed that night Mary wrote her notes up for the Mass Observation report. There was a lot to say today, what with the adoption going through and her letter from Fenella that had told of the sad news of the death of poor Margaret. But this time Mary had poured her heart out about Levi at last, and the idea that if Ruth and Bertie could adopt the orphaned evacuee children, then maybe she could apply to adopt her grandson and pretend to everyone back home in Wavertree that he was a war-orphaned brown baby whose mother had died without knowing where his father was now stationed.

The more Mary thought about the idea, the more she liked it. It would also mean that Bella could get on with her life and marry Bobby Harrison and he need never be told that the baby her mother brought back from the farm was Bella's. Molly and Ethel Hardy would be sworn to secrecy. Mary was sure that Molly could be bribed by letting her join ENSA and it would buy her silence.

And when Harry came home they would bring up the baby as their own, which he was, almost, well their own flesh and blood anyway – but at the moment, she didn't feel she could tell Harry that; there was no need. All that she really needed was for Bella to realise her mam's idea was for the best and to give her consent. Next time she saw her daughter, Mary would put the suggestion to her.

Chapter Eight

Bella pouted in front of the mirror and applied the red lipstick that matched her nails; it was the colour all the Bryant Sisters wore for their military-uniformed part of the show. Edie wasn't keen on the red; being blonde, she preferred a more pastel shade of pink, but she wore one in the second half, with their nice dresses. Basil said red was more glamorous and went well with the khaki. It suited Bella's dark hair and eyes and anyway, it was only for half an hour, so whatever it took to please the troops was all right by her and Fran.

Bella felt a bit nervous, as Earl's band was backing the show musically tonight. She hadn't worked with him since she'd told him she was expecting Levi, although they had kept in touch with occasional update letters and she'd sent him photographs of the baby. She hadn't even been sure that he'd be here at the base camp as he was more often than not flying planes across the Channel.

But Basil had warned her there was a chance he'd be leading the band tonight and on arrival they were told he was on site. She hadn't seen him yet, but he was probably doing other duties until later. She had an envelope of the recent photos of Levi she'd taken at the farm for him in her handbag and was hoping to catch up with him privately before the show started.

Bobby was also due to perform with them tonight and was on his way from Liverpool with his mother's driver for a quick rehearsal with Bella. Bella sighed heavily and hoped things wouldn't be too awkward and that she'd manage to keep her cool and not give anything away to Bobby about her past involvement with Earl. Everyone else who knew had been sworn to secrecy a long time ago. A ramp had been erected at the side of the temporary stage in the large NAAFI for Bobby's wheelchair to be pushed up and all was set.

'What was that big sigh for?' Fran said, brushing her hair and flicking up the ends.

'Oh, you know,' Bella said with a shrug. 'The bloody mess my life is in; and both of the menfolk here tonight under the same roof. It couldn't be worse timing. I half hoped Earl would be away.'

'You'll be fine,' Edie said, patting Bella's arm. 'Just let's get through the show and then maybe you could say you're too tired for the after-show refreshments. Bobby will no doubt be driven straight back to Liverpool afterwards anyway.'

'And if he's not, then what? He's bound to want to chat with Earl about band stuff and what have you. And he'll expect me to be around as it's weeks since we saw each other. I can't just dash away and leave him. He's really excited about tonight for some reason. Probably because he's glad to be getting up onstage again after so long.'

'Well if you make it clear that Bobby is your boyfriend, Earl will stay well clear, I expect,' Fran reasoned. 'Play it by ear and see how it goes. Right, let's go and have a quick cuppa before they rearrange the seats in the NAAFI theatre-style.'

Bella sipped her tea and watched several airmen putting seats in rows in front of the stage. She jumped as a hand fell on her shoulder. Thinking it was Basil, she whipped round, only to find

Earl Franklin Junior, looking his usual handsome self in his smart blue uniform, standing behind her. A warm smile lit up his brown eyes, so like Levi's. Bella returned his smile. It was good to see him again but she was relieved that she felt no physical attraction towards him. She'd remain his friend because of Levi and that was enough for her.

'May I?' He indicated the seat next to Bella as Fran and Edie stood up.

'Nice to see you again, Earl,' Fran said. 'We'll leave you two to catch up. See you later, Bella.'

Earl nodded and smiled. 'Good to see you ladies again too,' he said. 'See you onstage.' He sat down next to Bella. 'How you doin', girl?' he asked in his strong New Orleans drawl. 'How's my boy?'

Bella chewed her lip and dug into her handbag. She handed Earl the packet of photographs and studied his face as he looked at them. His features softened and a smile lit up his eyes. 'He's doing just fine, as you can see,' she said.

'He's a good-looking kid,' Earl said quietly, a catch in his voice. 'Real handsome. A credit to your mother's care and nurturing.'

Bella nodded, feeling proud. 'He is. Mam's besotted with him. I don't think she'll give him back to me without a fight when this war is over.'

'And who can blame her. Bella, I'm so sorry for the mess I landed you in. There's not a day goes by that I don't think about the pair of you and wish I could offer to marry you and look after you both.'

'Don't worry. We'll manage,' Bella said quickly. 'How are things back at home? And your little daughter, is she okay?' she asked, keen to change the subject.

'It's hard getting up-to-date news with all the postal delays,' he said. 'My sister is keeping an eye on my daughter to make sure that no-good wife of mine is taking proper care of her. But there are reports of other men, like I told you. I can't do anything until I get back to the USA.'

Bella nodded. No matter what happened to Earl's marriage eventually, she still wouldn't want to marry him. Bobby was the love of her life. She would have to pluck up the courage to tell him her secret about the baby soon and see if he then still wanted to be with her. 'Well when you do, I wish you all the luck in the world. If you still want updates on your son you can write to me care of my mother's house that we went to, err, that afternoon. Otherwise, just write to me care of ENSA for now.'

Earl smiled. 'I will always want updates on Levi, if that's okay with you.' He put the packet of photos into his jacket pocket and looked across to the stage, where the band was setting up ready for a quick run-through before the show began. 'Thank you for those. I'll send one to my sister Ruby; she'll appreciate being kept in the loop. I'd better go and join my band now. I'll see you up onstage later.' He got to his feet and gently squeezed her shoulder.

Bella watched him walk away and swallowed hard. He was a fine figure of a man, tall and good-looking with the same dark hair and eyes as Levi. As he took a seat at the piano onstage, ran his hands over the keys and began to sing, Bella shivered. Earl had a wonderful voice and when this war ended, if it ever did, she was sure he'd go back to doing what he loved most: singing and entertaining in his home city.

A noise by the doors made her look round and she saw Bobby and Martin, his mother's driver, coming into the room. She got to her feet, smiling, and waved to Bobby, who waved enthusiastically back from his wheelchair. He looked smart in his air force uniform, even though he had a blue tartan rug tucked round his remaining leg; although he wasn't officially a member any more since his accident, Basil had told him to wear his spare uniform onstage as the audience would appreciate it. Martin pushed him across to Bella and went to get them both a mug of tea.

She bent to Bobby's level and he pulled her into his arms and kissed her long and hard. When he released her Bella could see the love shining in his blue eyes. She pushed his blond hair off his forehead and hoped he could also see her love for him mirrored in her own eyes. 'It's so good to see you,' she told him.

'And it's good to see you too,' he said, holding her hand tightly. 'God I have missed you so much.'

'Not half as much as I've missed you,' she said. 'I wish you were up to coming with us all the time, but I know how hard it is for you.'

'Well…' Bobby's eyes twinkled. 'See how tonight goes and then we will see. Ah, here are the others,' he said as Fran and Edie came over and both gave him a hug. 'Good to see you again, girls.'

'Good to see you too, Bobby,' they chorused. 'Basil wants us on the stage to run through a couple of songs and then we can go and finish getting ready,' Fran added.

*

During the second half of the show Bobby, who was sitting in his wheelchair onstage with the girls and singing along with them, signalled to Basil in the wings. Basil winked and came and stood beside Bobby as the song came to an end. Bella frowned as Fran and Edie took a bow and ran off into the wings. As the band struck up with the opening bars of 'Over the Rainbow' Basil whipped the tartan rug off Bobby's leg and helped him to his feet. Bobby reached for Bella's hand. Her eyes opened wide with surprise as Bobby stood perfectly straight beside her and Basil moved away, taking Bobby's chair with him.

'For Betty,' Bobby whispered, nodding encouragingly at Bella before she got a chance to say anything about him being actually standing up. She smiled and began to sing the song they'd always sung for her late little sister, and her voice soared as he squeezed her hand gently and joined in with her. Bobby had been determined to do this tonight. He'd earlier spoken privately to Basil, who'd had a word with Earl and Fran and Edie, who were all in agreement. Only Bella had been kept in the dark as Bobby wanted to surprise her.

Tears streaming down her cheeks, Bella made it to the end of the song and the audience of airmen and women rose to their feet as one with cheers and clapping and shouts of 'More!' Edie and Fran ran back onstage and gave them both hugs and Bobby signalled to Basil to bring his wheelchair back for the next few songs. He'd achieved his goal of standing and singing alongside Bella, but wasn't taking any chances; he had another surprise planned for later and he wanted to be on top form for that.

Bella bent to kiss his cheek. 'You amaze me,' she whispered. 'I'd no idea you could stand. I know you told me in your letters you'd been fitted for a new leg, but you never told me you were actually using it yet.'

'I wanted to surprise you,' he said and patted his false limb. 'They fixed me properly a few weeks ago. It's not perfect, but I'm getting there.'

'Oh, Bobby, you most definitely are.'

Fran took the microphone and announced the next songs would be their Andrews Sisters set. They usually performed them in the first half of the show, but the set list had been changed tonight to allow Bobby to sing alongside them early, before he was too tired to stand.

The audience joined in and all of the artistes came back onstage for the finale, which had now become the favourite and most poignant song for everyone. Bella began to sing on her own and then encouraged everyone to sing along to 'We'll Meet Again.' Bobby always felt sad when he heard the Vera Lynn song, as the one person he'd loved and looked up to all his life, his father, his friend and his mentor, he would never meet again.

*

At the after-show get together Bella, Fran, Edie, Bobby, Basil and Martin all raised a glass.

'To all our lost heroes,' Basil said. 'Including Bobby's dad and all of the Dam Busters lads we lost back in May from RAF 617

Squadron.' Basil was referring to 'Operation Chastise', where several crews had flown to the Ruhr Valley in the industrial heartland of Germany to drop bouncing bombs on three dams in an attempt to bring about destruction. One of the dams generated electricity and it was hoped the damage to the region would cause mass disruption to the German war production. Sadly, the British air force had lost eight Lancaster Bombers during the raid and of the one hundred and thirty-three aircrew who took part, fifty-three members had lost their lives.

Bella sipped her sherry and looked around the NAAFI canteen. Earl and the members of his band were sitting at the top end of the room near the door and he caught her eye and raised his glass. She gave him a half smile and looked away. Basil, Fran and Edie were talking between themselves and kept glancing over at her and Bobby. Bella wondered what they were talking about. There was an odd air about them all tonight and she couldn't put her finger on it.

'Bella, come with us to the ladies',' Fran said, putting her glass down and pulling Edie up from her seat.

'I don't need the ladies',' Bella said, frowning.

'Yes you do,' Fran insisted. 'Basil, refill our glasses,' she ordered bossily, winking at him.

Bella rolled her eyes and got to her feet. 'What's going on?' she asked as Fran grabbed one arm and Edie the other and they frog-marched her towards the canteen doors. She was conscious of Earl trying to attract her attention but was through the doors and in the outside corridor before she could say anything to him.

She shook Fran and Edie off as she saw Earl's silhouette appear on the other side of the glass doors. 'I don't need the lavvy,' she said. 'I'll wait here for you.'

Fran tutted as the doors opened and Earl stuck his head outside. She pulled Edie into the ladies' as Earl joined Bella in the corridor.

'Don't know what's going on with them two tonight.' She nodded her head at the closed washroom door. 'They're acting really weird.'

Earl sighed. 'Well, it's not my place to say, but I overheard a conversation earlier that may have something to do with it,' he said.

'With what?' Bella asked, frowning. Earl had a sad look in his eyes and she wondered why.

'That young man in the wheelchair, your singing partner, is he also your boyfriend?'

Bella swallowed hard. 'Yes, he is. Bobby and I have been friends since we were kids. We sang together many times before his accident.'

'Basil told me he survived a tragic plane crash that killed his father.'

'Yes, he did,' Bella replied.

'He loves you very much, it's in his eyes and written all over his face.'

'He does. And I love him,' Bella admitted.

'Does he know about Levi?'

Bella shook her head and tears filled her eyes. 'I haven't told him yet. I'm scared he'll leave me. I don't want to lose him, Earl.'

'I understand. But if he loves you, you won't lose him. You need to tell him, and sooner rather than later. Whatever you decide to do, I will never stand in your way with regards to Levi. All I ask is that you keep in contact and let me know how my boy is doing from time to time, please, Bella.' His voice cracked and he turned away. 'I'll go back to my bandmates now. Tonight was wonderful. You get better each time I hear you sing.' He gave her a long look before turning and going back into the canteen, leaving Bella staring after him with her mouth open. She felt sad for Earl that he wouldn't see his son growing up, but she'd make sure he was always kept up to date with his progress.

She became aware that Fran and Edie were standing by her side again and allowed herself be led back into the canteen, where Bobby was standing beside Basil and Martin. *Now what?* Bella thought. *Why have they got him on his feet again? Can't they see he's tired?* Although when she got closer she could see Bobby's cheeks were pink and his eyes shining with excitement.

As she stood in front of him, he reached for her hand and, putting his other hand on the back of a chair to steady himself, Bobby lowered himself slowly down onto his good knee as Bella let out a shocked gasp.

He let go of the chair, reached into his pocket and pulled out a red box, opening it to reveal a pretty gold and diamond ring. 'Bella Rogers,' he began. 'You know how much I love you. Will you do me the honour of being my wife and marrying me as soon as possible?'

Bella looked at Bobby as though he'd gone mad. A proposal was the last thing she'd been expecting tonight. She stared at everyone as they stood round her and Bobby in a circle, waiting for her answer. She looked at Bobby and felt the tears falling. She wished with all her heart she could say yes, but until she'd told him about her son she could not accept a proposal of marriage from him. He was looking at her, a stricken expression in his eyes, as Basil helped him up and into his chair.

Bella shook her head and backed away. With a loud cry she turned and fled down the length of the room and out through the doors at the end. She didn't stop running until she'd reached the Nissen hut the girls were staying in; she opened the door and flung herself down on her bed, sobbing as though her heart would break. She wasn't sure how long she lay there before she heard voices and sat up as Fran and Edie came in. They closed the door and sat down on the bed opposite Bella's.

'What have I done?' Bella wailed. 'Was Bobby okay?'

Edie shook her head. 'Not really. He was very upset. Martin's taken him back to Liverpool. Basil got him a brandy to help calm him down. Look, Bella, *we* know why you said no, but Bobby doesn't and he deserves that at least. He's just told us that he thinks it's because he's a cripple and will hold you back in your career and you don't want the responsibility of looking after a man with so many ugly scars on his body.' She held up her hands. 'Bobby's words, not mine. You have got to tell him about Levi. You really can't leave it any longer. Bobby needs to know it's got nothing to do with his injuries, if nothing else.'

Fran nodded her agreement. 'He's broken, Bella. After all the effort he's made to stand onstage with you as well, and it must have been one heck of a struggle to get down on one knee like that. All the planning he's put into working towards it. Can you imagine how he's feeling right now?'

Bella sobbed into her hands. 'I've really hurt him, I know. But how could I say yes? I wasn't expecting him to propose tonight. It threw me completely. I just felt I had no choice but to say no. I'll have to try and get to Liverpool to see him. That's if he will want to see me after tonight.'

'He will,' Edie said. 'As he was leaving he said to tell you he loves you, no matter what.'

'Oh God,' Bella sobbed.

'Basil will take you over to Wavertree tomorrow morning,' Fran said. 'He said to tell you that. We're coming with you, but he'll drop us off to see our mams and we'll meet up with you later.'

Bella took a deep breath and nodded. 'Just keep everything crossed for me then. I spoke to Earl while you two were in the ladies'. I think he'd overheard Bobby talking to Basil and got wind of what he might be planning. He didn't tell me of course, but he said he wouldn't stand in my way over Levi and that I should tell Bobby about him right away. So this is it.' Bella paused and her eyes filled. 'No matter what the outcome will be, and I dread the worst, I just have to pray that Bobby will still feel the same about me.'

Chapter Nine

Wavertree, September 1943

Bobby looked out of the window and saw Basil's car pull up outside the house. His heart leapt as he spotted Bella sitting in the front passenger seat. He saw the pair exchange words and then Basil was running up the steps to the door and ringing the bell. Bobby heard footsteps in the hallway as his mother hurried to answer the door. He heard her invite Basil inside. Bella remained in the car, and his heart sank a little as he wondered if all Basil was calling for was to tell him when he would next be joining the ENSA tour. There was a light knock on his door and his mother popped her head inside the room.

'Basil would like a quick word with you, Robert,' she announced and stepped back to let Basil into Bobby's room. 'I'll just be next door in the dining room if you need me,' she said and closed the door as she left.

'Take a seat, Basil.' Bobby gestured to the small sofa under the window, next to his wheelchair.

Basil nodded and sat down. He placed his fingertips together, forming a steeple. 'How are you today, son?' he asked.

'I've felt better,' Bobby admitted.

'I'm sure.' Basil nodded. 'Well look,' he began. 'I've got Bella with me. She's waiting in the car in case you refused to see her.

She's got something she needs to discuss with you. Something she knows she should have done a long time ago.'

'Okay,' Bobby said, frowning. 'Sounds serious. Do you want to bring her in then? You could maybe join my mother while we talk privately. She might even offer you refreshments. She's getting quite good at making tea since our maid Margaret passed away.' Bobby tried to smile.

'Oh I'm sorry to hear that, I know she was like family to you. I'll fetch Bella in and then go and look for your mother. But, Bobby, listen carefully to everything Bella tells you, and be gentle with her, please. She's not had the easiest of times but she didn't want to burden you with her problems while you were recovering from your accident.'

Bobby nodded and Basil went to get Bella from the car, leaving him wondering what the heck was so awful that she felt she couldn't confide in him considering all they meant to each other. He chewed his lip anxiously as he heard their voices in the hallway; and then Bella walked into the room alone.

'Bobby, I'm so sorry for running away from you last night,' Bella began, looking at his worried face and wondering how she could have done that to him with no explanation. She felt sick at the thought of hurting him further, but until she told him what she'd come to say, they had no chance of sorting things out. She took a very deep breath as he indicated she should sit down on the sofa that Basil had just vacated. Her hands were shaking and she could feel tears welling.

'I love you, Bobby. I love you more than life itself, you must know that. Everything we've been through has brought us closer. But before I can accept your marriage proposal there's something I have to say to you. Believe me, I will understand if you tell me to go away and you want nothing more to do with me. It will break my heart, but I will understand.'

Bobby reached for her hand and squeezed it. 'Tell me, Bella. Nothing can be that bad, surely.'

'It can,' she said quietly. 'When you married Alicia I was very hurt and upset. But I tried to get on with my life. I met a man at Burtonwood. A US pilot. We became friendly. He is with the band and we worked together. We weren't really in a relationship but we became close and he asked me to write to him while we were touring the country. We exchanged the odd letter here and there.'

Bella looked down at their hands entwined on her lap. 'We had just one date where we were alone. I'm afraid that one date led to me getting pregnant.' She stopped and took another deep breath. He was still holding her hand tight. Hope soared through her. 'I gave birth to a baby boy, Levi, last Christmas. He's living with my mam and Molly at the farm they were evacuated to.'

'What about him, the baby's father?' Bobby spoke quietly. 'Where does he fit into your life now?'

Bella shook her head. 'He doesn't. He never really did. When I told him Levi was on the way he told me he was sorry and that he was married with a five-year-old daughter. I was shocked, at first. But even though I was terrified by the mess I'd got myself into, I wouldn't have wanted to marry him. He's a nice enough man, but I don't love him.'

She looked closely at Bobby. His face showed no anger and his blue eyes held only compassion and understanding.

'I'd thought about having my baby adopted, I was very mixed up and confused, but I changed my mind, and then when I saw him I knew I couldn't part with him. Mam agreed to help me and said she'd look after him so that I could go back to work. He's been in North Wales and I've only seen him once since March. So you see, Bobby, hiding that huge secret from just about everyone except Mam's friend Ethel, Fran, Edie and Basil has been really hard. Even my dad doesn't know yet. But there's no way I could have agreed to marry you before I told you about Levi. I was going to, but the time just never seemed right. Also, I was so scared of losing you.'

Bobby reached for her and held her close while she cried on his shoulder. She could feel him sobbing too and lifted her head to look at him. 'You don't seem angry with me.'

'Bella, how can I be angry with you? Look at the mess I made with Alicia. How badly I let you down that night and how hurt you must have felt for a very long time. Me and you, we're two of a kind. I love you. I want to marry you and I would love to help you bring up your son. By the way, I also love the name you've given him. It's unusual. How did you manage to choose that?'

Bella chewed her lip. *Bobby still wanted to marry her, but…* 'His father showed me a photograph of his brothers and sister one day. A couple of his brothers' names just stuck in my head. My baby's full name is Levi Scott Rogers.'

'You gave him your surname then?'

'Yes, I thought it would be better for him when we all settle back to normal life in Liverpool if he has our family surname.'

Bobby nodded. 'I think Harrison also goes well with Levi Scott,' he said quietly.

'Yes, it does indeed,' she agreed, wondering where this was leading.

'So, have I met his father then?' Bobby asked. 'Was he there last night if he's one of the band?'

Bella sighed heavily. This was it. This is where he told her to go away for good. 'Yes he was. Levi's father is Earl Franklin Junior. The band backing us last night is his band. The Earl Franklin band. Earl plays piano and trumpet.'

Bobby took in a deep breath. 'The tall black guy with the deep voice. I spoke to him with Basil about doing "Over the Rainbow" for you. He did tell me he knew about your sister Betty and I wondered how.'

Bella reached into her handbag and pulled out several photographs of Levi. She handed them to Bobby. 'He's not as dark-skinned as Earl. But as you can see, he has his brown eyes and curly hair.'

Bobby studied the photographs of the chubby, smiling baby boy. 'He has a look of you too, you know, Bella,' he said. 'You have very dark hair and your eyes are deep brown too.'

'Do you think he does?' Bella asked. She'd never really thought that Levi bore any resemblance to her but now, as she looked at the photographs, she saw that he smiled like she did, and held his head to one side just like she did.

'Yes, I do,' Bobby said. 'He's a lovely baby. When we are married, would I be able to take him on as my own, adopt him maybe?'

'Would you want to?'

'Bella, you come as a package, you're a pair.'

'Yes,' Bella agreed with a smile. 'Yes, I suppose we do.'

'Would Earl have any problems with me bringing up his boy?'

Bella shook her head. 'No, he wouldn't. We already had that conversation. He said he would never stand in my way and only wants what's best for Levi.'

Bobby nodded and reached into his jacket pocket. 'Then in that case, I'll ask you again,' he said, producing the ring box. 'But I can't get down on one knee today without help, so – Bella Rogers, will you marry me – please?'

Bella clapped her hand to her mouth to stop herself yelling out. She didn't want his mother rushing in and spoiling their special moment. She nodded, blinking back tears. 'Yes, Bobby, yes, I would love to marry you.'

'Thank God for that.' Bobby slid the ring onto her finger and the fit was perfect. 'That's pure fluke,' he said.

'It's beautiful.' Bella admired the solitaire diamond surrounded by a crown of tiny pearls. 'Absolutely beautiful.' She flung her arms round him and kissed him. 'Thank you so much. I know we have to wait ages for your divorce, but it gives us something to look forward to.'

'Ah, well,' Bobby began, smiling. 'About that. I'm already divorced. I was saving that to tell you last night along with the new-leg thing. I got the marriage annulled. So it was all sorted much quicker than I was expecting it to be. Alicia gets nothing from me, thank goodness.'

Bella sighed. 'Serves her right for what she did to you – to both of us. And I'm so glad there was no baby after all.'

'So am I. I'd have been trapped for life. Right, are we going to tell Basil and Mother now?'

'Yes, okay. But can we keep Levi a secret from your mother for a while longer? I don't feel confident enough to have the whole of Wavertree gossiping about me just yet. And she may let it slip accidentally.' She picked up the photographs of her son and made to put them away in her handbag, but Bobby stopped her.

'Can I keep one? I'll put it in my wallet so she won't see it.'

'Of course you can. Have this one. He's grinning like the Cheshire cat and he's showing his new teeth. I'll take you to see him when I next get a few days off. Maybe Martin or Basil will be able to drive us over to Wales.'

'I'd love that,' Bobby said, smiling, and then his face became suddenly serious. 'Bella, I need to tell you something quickly before we call Mother and Basil in.' He took a deep breath. 'Levi will be the only child we'll ever have. I was so badly burned round that area.' He indicated his nether regions with his hand. 'I'm okay in that I'm functioning like a normal man, so I'm sure I can be a proper husband to you, but I can't give you children. It's something the doctors told me when I was recovering. I, err, I know it's something we should maybe have talked about as well. But I was so made up that I could get down on one knee I wanted to propose right away. I guess I messed up the whole thing. But at least we can talk about this as time goes on.'

'Oh, Bobby, let's take things a day at a time,' Bella said, stroking his cheek. 'Just to have each other and Levi is enough. We've a war to win, troops to entertain, and we really should try and celebrate our engagement while we've still got a few hours before the ENSA troupe moves on to the next base camp. We could do that this afternoon. Fran and Edie are with their mams. Basil could go and get them while we tell your mother our news. The Kardomah will be open in the city, so let's go and have tea and cake and raise a mug or two.'

Bobby grinned and hugged her. 'Sounds like a great idea to me.'

*

Fenella sat by the window, looking out for the car that would bring her newly engaged son and future daughter-in-law back to the house. The excited young couple had been driven to the city by the ENSA leader, Basil, a very nice man of a similar age to herself. She'd spent an entertaining hour chatting with him while Robert and Bella had got themselves secretly engaged in her son's room this afternoon.

She felt so happy that Robert had proposed to Bella and that she'd accepted. And although she'd been initially delighted when he had married her god-daughter, Alicia, deep down she'd feared that their rushed marriage wouldn't work. And she'd been right – Alicia had turned her back on him. Bella would make him happy again and give him something to live for.

The lifestyle Basil talked about sounded like fun and Fenella needed some of that in her life. Since being widowed all she'd done was her work with the WI, tended to Bobby's needs and taken care of Margaret during her final weeks. She really missed Margaret, her calm and gentle nature and how she always kept the home and family so well organised. The place felt empty without her presence. She dreaded the day Bobby told her he was going back to work with ENSA full-time. The thought of being left on her own in Liverpool in this big house filled her with dread.

To think about the exciting life she'd led as a wing commander's wife during her time spent in Oxfordshire, with this emptiness she was feeling now, was painful. Most of her WI acquaintances had families and some had husbands at home still. They had full and satisfying lives and were often too busy to accept her invites to come over for coffee or tea. She sighed as the phone in the hallway rang out, and jumped up to answer it.

*

Bobby looked at his watch. 'What time do you need to set off on your travels, Basil?' he asked. They had just finished their lovely afternoon tea spread of sandwiches, cakes and scones, and Fran was pouring one last cuppa for her, Bella and Edie. The Kardomah café in the centre was a calm oasis in the middle of their war-torn city. The destruction had shocked the girls as they had been driven around, gazing open-mouthed at the piles of debris and partially demolished shops and houses. Their favourite stores, Lewis's and Blacklers, were badly damaged, schools and churches with windows missing; people, looking as cheerful as Liverpudlians always did, still going about their daily lives amidst the ruins and rubble as though it was normality.

The café was quiet this afternoon and the waitresses had been extra-attentive when they realised they had a newly engaged couple on the premises. The manager had been told and he'd apologised that they had no champagne, but said they could have unlimited tea or coffee on the house.

'As soon as the girls have finished this last drink we'll go,' Basil said. 'One last night in Warrington and then we're off up to Scotland with a quick stopover in Yorkshire on the way.'

'Wish I could come with you,' Bobby said. 'But I've several more appointments at the hospital to get my leg working at full capacity before I'm ready for that.'

'Hopefully by next year you'll be on top form, Bobby,' Basil said, clapping him on the shoulder. 'Right, come on, ladies. Let's be on the way back to Wavertree to drop Bobby off.' Basil got up to pay the bill and they all filed out to the car, Bella pushing Bobby's wheelchair.

'Oh no, why is Mother on the doorstep wringing her hands?' Bobby said as the car pulled onto Prince Alfred Road and stopped outside his home. 'She looks worried to death. What's wrong, Mum?' he called, opening the car door.

Fenella ran down the steps. 'I have an urgent message for Bella,' she gasped. 'Your mother called me on the telephone. She'd rung the base at Warrington and was told you had gone with Basil to see Bobby, so she called here. Call the farm right away, dear. Please hurry.'

Bella got out of the car, ran up the front path and bounded up the steps and into the house.

Bobby cursed his stupid injured leg and that he couldn't run after her. He hoped there was nothing wrong with her little boy. But why else would Bella's mother be ringing all over the place to contact her? Basil got his wheelchair out of the car boot and helped Bobby into it as Bella came out of the house, tears streaming down her cheeks. He grabbed her hand as she ran towards him and hugged him tightly.

'What's happened?' he asked. 'Bella, what is it?'

'Mam's had a telegram,' she sobbed. 'It came this afternoon. Oh, Bobby, my dad is m-mi-missing in action.'

Chapter Ten

North Wales, October 1943

'Bella, love, calm down, I've told you, there's no point in you coming here, chuck. There's nothing any of us can do until we hear something more, and I promise you as soon as I do I will track you down at whichever base camp you are staying at or heading off to, and tell you.'

Mary shook her head in Ruth's direction as she listened to her distraught eldest daughter, who was currently at RAF Grangemouth in Scotland, sobbing down the phone. This was so hard. Of course Bella wanted to come to Wales, but what was the point? There was not a thing anyone could do. Harry was missing in action in France and until there was more news from the authorities, they all had to just hope he'd eventually be found alive and well and meantime everyone just had to get on with their lives.

Hitler had recently lost out to the Russians after the Soviets had prepared a defence system that the German tanks had no chance against. The Russians had driven back the Germans, giving the rest of Europe some hope that all was not lost, but so far there was no let-up in their attacks on the UK.

It was all so worrying, Mary thought, and Bella was better off keeping herself busy and doing what she got paid to do, entertaining the troops. Her sitting around here moping about would make Molly more maudlin as well, and Mary had enough dealing with her own emotions at the moment. It might seem hard of her to want Bella to just keep working, but it was the only way she could cope herself and not fall apart. She had to stay strong for her girls.

She had Levi's needs to think about as well as helping Ruth with the twins. Georgie was now at school and Molly was doing more work around the farm, helping the land girls. She was still waiting to hear if she'd got a place with the dancing troupe. Basil had written to tell her that he might be able to take her on in time for Christmas. Mary didn't know how she felt about that; to have both her girls away at that time of year, as well as a missing husband, would be hard.

The day the telegram arrived, Bella had got engaged to Bobby. Her daughter didn't tell her when she'd spoken to her on the phone, as they were both too upset, but Bella had written that night and the letter had arrived two days later. In it she prayed her dad would be okay and would be home safe and sound to walk her down the aisle when the war was over. That line had broken Mary's heart.

But Bella had also written that she'd told Bobby about Levi and that he was okay about her having a son. Bella hadn't elaborated on that and Mary took it that he felt okay about it, but didn't want to take the baby on. She still had a plan in her head that she added a bit more to each day, about her adopting Levi and bringing him up as her own. She'd need to have the conversation with Bella at some point. But right now she had enough to worry about and as her grandson was doing fine and thriving, thanks to her care and attention, to Mary it made more sense for her to keep him than let Bella have him back.

*

Freddie Cagney groaned and rolled over on the pile of old rags he was trying to sleep on. He was cold, and fed up to the back teeth of the bloody hand-to-mouth existence that being expelled from the ENSA troupe had landed him in. He'd made his way back to his native Liverpool from North Wales and for months now had been sleeping rough in bombed-out houses. He'd been okay for a week or two as he'd been paid off, and he'd taken a room in a less-than-clean lodging house and had managed to get a bit of work in a few clubs, where he'd performed his magic act.

But most of the places he'd asked for work had looked him up and down and told him no thanks. He knew he stank to high heaven, as there was no bathroom where he was staying and the few bob he'd managed to earn had gone on the odd fish supper and bottles of whisky. He'd got into a fight last week and currently had a black eye and a missing bottom tooth, so knew he looked a right bloody mess. No one would want him hanging around their establishments in the state he was in.

Somewhere in Liverpool he still had a relative and he was hoping to find her. No use looking for his parents; they'd both died long ago. He and his younger brother Tommy had joined the army at the start of the war and Tommy had been immediately sent over to France. But he had been killed by a stray bullet within weeks. The shock of losing his brother had sent Freddie running scared and he'd gone AWOL before the army tried to pack him off to Europe too.

He'd always been good at magic tricks as a kid and young lad and had loved to see variety shows when he'd managed to sneak into the theatres. He'd altered his appearance by growing his hair, a beard and moustache, and had changed his name from George Carter to Freddie Cagney. After lying low for a while he'd managed to find work at a couple of clubs and had struck lucky. One Saturday night, a scout for ENSA happened to be in the club he was working in. He'd chatted with the man, Basil, who told him his regular magic act had recently retired and asked if Freddie would be interested in joining the show.

He'd jumped at the chance to get away and earn some money, and things had been fine for a while, until he was assigned to the tour the Bryant Sisters and that barmy Tina's Tappers lot were on. He'd been accused of improper misconduct and then fired. As far as he was concerned, those dancing girls had made a fuss over nothing. Half of them should have been grateful he'd made a pass at all; it was most likely the only one they'd ever get and it was just a bit of fun at the end of the day.

But one day he'd get his own back, especially on them bloody Bryant Sisters who thought they were a cut above everybody else. Bloody jumped-up match-factory workers is all they were, no better than he was. He'd found some old newspapers recently in one of the cellars he'd been dossing in and had been using them to keep him warm. In one of them he'd read about an accident in London where a man called Wing Commander Harrison had been killed when his plane was shot down by the Nazis.

The wing commander was from the Liverpool suburb of Wavertree. He'd left behind his widow, Fenella Harrison, and his son Robert, who had also been injured in the same crash. Freddie remembered that in the dim and distant past his younger sister Elsie had left home and had eventually married a Wing Commander Harrison. He was pretty sure he'd heard a rumour that she was living in a big house in Wavertree.

He also knew something that his sister had worked so hard to conceal all her newly acquired posh life – her big secret that she thought no one knew. *But more to the point, did her son know?* Well, there was only one way to find out. He'd have to try to track down Elsie. Wavertree would be a good start. If he could find the family home and she still lived there, then surely she wouldn't turn away her terrified brother who was on the run because their youngest brother had been shot dead. He smiled to himself. He was good at role-play. He should have gone into acting instead of the variety show circuit.

*

'Mam, Mam,' Molly yelled, dashing into the farmhouse kitchen with a snotty-nosed baby Levi on her hip, the twins Eric and Tony in her wake.

'She's gone down to the post office and bakers, Molly,' Ruth said. 'She went while you were out walking with the boys. What's the matter?' Ruth took hold of Levi, wiped his nose and took off his woollen bobble hat, running her fingers through his flattened curls.

'The telegram boy's on his way up the lane on his bike,' Molly gasped; her cheeks red from running. 'Oh God, Ruth, what if it's some bad news about me dad?' She burst into tears and Ruth set Levi down on the rug and took Molly in her arms as she sobbed.

'He could just as easily be bringing good news you know, 'she said softly as there was an urgent rap at the door. 'Sit down by the fire while I answer the door and then I'll make us a nice hot cuppa.'

Ruth took the telegram from the young man and thanked him, telling him that Mrs Rogers had just popped out but that she would be sure to let her see the telegram as soon as she came home.

He nodded solemnly and rode away, turning left up the lane rather than right to go down it. Ruth breathed a sigh of relief. At least he wouldn't pass Mary on the way back, which would mean she wouldn't panic and run when she saw him. She propped the envelope against the clock on the fireplace as Molly stared at it, tears pouring down her cheeks.

Ruth busied herself making a pot of tea and heating some milk for Levi and the little boys. She popped Levi in his high-chair and sat the boys at the table with a biscuit and a drink each. Mary had been a while but the walk down to the village would have done her some good, to stretch her legs as well as to see a few different faces to chat to.

The last few weeks had been hard for her friend, and Mary had spent ages just staring into space or holed up in the bedroom she shared with Molly and Levi, writing out her Mass Observation reports. She told Ruth that it helped her to focus on thinking that

Harry was safe wherever he was, and that if she concentrated on
writing about a future that she hoped to go back to it would all
come true. Ruth poured a mug of tea for Molly and herself. They
sat waiting patiently, the big clock on the fireplace ticking away
the minutes in the warm and cosy room.

'I can hear Mam talking to Bertie,' Molly said after a while.
She got to her feet and opened the door. 'Mam, come on inside,'
she called. Bertie had been in the top field with the sheep when
Molly had brought the children home, so he'd missed seeing the
telegram boy.

Mary looked round and waved at Molly. 'In a minute, chuck, I'm
just telling Bertie something funny that happened in the bakery.'

'Mam no, you have to come in now, please.'

'Why? Is something wrong?' Mary asked. 'Is Levi okay?' She
dashed indoors, almost knocking Molly flying in her haste.

'Mary, Levi's fine,' Ruth said. She pointed to the envelope by
the clock.

Mary's face drained and she dropped the bag of shopping on
the floor. 'Nooo!' she gasped as Ruth handed the telegram over
and gently pushed a shaking Mary by the shoulders onto a chair
next to the table. She quickly lifted the little boys down and sent
them outside to find Uncle Bertie for five minutes.

Mary's hands shook as she took out the sheet of paper headed
Post Office Telegram from the envelope. Her face crumpled and
Molly dropped to her knees by her mother's legs. 'A body has been
identified as Harry's,' Mary cried. 'He died from gunshot wounds.'
She got to her feet and handed the paper to Molly, her face ashen
and her eyes bright with unshed tears. 'Well at least we know now.'
She gave Molly a quick hug and hurried from the room without
another word, leaving Ruth and Molly staring after her.

Chapter Eleven

Wavertree, November 1943

Looking as clean and smelling as fresh as he'd been able to manage following a quick dip in the local swimming pool, Freddie Cagney swaggered up to the black gloss-painted front door of his sister's smart house on Prince Alfred Road. He lifted the brass knocker and rapped loudly. A cultured female voice called out, 'Just a moment,' and he rocked on his heels, waiting.

The door opened slightly and a slim, smartly dressed woman he would estimate to be in her early forties peered at him. *Was it Elsie?* It was hard to tell. But she had the same blonde hair and bright blue eyes that he remembered; the same colour as their brother Tommy's eyes. They'd been two peas in the same pod, their mam had always said.

'Yes,' the woman said. 'Can I help you?' Her voice held a note of disdain and that put Freddie's back up a bit. Here she was, his sister, no better than him, and she was looking at him like he was shit on her shoe. Well he was having none of that.

'Mrs Harrison, Mrs Fenella Harrison,' he began as she looked puzzled. 'Or should I say, Elsie Harrison, née Carter.' He smirked as a look of fear crossed her face and she drained of colour.

'Yes,' she whispered. 'But who are you?'

He laughed. 'Oh come on, queen, you're not telling me you don't recognise your big brother.'

Her eyes widened and her jaw dropped. 'George? George, is that really you?' she gasped.

'It is me, gel, but I calls meself Freddie these days. Well, are you going to invite me in then? I need some help, see, and I don't wish to discuss my business on the street.'

Fenella glanced up and down the road and then stood back and waved her hand for him to come indoors,

'Just making sure your nosy neighbours haven't clocked me, were you?' he said.

'Nothing of the sort.' Her tone was clipped as she led the way to the dining room.

He followed her, noting how elegant and smart the place was. There was money here all right. She'd certainly come up in the world since the tatty house they'd grown up in over Old Swan way, where most of the furniture had been chopped up and used for firewood and their mattresses had been old coal sacks stuffed with straw and tossed down onto the bare wooden floorboards; nothing as luxurious as a bed frame for them. No wonder Elsie had made her escape as soon as she could. He didn't blame her one bit for that.

'Please, take a seat,' she offered. 'Can I get you some refreshments? Tea?'

'That would be most welcome,' he said. 'I would have thought you employed staff, a big house like this.'

She nodded. 'I have a cook comes to the house three days a week, she's in the kitchen as we speak, but sadly I lost my housemaid to cancer several weeks ago. I haven't found anyone suitable to replace her yet. And I also have a driver-cum-handyman, Martin. He's taken my son Robert to the hospital for his physiotherapy appointment.' She swept out of the room leaving Freddie staring after her, scratching the top of his head.

So the son still lived at home. Mind you, from what he'd read in the newspaper report, he'd been badly injured and was lucky to have survived the accident. He must still need a fair bit of looking after.

His sister was back within minutes with a tray. The tea must have already been brewed, he thought, and she'd got a plate of scones on the tray that smelled freshly baked. His stomach rumbled. He was starving. He'd had nothing to eat since last night and that had been scraps he'd begged by knocking on doors.

'Help yourself to sugar,' Fenella said, handing him a mug and pushing the sugar bowl towards him. She gave him a small plate and indicated the scones. 'And there's jam and butter if you want it for your scone. So how did you find me and to what do I owe the pleasure of this visit, George or, err, Freddie, if you prefer it?'

'I do,' he said and took a large mouthful of the hot sweet tea. He told her how he'd found the accident report in a discarded newspaper and guessed that the wing commander was the man he'd heard she'd married. 'I'm so very sorry for your loss,' he said. 'It must have been really hard for you. I'm glad your boy survived though.'

'Thank you.' Fenella lowered her eyelashes and took a dainty sip of tea. 'I miss my husband very much, needless to say. But Robert is doing a lot better than we thought he would. He's determined to walk the best he can even with his false limb.' Her voice cracked.

Freddie nodded and reached out to gently pat her hand. 'I'm sorry, gel, but I'm afraid I have some more bad news for you. Our brother Tommy died in France almost four years ago now. He was caught up in Nazi gunfire. One of the first casualties over there. We were both in the army. I just couldn't handle things after that so at the first opportunity I'm afraid I went AWOL before they got the chance to ship me off to Europe. I changed my name and appearance.'

Fenella stared at him. Her hand flew to her mouth and her eyes filled. 'Not our Tommy?' she cried. 'Not my poor little brother.

I wasn't expecting that. So where did you go, what happened to you after you ran away?'

He told her about being a magician and working for ENSA but that he'd had an argument with the bosses and was told his act was no longer needed and he'd fallen on hard times. He didn't tell her why he'd lost his job though; he'd keep that to himself. 'I err, I just wondered if maybe you could help me out a bit until I get on my feet again.'

She chewed her lip and then half-smiled. 'Well, I do have a nice spare room in the attic I could let you stay in. You are my only living relative after all, apart from Robert. You'd need to help me clear the room out though. But there's a bed in there and a chest of drawers you could use. I may be able to help you job-wise as well. My son sometimes works with an ENSA troupe when he's feeling up to it. He sings with a group of young ladies known as the Bryant Sisters. I'm also acquainted with one of the scouts, Basil Jenkins is his name. Maybe I could put in a good word for you.'

Freddie tried to keep his face straight and not register any shock or recognition about the names she mentioned. He couldn't believe his ears. Just his bloody luck. The last thing he needed was for that lot to know he was here; certainly not for the minute anyway, until he'd got his feet properly under his sister's table.

'Right at this moment I'm not really up to doing my magic act,' he said. 'When I'm feeling better in my head and my mind's clearer maybe we can talk about it again. Also I need to keep a low profile as I don't want any of the authorities to come looking for me, so please don't let anyone know I'm here.'

Fenella frowned. 'Well what do I tell Robert? He will have to know, of course.'

Freddie screwed up his face as though thinking hard. 'What about telling him I'm a late acquaintance's husband who has been sent home from Europe because of injury? And I had no one to turn to as my home and family have been lost to the blitz. Or something along those lines anyway. Perhaps you and Robert could call me George – unless anyone in authority calls and then I'll be Freddie or make myself scarce; and it won't be for long, queen, just until I get on my feet again.'

Fenella sighed and then nodded. 'That sounds feasible I suppose, if not a bit confusing. We have few visitors anyway, so we'll leave it at that for now. Maybe as you say, you could go out when we know anyone is due to come to the house, or stay quietly upstairs in your room. Finish your snack and I'll show you the room and where the bathroom is.'

*

Early Monday morning Mary packed the last of her things into a suitcase and stepped back to cast an eye around the room, checking to make sure she'd left nothing behind. Since the telegram reporting the loss of her husband had arrived, all she'd wanted to do was go back home to Liverpool, to the house where her memories of Harry and Betty were still intact. She'd enjoyed herself here at the farm, but the urge to be back in Wavertree was overwhelming as the days went by. She glanced up as Molly popped her head round the door.

'Ruth's got the car loaded, Mam, ready to take us to the station. Bertie's sorted that wheel out on the trolley as well, so at least we don't have to carry Levi too far. Also we can pile our luggage on it on the platform.'

Mary smiled. 'I'll miss this place, but I feel it's time to go home now, chuck.'

Molly nodded. 'So will I, but I'm looking forward to seeing all my old pals again. I'll miss my little boys though.'

'Well you've got our Levi to teach now. He'll soon learn his colours and numbers. At least we'll be back for his first birthday and Christmas Day. It's a shame our Bella is down south right now. It would have been lovely to see her and for Levi to see her too.'

'What will we tell the neighbours when they ask where he's come from?' Molly asked. 'Bella doesn't want anyone to know he's hers until she's ready to say something.'

'I've got a plan,' Mary said. 'I'll tell you about it when we're on the train, if there's not too many people listening in. I've a lot to sort out when we get back, but we'll get Christmas and his birthday out of the way first and then I'll deal with it all in the New Year.'

'You all take care of each other,' Ruth said as they stood on the platform at Llandudno railway station. 'Don't forget to change at Crewe and then you can get the train direct to Liverpool from there. We'll miss you, but I understand the need to be in your own home at a time like this.'

'At least we've still got a home to go back to,' Mary said. 'We're one of the luckier families.'

'Indeed,' Ruth said. 'Now you must come back and spend a holiday with us, maybe when this blasted war is over. It can't go on for much longer, surely.'

'Thank you, Ruth. We'd love that, wouldn't we, Moll? You and Bertie enjoy your boys growing up. You'll have some fun with them, I'm sure.'

Ruth sighed. 'Well the little ones are fine so far, but we're a bit concerned about Georgie. He's the only one that really understands what's happened to his family. He gets a bit angry about it all at times, as you know. It'll take a while for him to come to terms with it. And at least he likes school and he's settled well there. He had a head start thanks to Molly. You should apply to become a teacher, Molly. You're very good with children.'

Molly smiled. 'I'd rather be in show business like our Bella. I'm hoping when I'm back in Liverpool I might stand a better chance of Basil asking me to join them.'

'You never know,' Ruth said. 'Good luck with everything. Whatever you decide to do.'

The train, whistling and belching steam from the big black engine, puffed towards them and they all hugged. A teary-eyed Mary and Molly boarded the train with a sleepy Levi and found a small compartment that was thankfully empty. Mary breathed a sigh of relief as she settled Levi down next to Molly and stowed their luggage to one side. Apart from a ticket inspector, they hopefully wouldn't be disturbed until they arrived at Crewe for their connecting train to Liverpool Lime Street. Mary sat down and looked out of the window to see Ruth standing close to the train and waving. As the train tooted loudly and belched its way slowly out of the station, Mary waved until she lost sight of Ruth.

*

As the taxi pulled up outside the terraced house on Victory Street, Ethel Hardy, who had been sitting in the front room looking out of the window, jumped to her feet and ran to open the front door. She watched as the driver unloaded cases and a trolley from the boot and then waved goodbye and drove away. Her friend Mary's face was a picture as she gazed up at her family home for the first time in ages.

'Hiya, Aunty Et,' Molly called dragging a suitcase to the door and dashing back to relieve her mam of the blanket-wrapped bundle that was Levi. She hurried him into the house and laid him down on the sofa, still asleep, and tucked the blanket around him. Mary pushed the trolley, loaded with the rest of their luggage, into the narrow hallway and breathed a sigh of relief.

'Come and sit down,' Ethel said, gazing at Levi with a fond expression on her face. 'Bless him. He just reminds me of my two when they were tiny. Now, the fires are lit in both rooms, so the house is lovely and warm, and I've plugged an electric fire in upstairs to take the chill off as well. My neighbour carried some coal and wood round and I've asked the coalman to drop you some nutty slack off tomorrow afternoon. There's enough wood left by the back door for tomorrow.'

'And everywhere looks so clean and fresh, and it smells really nice. Ethel, you are the best friend anybody could have, you really are.' Mary threw her arms round Ethel and gave her a big hug. 'Coming back to this warm welcome makes that awful, long journey all worthwhile.'

'Well, when you wrote to say you were coming home I couldn't let you walk into a freezing cold house with no food in. I'm just glad you made it back before blackout time,' Ethel said. 'Now I've made some spam sarnies and got a nice cake for your tea, so I'll go and put a light under the kettle and make a brew. I've got you some milk, bread and marge, to keep you going until you can go shopping tomorrow. It was hard to get much more when they'll only let me have my rations, but it's better than nothing. I've brought tea and a bit of sugar from home.'

'You are kind,' Mary said. 'I'll let you have some in return when I get my rations tomorrow.' She followed her into the back sitting room and kitchen, where Ethel lit the gas under the kettle. 'Is Ken next door still away?'

'As far as I know. A lot in this street are stopping with family out of the area.'

Mary nodded. 'Good, that means we'll have the carsey to ourselves.'

Ethel grinned. 'I borrowed some Lysol disinfectant from work and mixed it in a bucket of boiling water. It's fresh as a daisy in there now. I'd even let royalty use it if they was ever caught short on Victory Street.' She laughed at her own joke and Mary joined in.

'It's good to have you home, Mary,' Ethel said, spooning tea leaves into the brown earthenware pot that had been one of Mary's wedding presents many years ago. 'I've been proper lonely at times these last few years since my lads left home and you went away. Will you return to work, do you think?'

'That's something I need to think about,' Mary said. 'I'll have a bit of a war widow's pension to come, Bella sends enough to cover the rent and Molly's of working age so she'll be able to look for a job right away.' She lowered her voice. 'Although she's got these big ideas of following in Bella's footsteps and joining ENSA. But I've got the baby to think of and I'm not sure how I'll fare in getting a minder for him if I go back to work. Most women who would have done minding are working full-time or away stopping with relatives. I could do with the money of course, but I've a bit put by that should last me a couple of months.'

'I'm glad to hear that, chuck, it's been a hard few years for us all,' said Ethel, pouring a cuppa for them both.

'That it has. And now I'm back I can cash in Harry's penny policies with the insurers. That'll give me a few bob to help out. I've no funeral to pay for as I've been informed he's been buried out in France with many others.'

Mary's voice cracked and Ethel gently took her hand. She hiccupped and continued, 'But I'd like his name put on the family headstone in time. It's the least we can do for him. Maybe I can get a few late shifts somewhere, and Molly can see to Levi after work. I can manage until the New Year anyway, so we'll get Christmas over and done with and then sort something out.'

'You're doing a fine job with that boy, my love. He'll be a real credit to you. Harry would have adored him.' said Ethel.

Chapter Twelve

Oxfordshire, Christmas Eve 1943

Bella sat down on her bunk bed, opened the large envelope and pulled out a Christmas card from Bobby. She smiled at the satin robin redbreast sitting on a snow-covered log and her heart skipped a beat as she traced her fingers over his words in the accompanying letter.

My dearest Bella,

I hope this letter finds you well. Who would ever have thought that we are about to 'celebrate' our fifth Christmas at war? When will it ever end? I love you so much and I can't bear much more of us being apart like this but I'm sure you will have a better time than I. At least you have Fran and Edie for company and your singing to get you through. Sorry, I don't mean to complain or sound jealous and really I should just be thankful that I am still here to celebrate Christmas at all! But when I tell you that I will be spending mine with Mother, as usual, and a rather odd house guest that turned up out of the blue recently, I'm sure you will sympathise with me just a little bit.

Mother has told me that the man is the widowed husband of a late acquaintance, and had no one else to turn to when he'd arrived home from the war with an injury and found his home and family gone. He's okay and we get along all right but he drinks rather a lot. Well certainly more than I consider to be normal anyway. Mother excuses his behaviour and says he's had a lot of trauma and drinks to help him cope better.

My physiotherapy sessions are doing me the world of good and I spend as little time sitting in my wheelchair as possible. The new leg is quite comfortable now that the skin on my stump has toughened up and it doesn't rub as much as when I first started wearing it. I'm really missing you and I'm bored stiff doing nothing all day. I'm feeling raring to go on the bus again with you all, travelling up and down the country and singing with you. Let's hope it won't be too long now before I'm able to do that.

Please write back soon and tell me all your news. I hope to be able to speak to you at some point over the festive season. Please call me as and when you can. Enjoy your Christmas the best you can, my darling, and give my love to Fran and Edie and best wishes to Basil.

Take care of yourself. With all my love, Bobby. xxx

Bella smiled. The troupe were back up north again in early March, in Blackpool, so at least then she and Bobby would have time together, and he might even be ready to start touring with them a bit more often.

Fran and Edie also had cards and letters from their soldier boyfriends as well as their homes, and Bella was taken out of her reverie by Fran's raucous laughter from the other side of the Nissen hut they were sharing.

'What's so funny?' Bella asked as Fran rocked back and forth on her bed.

'Oh it's just a letter from me mam,' Fran said, tears running down her cheeks. 'Made me chuckle, that's all. Next door's dog ran off with Granny's teeth last week. And then he brought them back and dropped them at her feet and before Mam could stop her Granny only goes and puts them straight back into her bloody mouth without rinsing them first.'

'Ugh!' Bella said, grimacing, but, seeing the funny side, she joined in with Fran's laughter. 'She's always been one for taking her teeth in and out, your gran.'

'I know. She's a bugger with it. She'd put them down on the arm of her chair while she ate her dinner and the dog thought it was a treat. Bet he got a shock when he tried to crunch them. Surprised they were still in one piece after that.'

Edie shook her head and grinned. 'You can't leave anything lying around where our dog Rebel's concerned. He's a right scavenger. Sounds like they had a nice time at the old folks' Christmas party that the WI put on though – Fran, according to Mam, my granddad asked your gran to dance.'

'Oh, how nice is that,' Bella said. 'How sweet of him. My mam and Molly seem to have settled back in well on Victory Street and Levi has started walking around the furniture now. Molly's enclosed some photos. Look how much he's grown since the summer! This time last year I'd gone into labour. Oh I wish I was there to celebrate his birthday with them all. Molly said they are having a little party for him this afternoon, just her, Mam and Aunty Et.' Bella gazed at the chubby little boy staring at the camera. He was gorgeous; there was no doubt about that. Chunky little legs and arms, huge dark eyes and a big smile that lit up his face.

Fran and Edie looked at the photographs. 'Oh my God, Bella, look at his hair,' Edie cried. 'Those gorgeous curls are to die for. He's beautiful. Oh, I'd be on the next train home if he was mine.'

'There isn't one or I might be tempted,' Bella said wistfully. 'But we've got a job to do tonight right here, so that will keep me from getting too upset about it. We'll all celebrate his birthday next time we're up north.'

Fran nodded. 'And you'll get to spend time with Bobby again as well. Have you seen any signs of *her* yet? I'm surprised she's not come sniffing around. She must have seen we're here on the posters in the NAAFI.'

'She wasn't around when I nipped out to the shower block,' Bella said. 'But I've no doubt she'll be somewhere on site, more's the pity.'

The ENSA team were at the Brize Norton air force base in Oxfordshire; the same base where Bobby's ex-wife Alicia worked and where he had also been stationed. The same base where Bobby had told Bella that he loved her and wanted them to be together and also where Alicia, who had been hiding from them as they declared their love for each other, told him the lie that she was pregnant with his baby.

'Don't forget to flash your ring in her direction and name-drop Bobby in her hearing,' Fran said as Bella started to laugh. 'Right, let's go and get something to eat and then we'll leave ourselves plenty of time to get ready.'

Dressed in their smart khaki uniforms, hats sitting atop neatly styled waves, the Bryant Sisters, arms linked, crossed the grounds towards the NAAFI. Tina's Tappers, just in front of them, dressed in Christmas outfits of short red dresses edged with white fur, legs clad in shiny silk stockings and feet encased in red dancing shoes, were the subject of loud wolf whistles from a group of young airmen standing nearby. The two younger girls bringing up the rear giggled and shot the airmen coy looks. Bella shook her head at the giggling girls. 'Better keep an eye on that pair at the after-show party later. At least we've not got creepy Freddie around plying them with alcohol this year.'

'Thank God,' Fran said. 'Wonder what happened to him when he cleared off. Not had sight or sound of him on any theatre posters or variety show ads in newspapers. He seems to have vanished completely.'

'Yeah, bit odd that. I would have thought he'd still try and get variety work somewhere,' Bella said. 'But we've done the length and breadth since he was fired and his name hasn't cropped up anywhere, and I don't just mean with ENSA. We've stayed in theatre digs all over as well as the bases but not a sign or mention of him.'

'Maybe he's popped his clogs,' Edie said. 'Drunk himself to death, sort of thing. Wouldn't surprise me. Good riddance to him.'

'Hello, ladies. How lovely to see you again,' a dark-haired young woman in air force uniform greeted them.

'Oh, Marie,' Bella said, remembering the girl from last time they were at Brize Norton. 'Good to see you too.'

'I've been on manoeuvres for a couple of days,' Marie told them. 'I'm learning to fly and I was hoping to be back in time when I saw your names on the poster in the canteen earlier this week.'

'Wow, really? You're learning to fly?' Fran said. 'That's very brave of you.'

Marie smiled. 'Not really. To be honest I'm petrified when I'm up there. But we've lost so many of our men and when the opportunity came up I thought I'd ask if I could have lessons. It's a bit more taxing than telephony and postal duties of course, but I think I'm going to enjoy it once I'm fully trained.'

'Is, err, is Alicia still here?' Bella asked.

Marie nodded. 'Yes, but we're not really friends any more. I don't have a lot to do with her. After what she did to that poor Robert Harrison, she's lost a lot of friends round here. I often wonder how he is. The poor boy, he was so badly injured and losing his father like that as well, and then her being totally unsupportive and going with any man who crossed her path. Nobody wants to know her now, but she's only got herself to blame.'

Bella half-smiled. Sounded like Alicia wasn't having much fun lately. 'Can you keep a secret, Marie, for now anyway? Bobby is doing fine. He's recovered well. He's been fitted with a new limb and he's walking okay on it. He sings with us when we're near Liverpool in a show.' She held out her left hand. 'And err, he asked me to marry him earlier this year. We got engaged and as soon as this bloody war is over, we are getting married. You must come up to Liverpool for the wedding. We'll send you an invite.'

Marie's face lit up with a big smile. 'Congratulations, Bella! That is wonderful news. I most definitely will come up to Liverpool for your wedding. How exciting. I'm so glad Bobby is okay. I've often thought about him. Well that's one in the eye for Alicia. Did he manage to get a divorce?'

'Yes, well, he had the marriage annulled,' Bella said.

'Good for him. Oh I'm so happy for you and I can't wait to see the show later.'

*

Levi squealed with excitement and clapped his hands as they all sang 'Happy Birthday'. Molly helped him to blow out the candle on his cake. Ethel had made the fatless sponge, sandwiched together with jam, as a gift, and they'd managed to ice the top of it with some icing sugar she'd found at the back of her pantry cupboard. It had gone a bit solid but Mary bashed the box a few times with a rolling pin and it had reverted almost to its powdery form. Molly had some chocolate she'd saved from a slab she'd been given by a neighbour of Ruth's for helping with her little boy one afternoon, and they'd grated the chocolate and sprinkled the curls across the icing. A bit of light-blue crêpe paper fringing had finished the look.

'Well, considering we're on rations and watching our pennies I think we did him proud today,' Mary said, watching her little grandson ramming a slice of cake into his mouth and grinning with delight. 'Them sarnies and sausage rolls were lovely as well.'

'Molly's little buns were tasty,' Ethel said. 'We've had quite a spread. We make a good team. It's surprising what you can do with not a lot.'

'He can wear his new jumper you knitted him and the trousers I made, tomorrow when we come to you for our dinner,' Mary said to Ethel. 'Don't forget to take our potatoes, sprouts and carrots with you when you go, Et. They're in a bag in the kitchen.'

Ethel nodded. 'I'll peel them tonight to save me a job in the morning before the church service. The rabbit's all ready in the pantry. Not the same as a turkey but it's better than nowt. Now, have you made your mind up about coming to church tomorrow and bringing Levi with you? You've got to take him out at some point and face people, Mary.'

Molly raised an eyebrow in her mother's direction. On the train back from Wales Mam had confided to Molly her plans to adopt Levi as soon as she could. Pretending that he belonged to one of the land girls she'd worked alongside who couldn't keep him was the tale she'd decided to tell people.

But Molly had told her mother that wouldn't work as Bella would be sure to want her baby with her as soon as it was possible; her mam had argued that she knew best and she was sure Bella would be glad to leave his upbringing to her.

'I think tomorrow is a perfect time to take him to church, Mam,' she said pointedly. 'You can tell people whatever you want to tell them about where he came from, but you need to make sure you let Aunty Et and me know first if you decide to spin that pack of lies about him being a land girl's baby that you're looking after. Our Bella will be home one day and then the truth will be out. And anyway, didn't she say in her letter that she'd told already told Bobby? Because no doubt his mother will be at the church tomorrow and quite possibly Bobby will be there as well.'

Mary pursed her lips. 'Yes, Bella did tell Bobby, but she also said he would keep it to himself. He certainly won't have said anything to his mother. I've told both you and Ethel what my plans are and after the New Year I will make some enquiries with the children's department about adoption. I'm sure our Bella will think it's for the best as she and Bobby won't want to be tied down with a baby that neither of them really knows when they get married. You mark my words. They'll be glad to leave him with me. He's used to me, I do everything for him. Levi thinks I'm his mother.'

But you're not, Mam, Molly thought and chewed her lip. She didn't want to argue on Christmas Eve and spoil the nice time they'd enjoyed today. But her mam was setting herself up for a lot of heartache if she thought their Bella would give up all rights to her son just like that.

*

The finale of the Christmas show was just coming to an end when Bella spotted a blonde woman sneaking in by the doors right at the back of the room. Pretty certain it was Alicia come to have a nosy, Bella kept her eyes on the girl the best she could, but the stage lighting was blinding her. As the audience clapped and cheered, the main lights in the room were switched back on for a short time and Bella saw the girl slip into a seat at the end of a row. Fran nudged her while Basil was asking the audience if they all wanted more. She nodded in the direction of the blonde girl and Bella gave a slight nod to indicate she'd seen her.

Basil announced the final song of the night, which was, as always, 'We'll Meet Again.' The song was now such a favourite with all the forces lads that it couldn't be anything else. Bella stepped forward as the pianist played the opening bars, and fixed her mind on Bobby's face. At least they'd be meeting again in March, and she couldn't wait. She sang the first verse and then encouraged the enthusiastic audience to join in, which they did. They all got to their feet, clapping and cheering, all except the blonde girl. Bella smiled, took a bow and thanked everyone before filing offstage with the rest of the entertainers. There was no nicer feeling than to leave an audience wanting more and knowing they'd really enjoyed themselves.

After a quick visit to the ladies' the girls joined the after-party that was getting underway in the canteen. Glasses of something sparkling were placed in their hands.

'Champagne,' Fran gasped. 'Blimey.'

'Sort of champagne,' the airman who'd handed her the glass said with a grin. 'It's as near as damn it anyway.'

'It'll do me,' Fran said and clinked her glass with Bella's and Edie's. 'Cheers, girls, and happy first birthday to our gorgeous boy, Levi.'

Basil appeared by their side. 'Hear, hear,' he said. 'I hope he's had a good day.'

'Thank you, all of you. He'll have been spoiled rotten if I know my mam and Molly.' She stopped and turned as someone coughed by her shoulder. 'Oh, hello, Alicia,' she said and caught the eye of Marie, standing behind Alicia. Marie winked at her and nodded.

'I, err, I just wanted to say what a wonderful show you all put on tonight,' Alicia began.

'Oh, why, did you manage to see it all?' Fran said tartly. 'We only saw you sneak in right at the end.'

'I saw some of the first half,' Alicia said. 'Then I had to leave to do some work and I came back and caught the end.'

'Yeah right, if you say so.' Fran smiled sweetly, turned her back on the girl and began speaking to Basil.

'The lads I'm sat with had a fabulous time,' Marie said. 'We've really enjoyed ourselves tonight. Thank you so much.'

'It was our pleasure,' Bella said. 'Always a good audience down here at Brize Norton.' She turned to look at Alicia, who was clearing her throat, and raised an eyebrow.

'I err, I just wondered if you ever hear anything from Robert?' Alicia said, her cheeks turning pink as Fran spun back round and glared at her.

Bella dug Fran in the ribs before she had a chance to say anything. 'Yes, I do, actually,' she said. 'Every week in fact. He's doing very well. Making a great recovery from his injuries and walking well with his new limb.'

'Oh, really?' Alicia seemed shocked. 'I was under the impression he'd never walk again.'

'Well you didn't expect a fighter like Bobby to spend the rest of his life in a wheelchair, did you?' Fran said. 'You'll never believe this, but he gets up onstage and sings with us and he even got down on one knee to propose to Bella. Show her your ring, gel.'

Bella held out her left hand, her pretty diamond ring twinkling in the reflection from the lights overhead. Alicia's eyes were out on stalks as she stared at Bella's hand. Bella smiled as Marie put her hand over her mouth to stop herself laughing out loud.

'Well, I suppose congratulations are in order then.' Alicia almost choked on the words, her piping voice reaching its highest pitch. 'But of course you do realise that if I hadn't walked away from him, you wouldn't be engaged to him now.'

'But you did, you heartless bitch,' Fran cut in. 'You left Bobby when he most needed someone by his side. And don't think he wasn't aware of you dropping your knickers for all and sundry before his accident. Make no mistake, lady; he was ready to leave you anyway for the dirty trick you played on him at the beginning. We all know there was no bloody baby.'

Alicia stared open-mouthed at Fran and then, bursting into tears, she turned on her heel and ran.

'Crocodile tears,' Fran scoffed.

'Think you upset her, Fran,' Edie said with a hiccup, laughing. 'Oh dear, this sparkly stuff is very nice, but it's really strong and I feel quite tiddly.'

Bella laughed and gave both her friends a hug. 'What are you two like?'

'Well done, Fran,' Marie said, accepting a glass of the sparkly stuff. 'And here's to a very successful future for the Bryant Sisters, even after the war ends. And wishing you and Bobby all the very best, Bella, you both deserve nothing less.'

Chapter Thirteen

Wavertree, Christmas Day 1943

Molly tucked the red knitted blanket around Levi's chubby legs and pulled his bobble hat down over his ears. He gave her a big beaming smile and then tried to tug off his mittens with his teeth. 'No, no, don't do that,' she chastised him gently and tried to distract him with a knitted teddy bear. She pushed the trolley down the hallway towards the front door and looped their gas mask boxes over the handle. *What was taking Mam so long?* She'd been back and forth to the carsey nearly all flipping morning, well since breakfast anyway. They'd miss the start of the Christmas service at this rate if they didn't hurry up. The back door flew open and Molly breathed a sigh of relief as her mam dashed back inside, bringing a blast of icy cold air with her. 'Come on, Mam, get a move on,' she said as Mary washed her hands at the kitchen sink.

'Sorry, chuck. It's me nerves,' Mary said. 'Always sets me bladder off. If I'm honest, I'm dreading this. I hate telling lies. It's not really up to me to say anything to anyone. That's up to our Bella when she feels ready. She's going to have to bite the bullet when she's home in March. But what do I tell them all today?' She shook her head. 'I still think my way is best, but maybe for now we'll say we're minding him for a friend that's been taken poorly back in Wales.'

She fastened a woollen scarf over her hair and pulled on knitted gloves. 'Right, shall we make a move then? The pavements will be slippy with that bit of snow we had last night and we'll have to take our time or we'll be falling flat on our faces. Ethel should be there already, she'll have saved us a seat.'

'Let's just see what happens, eh, Mam?' Molly advised. 'Like we've said before, take a day at a time.'

*

Bobby stared out of the car window, watching people rushing by and going into church. Martin had parked close by so that they wouldn't have too far to walk, but Bobby wanted to wait until everyone was inside and then they could sneak in and sit at the back, hopefully unobserved. His mother was already inside doing her bit with the WI, handing out hymn books and preparing the after-service refreshments and what have you.

Bobby was determined to walk into church, although his wheelchair was in the boot just in case. His gaze fell on two ladies slipping and sliding along the snowy pavement, the younger one pushing a baby's trolley. As they drew close he recognised them and tapped on the window to gain their attention and the girl turned. Her brown eyes, so like Bella's, opened wide with recognition as he wound the window down and she smiled and stopped walking.

'It's Bobby, Mam, look,' she said, pointing to the car as Mary caught up behind her. 'Oh, Bobby, it's really good to see you again.'

Bobby opened the door and swung his legs round to the pavement. He grabbed the side of the door frame as Martin dashed round to steady him and helped him onto his feet. 'Thanks, Martin. Hello, Molly, Mrs Rogers, and it's lovely to see you again too. How are you both?'

'We're all fine,' Molly said, grinning broadly. 'And look at you now, walking again. Hey, I'm dead proud that I'm going to be your sister-in-law one day in the future as well. I hope our Bella asks me to be her bridesmaid.'

Bobby laughed and gave Molly a hug. 'I'm sure she will, and likewise I'm proud that I'm going to be your brother-in-law.'

'You're looking very well, Bobby,' Mary said. 'Very well indeed.'

'I feel it.' Bobby looked down at the baby, who was gazing up at him with big brown eyes. He put his hand to his mouth and swallowed hard. 'Hello, little one,' he said softly. 'I can't bend down to your level I'm afraid as I might not be able to get back up again.' He put his hand out and the baby grabbed it as though shaking hands. 'Nice to meet you, Levi,' he said with a smile as Levi squealed and grinned at him.

He turned to Mary. 'What a lovely child. His photos don't do him justice.' He showed them the one Bella had given him that he always carried in his wallet. 'I'm going to sit at the back of the church now everyone seems to have gone inside. I'm trying to avoid a fuss. You know what it's like round here. This is the first time I've been to church; well, since the accident anyway. I'm doing it to please Mother more than anything.'

'We're aiming for the back row as well,' Molly told him. 'Mam's friend is saving us seats.'

'Then shall we all sit together and I can get to know this young man a bit better? Might as well start how we mean to go on, eh, Levi? Then I can write and tell your mammy that we've met and made friends.' He smiled at Levi. 'And now you are all home, I hope we won't be strangers,' he said to Mary and Molly.

As the party, including Martin, filed into church and left Levi's trolley in the porch, Molly carrying him on her hip, Ethel waved them over to the back-row pew that she'd saved. She shuffled along to the end and Mary sat next to her. Martin sat next to Mary and then Molly with Levi on her knee, and Bobby squeezed in at the end as it was easier for him to get in and out. Heads turned as they all settled down and there were a few nods in their direction, which they responded to, but the pew directly in front of them was thankfully empty.

As the vicar began the service Levi squealed loudly. Molly rooted in her handbag and pulled out half a Farley's Rusk and handed it to him. She whipped off his bobble hat and ran her fingers through his curls. Bobby smiled at her and pulled a clean white handkerchief from his jacket pocket.

He handed it to Molly. 'Just in case,' he whispered, indicating Levi's sticky chin as he chomped loudly and blew raspberries, splattering Bobby's jacket with wet crumbs.

'Oh, God,' Molly said, trying not to laugh and rubbing at the marks. 'Wait until they start singing hymns. He likes music. He loves it when we have the wireless on. He'll be trying to join in.'

'He's going to be a singer like his mammy then,' Bobby said. 'He's a beautiful child. I can see Bella in his eyes and the way he puts his head to one side as though he's studying me. She does that too.'

'Shhh,' Molly warned in a whisper. 'Nobody knows he's Bella's except for us and me Aunty Et down there'.

Bobby raised an eyebrow and nodded. 'I understand, but we can't keep him a secret for long,' he said quietly. 'Bella knows I want to take him on and bring him up as my own child. I believe his father has already given permission for her to do what she feels is right for him.'

Molly looked down the pew at her mam, who was staring at the vicar but seemed miles away judging by the look on her face. Molly sighed. Mam's thoughts were probably with Dad as the vicar was blessing the families of all the lost soldiers, sailors and airmen who would never be coming back home. She felt a tear slide down her cheek and Bobby squeezed her hand tightly.

'I know,' he whispered, his eyes bright with unshed tears too. 'I understand. We'll never forget our dads.'

*

As the service came to an end Mary got to her feet. 'Molly, you take him home now and I'll go with Ethel for refreshments into the church hall so I can have a bit of a chat with people.' She raised a meaningful eyebrow as Molly opened her mouth to protest. 'Remember, we agreed this last night,' she finished in a whisper.

'Did we?' Molly shrugged and lifted Levi up onto her hip.

'I'll take Molly and the little fella home,' Martin offered. 'Bobby doesn't want to hang around, so it's no skin off my nose not to either.'

'Thank you, Martin. That's very kind of you,' Mary said as Bobby and Molly got ready to leave. 'I'll see you back at the house and then we'll walk round to Ethel's later,' she said to Molly.

'Okay, Mam. See you later,' Molly said, swinging Levi up on to her hip again as he began to wriggle to get down.

Mary watched as Molly followed Bobby out of the church. She knew Molly would have liked to stay and chat with her pals, but she could always catch up with them another time and it saved having to answer any awkward questions about Levi and where he'd come from. She turned as they left her view, and saw his mother right near the front talking animatedly to members of the congregation. No doubt she'd be collared by Fenella in the church hall, but best get it all over with and then she could go home and enjoy the rest of her day at Ethel's house.

Mary followed Ethel out to the nearby church hall. She glanced across the graveyard as they walked. Betty's grave looked nice and tidy after her quick visit early yesterday morning with some greenery and stems of holly that were heavy with berries. She'd found a length of red ribbon in the sideboard drawer that had once adorned her youngest daughter's hair, and fastened it round the stems with a bit of tinsel. Betty would have loved that, she thought.

'Looks lovely,' Ethel said, linking her arm through Mary's. 'Betty always liked a bit of sparkle.'

Mary smiled. 'She did. Oh dear, Et, who'd have thought that my family of five would be reduced to just me and Molly right now.'

'And the little fella,' Ethel reminded her. 'Don't forget him.'

'Of course,' Mary said. 'But looking at how nice Bobby was with Levi this morning, I can't see how I'll ever get permission from Bella and him to adopt him, can you?'

Ethel shook her head. 'My honest opinion, Mary? No, I really can't. As soon as those two are married they'll be making a home of their own and that will include the baby.'

Mary sighed as they walked into the warm and welcoming, brightly lit front porch of the church hall. 'I suppose you are right.'

After accepting mugs of tea and a piece of shortbread each from the WI ladies, who had set up tables and tea urns inside the hall, Mary and Ethel moved towards the side of the room and sat down at a table to enjoy their refreshments. Within seconds they were joined by two other women, both Victory Street neighbours of Mary's.

'It's good to see you back home, Mary,' one of the women said. 'Very sorry to hear about your Harry, love.'

'Thank you, Maude. I hope your boys are okay.'

'As far as we know,' Maude said. 'We get the odd letter, but you know what lads are like for keeping in touch. I have to keep telling meself that no news is good news.'

'Same with me,' Ethel said. 'I got Christmas cards off the pair of them though, which is a miracle in itself.'

'I'm glad mine are girls,' the other woman said. 'They just go to work at the munitions factory and then come home. Mind you, when they go to those forces' dances at the weekend, I worry myself to death wondering what those Yanks are getting up to. I've warned my girls, don't you go bringing any trouble to the door or your dad will tan your hides.'

'Oh your two are good girls, Florrie. Just like Mary's two are. They know right from wrong, I'm sure.'

Mary could feel her cheeks heating, and spluttered on her cup of tea. Ethel patted her on the back and got to her feet.

'Think we should make our way home now, Mary. I need to get that rabbit in the oven if we want to eat today. Do excuse us, ladies. Have a lovely day, well the best you can anyway. We'll see you again soon.'

'Yes, all the best to you two as well,' Florrie said and Maude nodded her agreement.

'Thanks for that,' Mary said to Ethel as they neared the doors. She'd just put her hand on the doorknob when a voice rang out, calling her name. She turned to see Fenella Harrison bearing down on her and groaned inwardly.

'Mary, my dear, it's so good to see you again,' Fenella gushed. 'I hope you are well and settled back into your own home. I thought I spotted you in church, sitting on the same pew as Robert and my driver.'

'Err, yes, nice to see you again too and yes, we were,' Mary said. 'We arrived late and your Bobby and Martin were just coming in, so we all sat together.'

'Was that your daughter Molly with the baby on her knee? I saw Robert talking to her.'

'Yes, it was Molly,' Mary said, her mind going into overdrive for a few seconds. 'We are looking after the little boy for a friend who's ill.' There, she'd said it. It was a lie but it would do for now until things got sorted out.

'Oh, well that's very kind of you, I'm sure your friend appreciates it. I was hoping to catch you here today and if not, I would have sent an invite round with Martin. I was wondering if you and Molly would like to come for Boxing Day tea tomorrow afternoon? About four o'clock if that's okay with you. And I thought it would be lovely to have a little celebratory sherry to toast Robert and Bella's engagement.'

Mary felt her jaw dropping and took a deep breath. She hadn't been expecting that. 'Oh, now that would be very nice indeed,' she said. 'Thank you for the invite. It's very kind of you.' And besides, she thought, it would help them if they ate at Fenella's as they could save the bit of corned beef she'd put aside for tomorrow's meal for the day after Boxing Day instead. 'I hope you don't mind, but I will have to bring the baby with me, of course.'

Fenella smiled. 'That's fine. It will be nice to have a little one toddling around. And also it will be lovely for Bobby to have some young company with Molly. We've a good set of board games that never gets used these days. I'll get him to dig it out.'

'Thank you, Fenella; we'll look forward to it.'

'Shall I send my driver to pick you up? The weather is really cold lately and we don't want the little one catching a chill.'

'A lift will be lovely,' Mary said. 'We'll be ready for ten to four then. I'll bring the high-chair. Martin can put it in the car boot. The little one, he's at that messy stage when eating.'

Fenella laughed. 'I remember it well with Robert. See you tomorrow then.' She dashed away, leaving Mary and Ethel staring after her.

'Has she mellowed a bit?' Ethel said. 'She doesn't seem half as snooty as she used to be.'

'Hmm,' Mary mused. 'Seems that way. I'll not hold me breath though. We shall see.'

Feeling well-fed, and as contented as she could be with half of her family no longer with them and her eldest working away, Mary relaxed on the sofa in her best sitting room in front of a blazing fire and counted her blessings. The curtains were closed against the cold dark night and the little pine tree she and Molly had decorated stood proudly on a small table in front of the window, the glass baubles twinkling as light from the fire reflected in them.

There were many more much worse off than she was. Some had no roof over their heads or food in their bellies, had no idea where various family members were and their only possessions were the clothes they stood up in. She'd poured herself a small glass of sherry that had been in the sideboard cupboard since last year and lifted the glass in a toast to her late husband Harry and her youngest daughter Betty.

Tears streamed down her cheeks and she didn't try to bat them away. There was no point; they'd only be replaced by more. She put her glass down next to the framed wedding photo of her and Harry on the mantelpiece and gave the fire a final poke. Not worth putting any more nutty slack on as she was going to bed in a few minutes. Molly and Levi were already tucked up, and flat out.

They'd had a lovely afternoon at Ethel's and the Christmas dinner she'd made them had been a real treat. The rabbit had been tasty and cooked to perfection and the roast potatoes crispy and golden, just how Mary liked them. Levi had tucked in with both hands in the dish, his patience with a small fork and spoon wearing thin as he couldn't keep the food from falling off. He was getting to the stage where he wanted to feed himself, but it wasn't always possible.

Molly had done her best to shovel as much down him as she could before he dived in with both hands. They'd listened to the king's speech at three o'clock and then exchanged a few presents, mainly things the three of them had made as both households had little spare money for gifts. Ethel was a good knitter and would even unpick clothes and wash and re-wind the wool to make new garments.

Molly's bright-pink hat, scarf and gloves from Ethel were just the job; they set off her dark-brown hair colour and contrasted nicely with her bottle-green woollen coat. Well, the coat had been bought at Paddy's Market a few years ago for Bella, but she'd hardly worn it. Ethel had made two embroidered cushion covers for Mary and they sat in pride of place on the sofa in the front room, the best room, which was only used for special occasions.

Maybe see how tomorrow goes at Fenella's and she might feel like inviting Fenella and Bobby round for a cuppa and a slice of cake in a week or two's time. She'd use the best room then. After all, when Bella and Bobby got wed, they'd all be related by marriage, whether Fenella liked it or not.

Chapter Fourteen

RAF Brize Norton, Oxfordshire, Christmas Day 1943

Bella put down the phone after speaking to Bobby. It was quite late in the day to be calling, but she'd promised to ring him as soon as she could get a turn on the public phone that everyone wanted to use to wish their families at home a Merry Christmas.

It had been a busy day and the ENSA troupe had all been invited to attend a morning service with the air force members at the local church, followed by a sumptuous Christmas dinner in the NAAFI. The afternoon had been a lazy one, with card games and charades and the luxury of shared boxes of chocolates and Christmas cake.

A gramophone had been set up on last night's makeshift stage and records had been played, with everyone joining in singing Christmas carols and festive songs. Some had got up to dance and Bella, Fran and Edie had been partnered around the floor several times. When news of Bella and Bobby's engagement broke, she was inundated with congratulations, the young airmen Bobby had been friends with seeming genuinely happy for them both.

Bella had passed on the good wishes during her phone call and she'd also told him about Alicia's little performance last night. He'd laughed and told her to take no notice of the girl. As far as he was concerned she no longer existed. Then he told her that he'd met her mam and Molly and Levi in church.

Bella had held her breath for a second or two. 'How was he?' she asked, choking on her words. 'And Mam and Molly, of course.'

'Well they're both fine as far as I could tell. But Levi is wonderful, Bella. He smiles all the time and he's so happy and noisy and likes to join in with the singing. I love him already and can't wait to be a proper father to him.'

Bella laughed and felt overwhelmed with relief, as well as love, for her little boy and her future husband. 'So, he's a noisy one, eh? That should be fun. Did Mam seem to be coping okay? I mean, with losing Dad I wasn't sure if she'd be all right, but she insisted she was and you don't argue with Mam.'

'She seemed a bit overwhelmed but the church service was mainly about our lost loved ones and that might have knocked her off kilter as it did me. But Molly is wonderful with Levi. She's a great aunty. Oh, and she wants to know if she can be your bridesmaid.'

Bella smiled. 'Of course she can. I would have asked her anyway.'

'My mother has asked them all to tea here tomorrow afternoon.'

Bella's heart almost stopped when he told her that bit of unexpected news. 'Levi as well? Does your mother know about him then?'

'Well, when we came home she said she'd invited your mam and Molly and that they would be bringing a baby they'd brought to church. But then Mum said she'd been told by your mam that he's the baby of a friend who is poorly and they are looking after him. So shall we stick to that story for now? It's up to you, Bella. There really is no need to be ashamed of Levi, you know. I'm so very proud that he'll be mine to take care of as soon as we're married.'

'Oh, Bobby,' she said, tears springing to her eyes. 'Is it any wonder I love you? I'm not ashamed of Levi. It's me I'm ashamed of for getting myself into such a mess.' She took a deep breath.

'I'm going to have to go now. People are starting to form a queue again for the phone.'

'Okay, well look, why don't you try and call again tomorrow, and you can speak to your family as well? That would be a lovely surprise for them.'

'I'll do my best. We're still here tomorrow and putting on a small show, but I'll try and use the phone before we start. I love you. Take care.'

'I love you too, Bella,' Bobby finished.

Bella made her way back to the Nissen hut, where Edie and Fran were already in bed reading and eating chocolates. Marie had brought them a few *Woman's Weekly* and *Woman's Own* magazines over to read as well as the box of chocolates, an unexpected gift from several of the airmen she was friendly with, who'd asked her to pass them on to the Bryant Sisters.

'Have you got a spare magazine for me?' Bella asked, stripping off her clothes and pulling on a nightdress. She put on her dressing gown and picked up her toiletry bag.

'Here you go. How was Bobby?' Fran asked.

'He's fine. He actually met Levi this morning and he's really taken with him. I'm just popping to the shower block, will tell you all when I get back. Save me a couple of those chocolates as well, you pair of gannets.' She dashed out of the hut, smiling at their shocked faces.

*

Freddie Cagney sat by the window in the attic bedroom of his sister's house and watched as her driver pulled up outside. The driver got out and helped a woman and young girl, who was carrying a wriggling kid in her arms, out of the car onto the pavement and then he walked to the back of the car, opened the boot and lifted out some sort of contraption and carried it up the front steps as the family followed him.

His sister had told him she and Bobby were expecting visitors for tea and would he mind either going out or staying quietly in his room until they left. She was always on edge in case the authorities came calling for him. He doubted it would ever happen now after all this time, and anyway, no one knew where he was, but it didn't stop her from being twitchy at times.

He knew she'd prefer him gone as soon as possible but he played on not feeling quite right in his head to be looking for a job again just yet. And as he was feeling definitely unsociable, he had no problems with staying in his room rather than wandering around the freezing cold streets of Liverpool for hours on end. Fenella had wrapped a parcel of food for him and brought it upstairs a few minutes ago so he wouldn't starve; turkey sarnies and sausage rolls plus a slice of cake would do him nicely, and she'd made him a flask of coffee to wash it all down.

He had a half-bottle of whisky to finish and a newspaper to read, so he'd be fine. The only problem as far as he could see would be if he needed a pee. The sound of the toilet flushing would alert them to there being someone else in the house. Mind you, he could leave it and flush after, when he heard them leaving. His sister said the visitors would use the downstairs shower room that had been converted for Robert after his accident.

He wondered who the visitors could be. They didn't look like any of the well-heeled people he imagined Fenella would have mixed with in the past. The woman looked quite dowdy, with her headscarf tied under her chin and heavy zipped-up boots on her feet. But the girl looked okay. Long dark hair that she flicked over her shoulders to stop the kiddie from pulling on it. Hard to see her features from up here in the half-light though, as it was getting dark and the street lights were all out due to the blackout. Although Hitler's lot seemed to be taking a couple of nights off for Christmas. But he still wouldn't trust the bugger.

He could hear voices in the hallway, greeting each other, Bobby's and then the younger girl's. Maybe she was Bobby's girlfriend. He'd told Freddie he was recently engaged but not much else. Just that his fiancée worked away. Perhaps she was home for the holidays. But whose was the kid? Not hers and his nephew's, surely. He hadn't seen the little one's face, just a red hat bobbing around as the kid wriggled.

Ah well, it was nowt to do with him anyway. Let them all get on with things. He swung his legs up on the bed and picked up his newspaper.

*

'Can I do anything to help in here?' Mary asked, following Fenella into the large, well-equipped kitchen that her own tiny scullery would fit into three times over. 'I bet you're missing Margaret, especially at this time of the year.'

'Oh, Mary, you've no idea,' Fenella said, pulling what Mary described to Molly later as her *woe is me* face. 'I miss her dreadfully. I mean, this is such a big house to look after and I know we have Cook here for a few days a week, and Martin for maintenance and the garden, but keeping on top of the cleaning and the laundry, well I have to admit I'm struggling. I've advertised for a new housekeeper but I've had no luck so far. I don't suppose you know of anyone looking for a full-time position, do you? Or even part-time would help me greatly.'

Mary shook her head. 'Not at the moment I don't, but I'll keep my ears open. Normally I'd be looking for work myself now I'm back in Liverpool, but I've got the baby to see to.'

'Well, how long do you think you'll need to look after him for? Is his mother seriously ill and hasn't she got a family that will take care of him? He's a beautiful child though, those gorgeous eyes.'

'They look right into your soul, don't they?' Mary said. 'And no, there is no one else his mother can rely on.'

'What about his father's family, are they in this country?'

'Not as far as I know,' Mary answered carefully. 'His mother got herself in a bit of a tangle with a US pilot.'

'Well let's hope she gets well soon,' Fenella said. 'I'm sure she must be missing such an entertaining little fellow. I know I would be.'

Mary smiled, knowing that Fenella was right. Bella would be missing Levi a lot. 'I'm sure she is.'

'Right, shall we take the trays Cook prepared for us through to the dining table and then we can eat buffet-style rather than sit down formally,' Fenella suggested.

'Good idea,' Mary said. 'Then I'll come back through for the teapot.'

Levi sat as good as gold in his white painted high-chair, a contribution from one of Ethel's neighbours, a colourful bib fastened under his chin, and ate his sandwiches and a sausage roll. Molly had cut everything into bite-sized pieces for him and now he had a mouthful of teeth he munched happily on everything that was put in front of him. He smiled at everyone in turn, especially Bobby and Molly. He pointed at the large Christmas tree that stood to one side of the marble fireplace in an alcove, and chuckled.

'He loves the lights,' Molly said, 'and he's into tinsel too, so we'd better watch him when he's finished eating or he'll be yanking on that tree and pulling it over.'

'It's a beautiful tree,' Mary said. 'In fact the whole room looks lovely and festive with all the greenery and red berries you've got swagged around, and it smells so nice.'

Fenella smiled. 'The greenery is thanks to Martin. He gathered bits and pieces from The Mystery Park and Robert and I fastened it on to the red ribbons and festooned it around the room. There's nothing nicer than the smell of fresh pine.'

Levi banged on the high-chair tray with his spoon and said something that sounded like 'All gone.'

'What an absolute delight he is,' Fenella gushed. 'And he's got such a good appetite. Not a crumb left in that dish. Now when I told Cook we had a young man coming for tea she made a special jelly. It's a red one just like Robert used to love when he was Levi's age.' She smiled. 'We don't have any ice cream to put with it, but Cook left some cold custard in the fridge in case he'd like some of that with the jelly.'

'Bobby or Levi?' Molly said with a giggle.

Bobby laughed and Levi joined in with a squeal for good measure. 'Both of us I think,' Bobby replied. 'Why not, eh, Levi? Let's live dangerously.'

'Shall I dish up?' Mary said. 'And, Molly, you'll have to feed it to him, love. We don't want jelly all over this nice carpet or splashed up the curtains. You know how handy he is with a full spoon.'

Fenella laughed. 'Indeed, Molly, if you wouldn't mind. Mary, there's a sherry trifle next to the jelly for us more mature people. Bobby will have what Levi's having,' she teased. 'There are some glass dishes in the wall cupboard next to the sink.'

Mary smiled to herself as she lifted the very posh cut-glass dishes down. It was nice to see Fenella relaxed and enjoying herself. Maybe now she didn't have to put on so many airs and graces, entertaining the people of money that were her late husband's friends and acquaintances, she was reverting to being someone a bit more fitting for the background she'd originally come from. Them both being widowed was a great leveller, Mary thought.

And you couldn't fault the way she'd brought up Bobby. He was the nicest young man Mary felt she'd ever have the pleasure to meet. Her Bella could do a lot worse, she thought, as she filled the dishes and placed them on another tray. *How many trays did one family need?* There were three on the dining table already. She had one single tray at home and that was it. Mind you, what she wouldn't give for a kitchen like this, never mind the room for half a dozen trays at least. She rooted around until she found a cutlery drawer and put some spoons on the tray, picked it up and carried it through to the dining room.

Molly was playing peek-a-boo behind her hands and Levi was chuckling with delight. Fenella was sitting beside the high-chair twiddling his curls around her fingers, looking totally besotted. Bobby was over by the piano rooting through a pile of sheet music that was sitting on top of the highly polished surface. Mary was struck by the perfect family scenario, thinking that if you swapped Molly for Bella, it was like she was looking at the future. It all seemed perfect, for now anyway. Bobby lifted the piano lid and ran his hands smoothly over the ivory keys.

'We're going to have a little sing-song, Mam,' Molly announced. 'When we've had our desserts that is.'

That made Mary smile. A bit of Fenella was rubbing off on her daughter. They always said puddings at home. *Desserts indeed!* And then a sudden thought struck her. Molly looked quite at home here. Would she be of any use as a housekeeper for Fenella and Bobby? It was handy to walk to, being just a few streets away, no tram fares, and she would be well looked after under this roof as well as fed while on duty. It was worth thinking about.

She needed a proper job, never mind dancing for a living. Molly was bright and Mary would love her to train for something for the future. But their current finances wouldn't allow for that. Factory or domestic work was the best Molly could hope for until this war was over. And then like as not she'd meet a lad and settle down with a family of her own. She'd have a talk with her when they got home, see what she thought.

Molly gave Levi his jelly and custard and he smacked his lips at each mouthful, pushing his fingers into his mouth and saying, 'Ummm, ummm.' Mary laughed and wiped his face and hands and then lifted him down. The last thing Fenella needed on her light-coloured damask sofas was red sticky finger-marks. Molly cleared the table and Mary whispered to her as she carried the empty teapot into the kitchen, 'Wash the dishes for Fenella, love, and make a good job of it. Leave the kitchen nice and tidy. I'll tell you why when we get home.'

Back in the dining room Mary quickly picked up her grandson and dashed to the downstairs shower room to change his damp nappy. She let him walk back up the hall, holding onto one of her fingers. He was almost ready to go but needed that last bit of confidence. Bobby was sitting at the piano stool, tinkling the ivories as he put it. Molly came back into the room and they all relaxed onto comfortable chairs and the sofa, except for Levi, who went to stand beside Bobby, his eyes wide with curiosity, his thumb in his mouth. As Bobby began to play a tune Levi grabbed hold of one of the piano stool legs and started to jig up and down.

'He loves to dance,' Molly said. 'And sing, in his own style of course.'

They all joined in with 'Jingle Bells' and 'White Christmas' and then Bobby played 'Winter Wonderland' and Mary felt the tears running down her cheeks. Harry's favourite Christmas song. He'd always join in and sing along when he heard it on the wireless and Bella would often sing along with him. Fenella, sitting next to her, reached out and squeezed her hand.

'Memories?' she said softly. 'This Christmas is going to be the hardest year for us all. It will get easier as time goes by. We've got some better times to look forward to. Robert and Bella's wedding to plan for. We'll get there, Mary.' As she spoke Levi let go of the piano stool and wobbled across the room towards them on his own, grabbing Mary's knee as he drew close to her.

'Oh my God, Mam, look, he's walking.' Molly laughed at her nephew's look of surprise. He turned to look at her and giggled, then let go of Mary's knee and wobbled back towards Bobby, who scooped him up and tickled him.

'Well done, Levi. Well done.' Bobby turned him round to face the piano keys and showed him how to hit them gently to produce a noise. He loved it and moved his hands up and down, giggling to himself. 'See, this boy is going to be an all-round entertainer. He can dance, sing and play the piano. Multi-talented, that's what he is.'

They all clapped Levi's efforts and then Fenella got to her feet. 'Is that the telephone I can hear ringing?'

Molly cocked her head to one side. 'Yes, it is.'

Fenella rushed to answer it. 'Bobby, it's for you,' she called. 'A lady by the name of Marie calling from Brize Norton.'

'Oh, on my way.' Bobby struggled to stand up and Molly gave him a hand.

'Thank you, Molly. I'm fine once I'm upright,' he said and went to the hall and took the phone from his mother's hand. Fenella went back into the dining room and discreetly closed the door.

'Marie, hello, how are you? How lovely of you to call.'

'Hi Bobby, nice to hear your voice and I'm glad to hear that you're doing well. I'm in the telephone exchange room and I've got Bella here with me. I thought it would be nice if she had a bit of privacy rather than be standing in the corridor talking to you with a crowd queuing behind her. Here she is now and all being well I'll see you at your wedding.'

Bobby laughed as Bella's voice came down the line. 'How kind is Marie to let me do this?' she said. 'Have you had a lovely day with my family?'

'We have all enjoyed ourselves,' he replied. 'And your little star has just walked across the dining room, twice, on his own. He's also been sitting on my knee playing the piano and dancing and singing. I don't think there's any doubt about his future being on the stage, do you?'

'He walked? On his own? Oh, Bobby, I wish I was there with you all. I'm missing all his first things, his first tooth and words and now his first steps. I want to see you so badly too, it hurts.'

'It hurts me too, my darling,' Bobby said. 'But at least now I've got a piece of you here in Liverpool and I can see him every day if your mam will let me. He'll be really used to me by the time we get married. I already love him so much, Bella.'

'Bobby, I'm bawling my eyes out here,' she said, a sob in her voice. 'I can't wait for March. Has Mam told your mam I'm Levi's mother yet?'

'Not yet, but I have a feeling it won't be too long now. She has to do it in her own time, Bella, and she will. I'll get your mam and Molly now and close the door so they can talk privately to you. I'll come back and say goodbye when they've finished.'

*

Freddie had just crept out of the bathroom when the phone rang two flights of stairs down in the hallway. He sat down on the top stair and cocked his ear as his sister answered, and then he heard her calling out to Bobby. Then he heard Bella's name being mentioned and strained to listen the best he could. He nodded thoughtfully to himself as Bobby's conversation came to an end and he heard the women visitors speaking.

After they had finished, Bobby came back to the phone and told her he was looking forward to seeing her in March when they were all back up this way. By piecing it all together, he deduced that Bella was THE Bella from the Bryant Sisters.

So she was the girl Fenella told him Bobby sang with occasionally and was also engaged to; the visitors downstairs were her mam and sister and the kid was also hers, but Bobby's mother didn't know that yet. From what his nephew had said about getting the baby used to being with him for when they got married, Bobby wasn't the father. That would have been impossible anyway as his nephew would have been married to his first wife at that time, just before his accident.

Now if the kid had just started walking that would put him at about a year old, and he knew for a fact that Bella had taken time off from touring for a few months, until March this year. No doubt to have the kid that no one on the ENSA team talked about. She'd dumped him with her mam and come back to work like the golden girl everyone thought she was, keeping her dirty little secret to herself.

Freddie smiled as he made his way back into his room and took out a pad and pen. He wrote down everything he'd heard so that he wouldn't forget it if his mind got fuddled after he finished the bottle of whisky. *So who was the kid's father?* Basil? No, he was too old for a young girl to be interested in. Most likely one of the soldiers or airmen she'd met while on tour.

And the name Levi was unusual. It was of Jewish origin and used a lot in the States. Where would a Liverpool backstreet girl like Bella hear of a mainly American name like Levi? So the father was most probably a Yank. Freddie hadn't been with ENSA at the time Bella would have copped for the kid, but he'd bet his life it would be one of the Yanks from Burtonwood as that's where the troupe seemed to play a lot.

That black bandleader Earl Franklin Junior was quite friendly with the Bryant Sisters, he recalled. He also remembered that he'd never taken his eyes off Bella while she sang. Freddie needed to clap eyes on the baby close to. If he was a dark-skinned kid then Freddie knew he had his man. He had a close mate who was a newspaper reporter, who would pay handsomely for a juicy story like this one. Freddie had heard it said once too often that Bella had the voice of an angel. *Hah! Angel my arse*, he thought and smirked.

There was nothing angelic about that little tart, as the nation was about to find out. He rubbed his hands together with glee and crept quietly down the stairs onto the lower landing so that he could peer through the banisters when the guests were leaving.

*

'Thank you so much for a very entertaining time, Fenella,' Mary said. 'You and Bobby have helped us to get through this first Christmas after losing Harry and with our Bella being away down south.'

'It's our pleasure,' Fenella replied. 'You've also helped me and Bobby to cope better as well. And it's been such a joy to have little Levi here. I bet you'll miss him when you have to give him back.'

'Oh I will,' Mary replied, looking round for her little grandson. 'Molly, grab hold of him quick. He's halfway up the stairs.' She shook her head. 'You need eyes in your backside with a toddler. I'm going to have to get a gate made to stop him going up ours. That's another expense I could do without.'

Molly grabbed her nephew, who was smiling at something out of her view, and carried him back to the hall. 'Little devil,' she said, sitting him on her hip. 'Say bye-bye now to Bobby and Aunty Fenella. Thank you for a lovely time.'

'We hope to see you again very soon,' Bobby said as Martin carried the high-chair out to the car. 'Take care getting inside at home with it being so dark out there.'

'We will. Goodbye,' Mary said as they followed Martin out to the car.

*

Freddie waited until he heard the front door close, then crept silently back up to his room in the attic. That couldn't have been more perfect than if he'd called the little one's name and he'd climbed the stairs to answer to it. Freddie had seen him on the first stair and then swung his pocket watch on a chain over the banister railing to catch his eye. The kid had spotted it right away and looked up. His big brown eyes and thick mop of dark curls, as well as his skin that was lighter than Earl's, but still dark enough for Freddie to see that he had mixed parentage, told him for certain that his suspicions of Earl Franklin being Bella's child's father were right on the nail.

Tomorrow, when his sister and Bobby were out of the house he would write to his reporter mate and ask to meet him. He planned to tell all he knew, but would ask him to save the story for when the Bryant Sisters were next up north, which he believed was March next year. It would make an even bigger impact in the local community and would help to ruin the trio's snow-white reputation, like they'd ruined his when they got him fired.

Chapter Fifteen

Wavertree, January 1944

'Are you sure this is a good idea, Mam?' Molly asked, brushing her hair in front of the mirror over the back sitting room fireplace. 'I mean, she won't be expecting me or anything and I'll feel a bit cheeky, like I'm just barging in.'

Mary looked at her daughter, head on one side. 'Well I can't just pick up the phone to warn her you're popping round, can I? It means I'd have to go out to the phone box and I haven't got the time. The worst thing that can happen is she'll say no. But I tell you, she's desperate for some help and I bet she'll pay you well if she takes you on.'

Molly sighed and put on her warm coat, best hat and scarf and boots. 'I'm not that keen on cleaning at the best of times.'

Mary laughed. 'None of us are, but it puts food on the table and coal on the fire. And we really need you to be working, love. I've not got much money left from your dad's penny polices and my army widow's pension still hasn't come through, so we haven't got much choice. It's either that or you'll have to see if the match factory where Bella worked could take you on.'

Molly tutted. 'It's not fair. Here we are stuck in Wavertree looking after Bella's baby and she's having the time of her life

doing exactly what she wants to do up and down the country.'
She folded her arms and glared at Levi, who was sitting on the
rug playing with his building bricks. 'It should be her back here
and me doing her job.'

'Yes, well it's not.' Mary pursed her lips. 'And it's not Levi's
fault either. He's missing out and so is Bella. So stop being selfish
and let's all do what we can to help one another until this bloody
war is over. Arguing is not doing anyone any good. Now off you
go to Fenella's and tell her you'd like to be considered for the job.'

Mary watched as Molly flounced off down the hall and slammed
the front door. She couldn't really blame Molly for her outburst.
She'd have felt the same at her age, seeing her sister doing all those
glamorous things while all there was for her to look forward to was
a dustpan and broom and maybe a new mop and bucket.

She turned to look at Levi, who got to his feet and toddled
over to her. He grabbed the edge of her wrap-around pinny and
wiped his snotty nose against it. 'Oh you mucky little boy,' she
said, laughing. 'Time for your morning milk and biscuit I think.'
She picked him up and sat him in his high-chair by the window
and wiped his nose. He gave her a big grin and she ruffled his curls.
'Good job you're so bloody lovely, little man.'

She brought his snack to him and sat at the table with a pad
and pen to make a shopping list. It would have to be a carefully
planned shop today as the few shillings she had left after Christmas
would need to feed them all for a week. Bella was due to send
some money but that would go on the rent and feeding the gas
and electric meters. At least if Molly got the job today, she'd get
paid at the end of the week and with a bit of luck Fenella might
let her bring the odd treat home. Fingers crossed.

*

Molly took a short cut across the snowy Mystery Park, thinking how pretty the trees looked with their laden white branches, twinkling in the bright winter sunshine. She banged her feet against the step to get rid of the worst of the compacted snow from her boots and rang the Harrisons' doorbell. She stepped back, waiting for a response. She rang again and was just about to give up when the door opened a crack and a man with a moustache, who she didn't recognise, peered at her and frowned.

'Can I help you, young lady?' he asked.

'Is Mrs Harrison in please?' Molly asked, wondering who the man was. He wasn't smartly dressed, so she thought he might be a workman or gardener or something.

'I'm afraid she's out at the moment. She'll be back in about ten minutes, I believe.'

Molly nodded. 'Well is Bobby in then? Maybe I could talk to him.'

'He's not here either,' the man said. 'He's at the hospital having physiotherapy on his leg. Would you like to come in and wait?'

Molly chewed her lip. The man was a stranger and she felt a bit unsure.

'I'm Mrs Harrison's house guest, if you're wondering. I'm staying here with the family for a few days. We're old acquaintances from way back,' he said by way of an explanation.

'Oh, okay, well if you're sure that will be all right, I will come in and wait. Save me walking home and then having to come back later.'

The man stood to one side while she entered, then closed the door and gestured for her to follow him down the hallway to the dining room at the back of the property. 'Please take a seat,' he said. 'The kettle has just boiled and I was about to make a pot of tea. Will you join me? My name is Freddie, by the way, and I don't bite so there's no need to look so worried.' He smiled.

Molly grinned and sat down on the sofa, feeling a bit more reassured. 'Thank you. I would love a cuppa.'

He was back within minutes, carrying a tray with two china mugs and a plate of ginger snaps. 'Sorry we've no fresh scones but Cook has phoned in sick this morning and Mrs Harrison has had to take herself off to the shops to buy some supplies. Not something she's used to doing. Sadly her housekeeper passed away and there's been a struggle to find a new one.'

Molly smiled as she helped herself to sugar. 'Hmm, well funnily enough that's why I'm here. Mrs Harrison told my mam she needs domestic help, so Mam suggested I apply for the job, and here I am.'

Freddie nodded. 'Then it's a good job I was here to let you in.'

'It is indeed.' Molly picked up a ginger snap and dunked it in her tea. She grinned. 'That's not very ladylike is it? But I love them nice and soft to eat.' She stopped as she heard the door opening and footsteps in the hallway and Mrs Harrison calling, 'It's only me.' She shoved the ginger snap in her mouth quickly as Freddie grinned and put a finger to his lips.

'I won't tell if you don't,' he said.

Mrs Harrison came hurrying into the dining room, carrying two loaded shopping bags, and stopped in her tracks, her mouth open. 'Molly, what a lovely surprise,' she said.

'Sit down, Fenella dear, and I'll get you a cup of tea,' Freddie said. 'Then I'll leave you two alone. The young lady has something she wants to discuss with you.' He was back within seconds, bearing a dainty white bone china cup and saucer. 'There you are. I know you prefer a cup to a mug, unlike us heathens.' He laughed at his own joke and left the room, closing the door behind him.

Mrs Harrison stared after him and then turned her attention to Molly. 'I'm so sorry I wasn't here to greet you,' she began. 'But it seems Freddie has taken care of you very well.'

'Yes, he did, thank you. He seems a very nice man; he said he's an old family friend.'

Mrs Harrison nodded her agreement. 'Now what can I do for you, dear? I hope there's nothing wrong at home. Your mother and the little one are okay I presume?'

Molly nodded. 'Yes they're both fine, thank you.' She went on to explain the reason for her visit and smiled at the look of relief that crossed the other woman's face.

'That would be a godsend,' Mrs Harrison said. 'Oh I can't believe my luck. I only said to Robert what a good job you did of tidying the kitchen on Boxing Day after tea. I can give you full-time hours if you'd like them. That would leave me more free time to oversee my work with the WI. As the president of the Wavertree branch I feel I've sadly neglected my duties since Robert's long convalescence and the loss of Margaret. It would be a tremendous weight off my mind to know I have someone at home I can rely on while I get things back into shape at the church hall.'

Molly smiled, shyly.

Mrs Harrison continued. 'We are in the middle of trying to send our troops comfort packages from the homeland but it all needs a proper rethink and an overhaul. Those poor boys are suffering all sorts of problems. I've heard of at least a couple who have a terrible case of foot rot because they have no spare socks. As if they haven't enough to contend with, trying to avoid being blown to bits by the enemy. Then we've got families here who have lost everything including the roofs over their heads. We need to try to collect contributions of clothing and food from people who can spare at least something.'

Molly nodded as Mrs Harrison paused for breath and took a sip of tea.

'I can pay you two guineas a week to start; provide meals while you are on duty, and a nice uniform. How does that sound to you?'

Mam had told Molly she'd need to ask for about two pounds, so this offer was more than she'd been expecting.

'Of course there will be pay rises if we find we suit one another,' Mrs Harrison continued. 'And I'm quite sure we shall.'

Molly nodded. 'That all sounds fine to me.'

'Oh I'm so glad. Now if you write me down your size I will order a uniform today and it will no doubt be delivered this week, but if you want to start working tomorrow morning then maybe just wear something suitable to clean and tidy in that won't get spoiled. I expect Freddie told you my cook is off ill, so that's an extra headache for me as well. I'm not the world's best but I'll manage for now.'

'Don't worry about it,' Molly said. 'I quite enjoy cooking and I love to bake as well. I'm sure you won't starve and we'll manage all this between us.'

'I'm so grateful, I really am,' Mrs Harrison said. 'Obviously we have our house guest staying for a short time, but he's out of the way in the attic for now, so you don't need to bother doing his room. We'll wait until he's moved out, which hopefully won't be too much longer. There's just my room and Robert's room, which is the converted lounge, and the two spare bedrooms on the first floor, two bathrooms, the dining room, kitchen and parlour. Oh dear, it does sound a lot, but a bit at a time until it's got on top of will be ideal.'

Molly smiled. It all sounded fine to her and if she was left alone most of the time she'd be her own boss. 'I'll work out a routine as we go,' she said. 'Shall we start by putting those bags of shopping away and then I'll get back to Mam and tell her the good news.'

*

Freddie watched Molly walk away from the house and stroll across The Mystery Park. *So, she was the new maid eh?* He hoped the uniform she'd be wearing was a bit more sexy than the drab attire he'd seen his sister clear out from Margaret's room. Be nice to have a bit of young blood around the house for company, besides Bobby. And of course, her being Bella's sister, she was bound to talk about her and the other girls. He might be able to find out a bit more information so that the facts he'd already gleaned from eavesdropping could be strengthened to help sell his story. He'd written to his reporter friend and was hoping to hear from him to arrange a meeting soon.

He saw the car pull up and Martin help young Bobby out of the passenger seat. His nephew was doing well and there was talk of him going out with the ENSA team soon. Bobby still hadn't been told of Freddie's past work with ENSA, nor that he was his uncle. He'd warned Fenella not to give him away, saying that he'd get in trouble with the authorities and so would she for harbouring a soldier who had gone AWOL. Freddie wished with all his heart he could get back on to the variety show circuit again. He'd been perfecting a few new tricks while he was ensconced in his room out of the way. He was feeling much better about life at the moment. He was worried about moving on until he had some money in his pocket; but that would come when he sold his story, in the not-too-distant future.

Chapter Sixteen

Wavertree, March 1944

'Have you seen my wallet, Molly?' Bobby called. She turned round to look at him from the stairs, a dustpan and brush in her hands. He'd just got back from his regular hospital visit and realised he'd not got his wallet in his jacket pocket.

'Yes, I put it in the top drawer of your chest of drawers,' she replied. 'It's right on top of your socks. It was on the floor near the window when I cleaned your room. You need to be more careful or you'll be losing it outside the house.'

'Yes, Mother,' he teased and gave her a mock salute. Back in his room he checked the drawers and there it was, just as Molly had said. He always talked to his photo of Levi in the morning after his shower. Seeing that little face made him smile and dream of the future he was going to spend with him and Bella. He must have put the wallet down and then forgotten all about it when Martin came to pick him up.

He came back out to the hallway. 'Thank you,' he said. 'I'm going out again in a few minutes to spend an hour with an old school pal. He's a soldier who's been sent home from Europe following a bad accident. Martin is going to come back for me after he's run Mother across to the church hall. Will you be okay in the house on your own for a while? I believe Freddie took a tram down to the city centre – he'll be out for a few hours, no doubt.'

'I'll be fine,' Molly said. 'Cook's not here again so I'll get your evening meal prepared and leave it in the oven for when your mother comes home.'

'Seems Cook's quite poorly,' Bobby said. 'She might not come back at all according to Mother. We'll have to get someone in to give you a hand if that happens.'

Molly nodded. 'We'll see. We're okay for now though. Enjoy your time with your friend. See you later.'

*

Shaking his head with shock at the destruction he'd seen on the way into the city centre, the vast empty spaces and piles of demolished rubble where houses, shops and factories had once stood, Freddie got off the tram near Hope Street and walked across to the miraculously undamaged Philharmonic Dining Rooms, or the Phil, as the pub was affectionately known in the area, where he'd arranged to meet his reporter friend. He couldn't believe how lucky he was with what he'd found this morning. Bobby had left the house earlier and Fenella was upstairs getting herself titivated for her WI good works, and he'd gone downstairs to make a cuppa and spotted Bobby's door wide open.

The catch mustn't have caught. It always swung back open again if that happened. As he reached out to close the door he spotted a wallet on the floor by the window and was tempted to see if there was any money inside. But as he bent to pick it up, on the arm of the chair nearby he saw a small photograph. He reached for it and realised it was a photo of the child, Levi. He turned the photo over. On the back was written, 'Levi Scott Rogers age seven months'. He smiled. That kid was the spitting image of Earl Franklin Junior, the Yankee bandleader. Rogers was Bella's surname, and here was the photographic proof to show his reporter mate.

Stealing money forgotten for the moment, Freddie shoved the photo in his trouser pocket and hurried from the room, closing the door firmly. He made a mug of tea and a slice of toast in the kitchen and then dashed upstairs to get ready.

Inside the Phil, Freddie patted his pocket containing all his carefully written notes and waved as he saw his friend Colin Makem sitting at a table with two pints of ale in front of him. That was good, because Freddie was very short of cash at the moment.

'Freddie, it's good to see you again, matey.' Colin stood up and shook him by the hand.

'Good to see you too, Col.' Freddie sat down and took a long slug of ale. He smacked his lips. 'That's a good pint. Perfect in fact.'

'Always is in here. How are things going with you? Are you still doing the magic act?'

Freddie shrugged his shoulders and pulled a face. 'I'm going through a bit of a bad spell at the moment, if you'll pardon the pun.' He told Colin what had happened in Anglesey and how he'd been without work ever since. 'And that's why I wanted to see you, Col. I've found out something very interesting that might make good news. A bit of scandal to make a change from the war.'

'Have you indeed? We love a bit of scandal. I'm all ears, let's have it.'

Freddie took out his sheaf of notes and the photo of Levi, as well as a publicity photo of the Bryant Sisters, and handed them over to Colin. He'd exaggerated a wee bit, but Colin could check for himself that most of what he'd written was fact. Colin also had friends in most places within the military, so he'd have no problem clarifying details.

Colin had a quick scan through the notes and smiled. 'So, this girl Bella is portrayed pretty much as innocence personified to the public?' he said. Freddie nodded his agreement.

Colin raised his eyebrows. 'They're very popular. Highly thought of on the ENSA circuit. They've even starred with George Formby here in Liverpool and I've heard a recent rumour that they may star in a show with Glenn Miller later this year. I've seen reviews of some of the theatre shows where they're billed as Britain's answer to the Andrews Sisters, and a few more that say Bella's the next Vera Lynn. But this Earl guy, the baby's alleged father, what do you know about him and why is she not engaged to him instead of to this Bobby Harrison?'

'That's what I'd like to know. I've no doubt the kid is Earl's though. They are both in the same entertainment business; I would have thought they'd make an ideal couple. That's why I wondered if you could find out a bit about his background, and why she's keeping the kid a secret from nearly everyone. What have they got to hide?'

Colin smiled. 'Leave it with me, mate. This has the makings of a front-page story. And like you say, it's a change from war news. Nothing sells a paper like a bit of juicy scandal.'

'Well if you can pull it off in time, the Bryant Sisters are coming up north to appear in Blackpool the last week of March,' Freddie said. 'It would be good if it could hit the local papers that week. See how they like *their* careers ruined. It would serve the bitches right after all the untrue complaints they made about me. Them three and a dancing troupe they travel with. A right bunch of witches.' He tapped the notes. 'It's all facts and that kid is the living proof of it.'

Freddie didn't add the extra facts that Bobby was his nephew and that he was staying at his sister's house. That was no one's business anyway. He just made out that he was staying with old friends and could be reached on the phone number he'd written on the notes he'd handed over, but that he might be moving on from there very soon.

'Well if you do move on you can ring me at the office and let me know,' Colin said. 'And once I've got everything sorted, we'll agree a fee for you. I'll need to read these through from start to finish and make my own notes on the matter.'

Freddie smiled. 'You're the expert, so I'll leave it up to you to put your own spin on things. Cheers, mate.' They laughed and clinked their glasses together.

*

Molly was singing along to something on the wireless, totally oblivious to the fact that she was being closely observed from beyond the open kitchen doorway. She finished mashing the potatoes and spread the mash over the mince and onion mix she'd laid at the bottom of a dish. She fluffed the potatoes with a fork, bringing them to a peak in the middle, and stepped back to admire her cottage pie.

Ruth's voice echoed in her head. 'It's all about the presentation, Molly.' That advice had stood her in good stead for the last few weeks while she'd been working for the Harrisons. A pan of carrots and another of cabbage was simmering gently on the gas hob. Molly lifted the cottage pie into the oven and sighed with pleasure. To her surprise, she loved running this household. Fenella Harrison pretty much left her to it and Bobby hardly ever got under her feet, but if he did he was good company and often made her a cup of tea and insisted she take a break.

Neither of them made her feel she was lower class than they were just because she did their cleaning. In fact, she felt like a family member. The only one she was unsure about was the house guest, Freddie; he was okay and very polite but she found him a bit weird at times, the way he stared at her. She always hoped he would go out or up to his room on the odd time she was alone in the house with him. She couldn't put her finger on what it was she didn't really like about him though, it was just an inner feeling.

As the song on the radio came to an end and 'Don't Sit Under the Apple Tree' came on, she thought about her sister and how the

Bryant Sisters had sung this at the theatre in Llandudno. She began to sing along and danced around the kitchen while she tidied up. She made herself a cup of tea and was about to sit down when a voice made her jump.

'Well that was a very nice performance,' Freddie said, stepping into the kitchen and clapping. 'Has anyone ever told you that you move well, you're very natural? You'd make a good dancer. Be a nicer career for you than being stuck in a kitchen.'

Molly could feel her cheeks heating. How long had he been watching her? She was struck dumb for a few seconds and he continued. 'I have show business connections, you know. I might be able to put in a good word if it was something you fancied doing. Why don't you pour me a cuppa and we'll talk some more?'

He pulled out a chair from under the kitchen table and sat down. She was conscious of his eyes on her back and her hands shook as she poured his tea and spooned two sugars in it.

'There you are,' she said, putting the drink on the table, her hands trembling.

She sat down opposite him and took a sip of her tea. 'I was supposed to be joining the same ENSA troupe that my sister Bella travels with,' she began. 'They have a team of dancers and I was told I might be able to work with them, but it's not happened yet.'

'You don't want to join a dancing troupe like that,' Freddie said, shaking his head dismissively. 'They're ten a penny. You need to think bigger; a solo dancer, or maybe become part of an act that incorporates dancing as well as other things. Like a magician who uses a glamorous assistant to dance around and hand him things.'

Molly's face lit up. 'I once saw that sort of act at a theatre before the war started and the magician put the woman in a long box and sawed her in half but she wasn't dead or injured. I don't know how he did it, but it was very good.'

'It's all an illusion,' Freddie told her. '*I* do magic tricks too. I can make people seem to vanish, but they don't really.'

Molly's jaw dropped. 'Honestly, you can do that?'

He nodded. 'Tell you what. Next time we have the house to ourselves, we'll give it a go. I'll show you some of my tricks and you can practise your dancing around me and we'll see how we're suited. I've been looking for a new partner to work with. But it's so hard to find the perfect girl who's not either in the forces or getting married and doesn't want to try anything new. Now what about you, Molly, do you have any plans like that?'

She shook her head. 'I wouldn't join up, and I don't have a boyfriend yet.'

He raised his eyebrows. 'Now that does surprise me, a pretty girl like you. I thought you'd have had plenty of lads after you. Well in that case we might be able to make this work. There's a chance of fame for us both here, Molly, if we do things right.'

Molly swallowed hard. Could she really do that, go off to do what she wanted and seek fame and fortune with Freddie? It would leave her mam in the lurch. But her mam could easily work here and then they could all look after Levi between them. It wasn't fair that Bella should have all the fame and not have to worry about him. It was Molly's turn to be a star now and if Freddie could make it happen for her then she was going to take that opportunity.

'We need to keep this to ourselves for now,' Freddie warned. 'It will be our little secret. There are too many rivals out there that can cause trouble. Is that okay with you, Molly? You mustn't tell a soul. Are you good at keeping secrets?'

Molly nodded and smiled. 'Cross my heart and hope to die,' she promised. A little bubble of excitement began to grow in her stomach. He must have his reasons to want to keep things a secret and it wasn't up to her to question him. At long last she was going to get a chance to be famous; even a little bit of what her sister had would be better than nothing.

'Well it's good to know I can trust you.' Freddie reached out, squeezed her hand and smiled.

*

Mary frowned as Molly came hurrying downstairs later than usual. 'Come on,' she said. 'You're going to be late for work.'

Molly tutted and shrugged into her coat. 'I'm not. It doesn't take me long to walk across the park.'

Mary pursed her lips. 'Have you got make-up on? Why do you need to wear make-up to go out cleaning? *And* you've curled your hair.'

Molly's cheeks went pink and she replied snappily. 'Because sometimes I have to answer the door and it's better if I look smart when we have visitors. There's no need for me to go out looking like a scruffy tramp with my hair a mess and a turban on. Some of us like to keep to a certain standard.' She picked up her handbag and opened the front door. 'I'll see you later. But don't forget, I'll be staying on to do a couple of extra hours this evening as the Harrisons are having friends over.'

Mary nodded. 'Yes, you already told me. What about your tea, do you want me to keep something warm for you?'

Molly shook her head. 'I'll have some supper before I come home.'

She left the house and Mary closed the door behind her and went back into the sitting room. She'd swear her daughter was turning into another Fenella, the airs and graces she'd started to pick up lately. Fenella was losing hers and Molly was collecting them. Over the last couple of weeks she'd noticed a change in her girl, but couldn't put her finger on it. 'Ah well, what will be and all that, she's growing up and I need to let her be,' Mary muttered as she sat down at the table with a cuppa, savouring the last few minutes of peace before Levi woke up and started demanding her attention.

*

Molly hurried across The Mystery Park, glad to be out of the house and away from her mam's close scrutiny. Freddie had given her the make-up so that she could look glamorous when they practised some of his tricks. He'd also given her fancy underwear and silk stockings, as well as skimpy little outfits that he liked her to wear when they were ensconced in his room upstairs. He told her to get used to them as she would need to wear them when they performed onstage.

She left the outfits at the house with him, as Mam would have a hairy fit at her wearing anything quite so revealing, but she was wearing some of the underwear now so that she could get changed quickly after work. The Harrisons were actually going out today, not having visitors, and would be staying overnight with friends, but Mam didn't need to know that and it was only a little white lie.

She and Freddie would have hours to practise the routines he'd been trying to teach her for the last couple of weeks. She enjoyed working with him and he made her feel special and quite grown up as he instructed her on what to do. She wasn't sure about the way he constantly touched her and put his arms round her while they were doing the routines, but she supposed she'd get used to it. He'd promised to look after her and make sure that the men in the audiences where they'd be performing didn't bother her. Molly trusted him; she had no choice if she wanted to be famous.

Freddie was on the phone as she let herself in at the front door. He hadn't heard her come in but was shouting at someone on the other end of the line. He sounded angry – but then he turned and caught her eye, lifted his hand in a wave and softened his tone. He said goodbye to whoever he was speaking to and hung up. He smiled and came over to give her a hug.

'Are you okay?' she asked as he held her tight. She wished he'd loosen his hold and remove his hand from groping her backside. But he just stayed there, holding on, and spoke into her hair. She could smell whisky on his breath. *It's too early to be drinking*, she thought, but he seemed to do it quite often.

'Yes, I'm fine. I was just speaking to a steward at a Liverpool club, trying to book us in for a night or two next week to get us started, but he's fully booked for the next few months. He just annoyed me with his cocky attitude, that's why I raised my voice. We're going to have to go further afield if we want to work, Molly. And that will mean travelling and staying in hotels. I hope you're okay with that after all the work we've put in. It's time I was moving on from here anyway and I want to take you with me.'

Molly stared up at him, her mouth open. 'What about me mam?' she stuttered.

'Well what about her?' he teased. 'I'm buggered if I'm taking her with us.'

She shook her head. 'I didn't mean that. But what will I tell her? She'll say no, I can't go with you.'

'Well, if that's the case you'll just have to forget it then. Or we'll just have to go without telling her. You can write to her when we get to a city we find work in and tell her you're not coming back, ever.'

Molly swallowed hard. She felt a bit scared. Freddie was still holding on tight to her and she knew if she pulled away, he might hurt her. He'd bruised her a couple of times recently by handling her roughly. She'd complained, but he'd threatened that she'd never work again if she told anyone he'd done that, not with him or his friends, the Harrisons. She couldn't afford to lose her job; Mam needed her wages. And this was also her only chance of achieving her dreams of fame. She nodded her head. 'Okay. If that's what you think is best, then we will do what we have to do.'

'Good girl, my little Molly Dolly. Now let's have some breakfast and we can get a bit of rehearsing done. Fenella told me to let you know that you can have a day off today as they're away. She forgot to tell you yesterday. So we've got all the time in the world to perfect that trick we've been working on this week. I just need to pop up to my room for a few minutes. Meantime you can make me a nice mug of coffee if you will, please.'

*

Freddie finished packing his bags and made sure everything he owned was safely stowed away. The shit was hitting the fan right now thanks to bloody Colin. He'd been speaking to him just as Molly arrived. Colin had called him to tell him the scandal article was front-page news today. It was in every paper and he would be paid handsomely.

But far from being thrilled by this, Freddie was fuming. The ENSA troupe were not in Blackpool until the end of the week and the impact on the locals, getting them tongue-wagging and gossipmongering, would have been far greater then and the shows in Blackpool would have most likely been cancelled. Also, he'd specifically asked for that date as he'd planned to be out of the area by then so no one could point any fingers in his direction. Now he would have to change his plans and move on sooner.

As Fenella had dashed out of the house this morning, she had mentioned that Martin the driver was due to come back to the house later to collect a case of clothes to drop off at the dry-cleaners, and to make sure he was at home to let him in. So instead of disappearing at the end of the week, Freddie planned to get the car keys off Martin today, by fair means or foul, and use the family car to make his escape, leaving Molly behind.

He also needed to collect his payout from Colin, but he could do that once he was on his way. Satisfied that he'd thought of everything, Freddie shoved the half-bottle with what was left of his whisky in his pocket and went back downstairs to have his coffee and to enjoy a little bit of fun with Molly before he left the house. As he passed the telephone, he lifted the receiver off its cradle and laid it to one side. *There*, he thought. *Don't want that bloody thing ringing out and disturbing us.*

Chapter Seventeen

Basil dashed into the NAAFI. He scanned the room and spotted his trio of Bryant Sisters finishing their breakfast at a table at the far end near the windows. He hurried across to them. 'Hurry up, girls,' he said as they all looked up to greet him. 'Get back to your hut and I'll meet you there. We need to talk, urgently. I'm just nipping out to get a newspaper, but like I say, hurry.'

Aware of their curious eyes on his back, he left the building and jumped into his car. The newsagent's shop in the village was open and he dashed inside and bought copies of all the day's papers, wincing as he glanced briefly at the headlines. He drove back and walked around the camp to the girls' Nissen hut, knocked on the door and walked in without being invited.

Three worried pairs of eyes turned towards him.

'What's happened, Basil?' Fran asked as he threw a batch of newspapers down on the nearest bunk bed.

He swept his arm towards the papers. 'Trouble, I'm afraid. Scandal, gossip, call it what you like. It's not nice. Where the heck have these reporters got their information from? That's what I'd like to know. Most of it's lies anyway, but the fact is, it's there and it could do the Bryant Sisters' reputation a lot of damage.'

The girls picked up a newspaper each and stared in horror at the headlines above a promotional photograph that was taken at a show last year.

ENSA SCANDAL. SECRET SHAME OF THE BRYANT SISTERS seemed to be the favourite. But in the middle of the report was also a photograph of Levi.

Bella gasped as she stared at the page, the words swimming before her eyes. 'I gave that photo to Bobby. He misplaced it recently,' she said. 'He was really upset and couldn't understand where it had gone, as he was keeping it in his room. He wrote and asked me for another.'

Fran shook her head, her eyes full of disbelief. 'Half of this rubbish is just not true,' she said. 'Why are they allowed to print such nonsense?'

Edie's eyes filled with tears. 'This makes us sound like out-of-control tarts, like we mess with every serviceman we meet. Oh, my mam will go barmy when she reads this. Will it be in the *Echo* do you think, Basil?'

Basil nodded, his heart going out to his girls. 'Sadly, yes. I was alerted to this by someone in London from HQ who called this morning.'

'London?' Bella sobbed. 'Oh, God this is just awful. What are we going to do? I mean, hardly anyone knew about Levi and Earl. Now the whole world and his mother will know. But how has this happened? We've been so careful. Not even Bobby's mother knows. Well, she will now as soon as she sees the papers, of course. Oh God and my poor mam too.'

'Look, let's calm down a bit,' Basil advised. 'Now I really don't want to do this, but there's a good chance I might have to pull you from the Blackpool theatre shows until this is sorted out. I think the best thing for me to do right now is take you all home to Liverpool so you can stay with your families and lie low for a few days. I'll get to the bottom of this if it's the last thing I do.'

Bella shook her head and wiped her eyes. 'I feel this is all my fault. I'm so sorry for all the problems I've caused.'

Fran and Edie each took a hand. 'No it's not,' Fran reassured her. Edie squeezed her hand gently and Basil nodded in agreement.

'Somewhere out there is a weasel who will have made a lot of money from this story,' he said. 'These reporter guys who've put their own spin on it will have been given basic information from someone. Now who do we know that bears a grudge against Bella? Or the Bryant Sisters, as a whole.'

'Alicia,' all three girls said at once.

Basil nodded slowly. 'The thought did cross my mind. But then I also thought, how would she have got all that information about Earl and his wife and daughter? Or even about Levi being looked after by Bella's mother, or abandoned with Bella's mother, as the more dramatic piece reports.'

Fran shrugged. 'Maybe she knows someone at Burtonwood,' she suggested, 'after all she works for the air force and the various bases will communicate; she's on telephony as well. All it would take is a phone call to a mate there – if she has any. 'And that mate could have rooted out personal information and passed it on.'

Basil sighed. 'Well, apart from her jealousy over Bella being engaged to Bobby, how did she find out about the baby? And how did she get her hands on that photo of Levi and why would she want to hurt you and Edie, Fran? It doesn't really add up. This mess smacks to me more of professional jealousy, someone wanting to damage our ENSA team. Ruin any future shows for us by pulling apart the reputation of my star act. Now apart from Marvo and Gloria retiring last year, I currently have the same acts with me that I've had for the last few years. Everyone gets on well and looks out for each other. That's the way it's always been. The only act I've had to let go over wrongdoing was Freddie Cagney, who for some reason seems to have disappeared from the surface of the earth.'

Bella stared at him. 'I know he was a right creep, but why would he do something as horrible as this? And how on earth could he possibly get his hands on that picture of Levi and, and… oh God, I don't know.' She burst into tears. 'It's all such a muddle in my head.'

Basil scanned down the report in the *Guardian*, which stated that Wing Commander Earl Franklin Junior was unavailable for comment. 'I bet he was,' he muttered. 'And who can blame him? What a mess this is. If someone gets this news to his wife it will cause him no end of problems.'

Bella nodded. 'He's worried about his little daughter and wants to fight for custody of her when the war is over. The wife seems to be a bit unstable and something like this might tip her over the edge. It's one thing knowing he's had an affair, but the fact that he's got a son with me might be a bit too much.'

Fran rolled her eyes. 'The evil swine that's done this doesn't have a clue what a nightmare they've created for everyone involved.'

Basil sighed. 'Right, let's make a move. Get your things packed up, and I'll run you three home. I'll come back to the camp afterwards and make a few phone calls, find out what's going to happen with the Blackpool shows. I should have you back in Wavertree just before eleven, all being well.'

*

With the wireless playing quietly in the background, Freddie watched as Molly placed two mugs of coffee on the table. Humming to herself as she turned to get the sugar basin from the cupboard, she didn't see him tip some whisky into both mugs and shove the bottle back into his pocket.

'I'll just top this bowl up with some sugar cubes from the pantry,' she said, walking into the big deep cupboard where the spare grocery supplies were kept. 'We've nothing like this at home,' she shouted back. 'It's got more stuff than the corner shop. Mam just buys what we need on a day-to-day basis.'

Freddie took another chance while she waffled on, out of his sight, and swigged some of the coffee, topped it up a bit more and added a crushed sleeping tablet that he'd had wrapped in paper in his pocket. He poured in milk from the jug and pushed the mug with extra whisky and tablet over to Molly's place. She brought the full sugar bowl to the table and smiled.

'Thanks for pouring the milk.'

'My pleasure,' he said, grinning. 'I'm going to be a devil and have three sugar cubes, but don't tell Mrs Harrison. I suggest you do the same. We never know when we'll be able to get any more with all the rations imposed on us now.'

Molly smiled and helped herself to three cubes. She stirred her coffee, took a sip and grimaced.

'Something wrong?' Freddie asked, raising an eyebrow.

'No, it's just very sweet. I'm not keen on this proper coffee really. It has a funny taste. Mam buys Camp coffee and it's much nicer.'

'Nothing wrong with this,' he said. 'Your palate needs refining. We'll soon sort that out once we're dining in London's finest restaurants. Get it down you. Start as we mean to go on.'

'Do you really think we'll be doing that?' she asked, her brown eyes dreamy. 'Dining in nice places I mean?'

'I can assure you we will. And once this war is over we'll be in great demand to work on variety shows all over the country. None of that ENSA stuff and nonsense will exist beyond the end of the war. But good professional acts like us, we'll go far.'

Molly smiled and finished the rest of her coffee. She got up to put the empty mugs in the sink and ran some water in the bowl. She blinked hard and tried to focus on grating a bit of soap into the hot water, then whisked it around with her hand.

'I feel a bit strange,' she said, 'but it's a sort of nice floaty feeling.' She turned as Freddie went to stand behind her, slipped his hands round her waist and nibbled her neck, pressing her right up against the sink. His hand slid upwards and cupped her right breast, squeezing it gently, while his other hand caressed her backside.

Molly gasped as he turned her slowly round and swept her into his arms. His lips came down heavy on hers and he forced his tongue inside her mouth. She tried to push him away, but he was too strong for her and he pulled her into the dining room and pushed her back onto the sofa, his weight pinning her down.

'Come on, my Molly Dolly,' he whispered, using the name he'd started calling her when they were practising the act in his bedroom. 'Stop playing hard to get. You know what will happen if you do that, don't you? I'll have to leave you behind when I go away and you'll never get to perform onstage.'

She stopped struggling and went limp in his arms, 'I'm sorry,' she mumbled.

He picked her up and carried her up the two flights of stairs to his room. Good job she was light as a feather, he thought as he set her down on the floor, where she swayed slightly and grabbed hold of the wooden end of the bed. She eased off her working shoes and kicked them under the bed out of the way. 'I feel a bit funny,' she said, her face draining of colour.

He held her close for a moment to steady her as she wobbled. 'Right, let's have that ugly uniform off as well, shall we?' He unbuttoned the plain black dress and lifted it over her head, throwing it down on the floor. 'Oh, yes' – he nodded approvingly, his eyes narrowing – 'it's nice to see you've got your special lacy underwear on for me today *and* your silky stockings. Good girl. Now put your stage outfit on for me and we'll have a dance first before we do a rehearsal. The red sparkly one if you don't mind, it will go nice with the white lace.'

Molly slipped the low-cut, short, red dress over her head and turned to face him, her cheeks flushing pink. He flicked her long hair away from her face and spun her round, looking at her from every angle. He'd brought Fenella's gramophone up to his room and a selection of records. He placed Billie Holiday's 'I'm Yours' on the turntable and as the song began he took Molly in his arms and swayed around the room with her.

'Nice to have a slow, smoochy dance, I think,' he said. 'Now isn't this lovely, just you and me and the music. I promise you it will always be like this, Molly Dolly, and we'll spend every night together from now on.' He put the record back on to replay over and over and turned up the volume slightly. Molly had her eyes closed now, and she grew heavy in his arms.

He lifted her onto the bed, lay beside her and ran a finger down her cheek. *Spark out*, he thought. Pity really, he would have liked her to enjoy her first time, but he knew she'd put up a resistance and he'd have to hurt her if she did. Shame she wasn't more like that tart of a sister, dropping them for anybody, it would appear. The red sparkly dress had ridden up round her waist and he ran his hand up her silk-clad legs and cuddled her to him.

He removed her clothes gently so as not to wake her, and had her stripped naked in minutes, fondling and kissing every inch of her as he did so. She was so beautiful with her soft creamy skin, pert breasts and neat little nipples that fitted his mouth perfectly. He'd waited a while for this and he was going to savour every single minute. He got to his feet and took off his clothes, throwing them onto the floor on top of hers.

As he knelt between Molly's legs he felt a momentary pang of regret that she wouldn't remember this, but *he* would and that's all that mattered really. It wasn't the first time he'd taken a young girl's virginity while she was out cold and it certainly wouldn't be the last. He'd be long gone from here before Molly woke up. He'd have the car, money in his pocket, a different name and the world at his feet.

As Billie Holiday continued to warble he thought he heard a sound downstairs, like voices; he cocked an ear, but decided he was mistaken – it was probably somebody walking past the house and talking loudly, their voices carrying through the slightly open window. It was too early for Martin to be coming back yet and anyway, he wasn't one for talking to himself. He closed his eyes and prepared himself to push into Molly and savour those first few moments of stolen bliss.

*

Martin pulled up outside the house and leapt out to open the car doors to help Fenella and Bobby out of the vehicle. Fenella unlocked the front door and they all trooped inside. The friends they'd gone to visit had unfortunately been taken ill in the night with a serious stomach bug. They had tried to warn them by phone before they left the house, but said they couldn't get through as the line was constantly engaged. Fenella reasoned that they'd just missed their friends' first call as they set off and that Freddie must have used the phone immediately following their departure.

'It's such a shame. I was looking forward to spending time with Frances and David,' she said. 'We'll just have to go again once they're recovered.'

'We will, Mum,' Bobby agreed. 'Hopefully they won't be ill for too long.'

Martin deposited their baggage in the hall and they made their way into the kitchen.

Fenella looked around and frowned. 'I wonder where Molly is? I thought she'd be busy in here and might have a nice pot of tea on the go. I'm certainly ready for one. Not like her to be late.'

Bobby pointed to a chair in the corner. 'Well she's definitely here. Her coat and handbag are over there. She might be upstairs doing the bedrooms.'

'In that case I would have thought she'd hear the door opening and come downstairs to see who was coming in,' Fenella said.

Martin cocked his head. 'I can hear music; I thought I could when we came inside. It's quite loud as well. Billie Holiday, if I'm not mistaken. Molly probably wouldn't have heard anything over that noise.' He went into the hall and called, 'Molly, are you up there?'

Bobby came to stand behind him. 'Where's Freddie?' he asked.

'No idea,' Martin said. 'Freddie?' he called above the sound of the music.

'What's going on?' Fenella appeared behind them. 'Oh, that is loud.'

Bobby shrugged and then his eyes widened as he spotted the telephone, off the receiver. He pointed. 'Why is that off the hook? And where is Molly?'

Fenella shook her head but a cold feeling crept over her. 'Molly?' she called. 'I don't like this,' she said when there was no reply, just the music still droning on. 'Why are they not answering us? Martin, hurry please, follow the noise and see who's up there. I'm scared.'

Martin shot up the two flights of stairs, located which room the music was coming from and flung the door of the attic room open, with Fenella puffing several stairs behind him. He knocked the needle off the gramophone record and took in the scene before him. Molly was flat out and naked on the bed. She appeared to be unconscious. Freddie, also naked, was just about to get on top of her. Martin sprang forward, grabbed hold of Freddie's arms and pulled him backwards off the bed as Fenella dashed into the room and screamed.

'George, what the hell do you think you're doing?' she yelled. 'You disgusting excuse of a man.' She hurried to the bed and threw a discarded blanket over Molly as Martin wrestled Freddie onto the floor.

'Get dressed and get out of my house!' Fenella screamed at him. She patted Molly's white face. 'What have you done to her? Why is she unconscious? Molly, Molly, love, wake up.' She shook Molly gently but there was still no response. 'Martin, we need an ambulance.'

'No you don't,' Freddie said, pulling on his clothes. 'She's been drinking my whisky. Her choice. She's just fallen asleep, that's all.'

He pushed his feet into his shoes and picked up the suitcase he'd packed earlier. 'She was willing. She's a tart, like most women are. Led me on all along.'

'Don't be ridiculous,' Fenella snarled. 'She's just a young girl. You've given her drink so you could have your way with her, haven't you?' She glanced at the clothes on the floor; Molly's uniform dress, but also the red sparkly outfit and the fancy lace underwear. She shook her head. Molly wasn't the sort of girl to buy something like those; she had no money to spare, for one thing. 'Where did those clothes come from? They're not Molly's. Did you make her wear them for your own perverted pleasure?' She pulled a disgusted face. He ignored her and shoved his wallet and house keys in his trouser pocket.

'And you can leave those keys here,' Fenella said. 'They are mine. You are no longer welcome in my home. I want you out of here now.'

'Don't threaten me, lady. You don't know what I'm capable of.' He glared at Martin, who was standing by the bedroom door as though barring his way. 'Now tell your driver to give me the car keys and I'll go.'

'Not a chance, George,' she said. 'Go now, before I phone the police and report you for desertion and attempted rape.'

George laughed in her face. 'Do that and I'll land you in it as well for letting me stay here knowing I'm a deserter. Not only that, I think it's time people learned what a liar you are, don't you?'

Fenella's face blanched. 'W-what do you mean?' she stuttered.

George grinned again. 'You know full well what I mean. It's time young Robert knew about his roots. Where he really comes from. Now, keys, if you don't mind. Or I'll tell him myself.'

'Martin, just give him the car keys, please,' Fenella said, tears running down her cheeks as Martin, looking puzzled, handed over the car keys. 'Now just get out, go.' But he just stood there, leering at her.

Suddenly, Fenella leapt up and pushed Freddie so hard he cracked his head on the door. 'Ouch, you vicious little mare,' he growled, snatching up his suitcase and giving her a hard shove backwards. 'Now keep your trap shut or all your pigeons will come home to roost.' He ran down the first flight of stairs and bumped into Bobby, who was making his way slowly up the stairs to see what was going on. 'Get out of my way, you useless cripple,' he snarled, barging into Bobby, who lost his footing and fell down the stairs to the hallway, where he yelled in pain as Freddie left the house, leaving the front door wide open.

Hearing Bobby's distressed yells, Martin hurried down the stairs and saw the car pulling away. He closed the door and went to help Bobby. He had cut his forehead on the corner of the hall table and blood was dripping profusely on to the carpet. Martin pulled a handkerchief from his pocket and held it over the cut on Bobby's head as Fenella joined them and dropped to her knees, cradling Bobby in her arms.

'Do we need a doctor?' Martin asked. 'For Molly as well as Bobby. What the hell was that all about – and why did you call Freddie George, Mrs Harrison? He's taken the car, so that's stealing. We should get the police involved and have him arrested.'

'Later, Martin,' she said. 'Help me to get Robert to his feet. I'll check his head when we get him onto his bed. Hopefully he won't need stitches. There's a first aid kit in the big pantry cupboard if you can get it for me please. I'll explain everything to you the best I can when we've seen to Robert and Molly.'

Chapter Eighteen

Wavertree, March 1944

Feeling shocked to her core, Fenella sat on the sofa in the dining room while Martin made hot tea in the kitchen and added plenty of sugar as she'd instructed him. Bobby was sitting beside her looking pale; his head wound was cleaned and dressed. As she'd suspected, it wasn't deep enough to require stitches.

He had insisted on not being put to bed as his mother had suggested, and that he'd be fine joining them for tea. He was still a bit shaken but fortunately had suffered no real damage apart from the cut on his head. Molly was still out cold but Martin, who had done a first aid course a few years ago, assured them that her pulse was regular and her breathing, although sounding shallow, was normal for someone in a deep sleep. They were taking turns on checking her every ten minutes.

'I'm sure she'll call out when she wakes up,' Martin said. 'I think she's been given a sleeping pill as well as the whisky. We'll need to catch her as soon as she rouses or she'll be a bit woozy. She may stumble on the stairs.'

'What an awful thing to happen,' Bobby said. 'Thank God we came home when we did. He was obviously packed and ready to clear off as soon as he'd finished what he started.'

Fenella nodded. 'He knew Martin would be coming back to the house after dropping us off, so he was no doubt planning an attack or something to gain access to the car keys. I dread to think what might have happened. Poor little Molly would have been so confused, and might have wandered downstairs to find Martin unconscious, or even worse. Oh it really doesn't bear thinking about.'

Bobby nodded. 'Mum, when you were yelling at him upstairs, I heard you call him George instead of Freddie. Where do you know him from? He's not the sort of person you'd normally mix with. I just have a feeling you're hiding something from me and it's worrying. I heard him threatening you as well and I know Martin heard him too. We're concerned, Mum.'

Fenella took a deep breath, looking truly scared. 'I have a confession to make,' she began. 'Please don't think badly of me; I felt I had no choice at the time. I was put on the spot. George is my oldest brother. He came to the house a few weeks ago in a dreadful state and he asked me for help. He'd deserted from the army after our younger brother Tommy was killed in France. He told me he was scared and he couldn't go back. He said he'd changed his name to Freddie.'

She paused for a moment as her voice wavered. 'He is the only member of my family still alive, apart from you, Robert. I hadn't seen him for many years as we were estranged. I left my family home when I was sixteen years old and I never went back. I couldn't leave him on the streets, but I know I did wrong taking him in and I should have let the police know. However, as you can see, he's a nasty piece of work and I was terrified of him and what he might do to me and to you too, Robert, if he felt under threat.'

Martin and Bobby were quiet for a moment while they digested this news. Then Martin got to his feet. 'I'll leave you two alone while you talk about this. It's personal family stuff. Nothing will pass my lips about your brother, Mrs Harrison, you have my word. I think we should let Molly's mother know what's happened.'

'Thank you, Martin. And yes, you're right, we should let Mary know.'

'Then I'll walk across The Mystery Park and see if she's in. I'll bring her back here.'

Fenella nodded. 'Please do, Martin. She'll go mad and I feel so guilty. Molly was my responsibility while she was here.'

'Mum, we need to phone the police,' Bobby insisted. 'He tried to rape Molly, he's stolen our car, injured me and he's a bloody army deserter to boot. You can't let this go. Your brother or not, he should be arrested and chucked in prison.'

Fenella felt like her life and closely guarded secrets were beginning to spin out of control, but she nodded. 'I know, son. I know. Let's just get Molly's mother over here first and make sure she's going to be all right and then I'll deal with the rest later like I said I would. He won't get far. Martin was going to put some petrol in the car today. There's hardly any left and I doubt George would have much money on him to buy more. Plus with rationing he'd struggle to get any anyway. He's got no income apart from the bit I gave him. He used to have a variety show act but he hasn't worked for weeks since he lost his job.' She got to her feet and followed Martin to the door. 'I'll go and check on Molly. Don't tell Mary what's happened until you get her back here, Martin. I don't want her panicking. Just tell her Molly's not too good and that I need to see her.'

'Will do, Mrs Harrison. Back in a while.'

*

'Hey, who's that fella knocking on your mam's door?' Fran said as the car carrying Basil and the girls pulled round the corner onto Victory Street.

Bella gazed out of the window and frowned. 'Looks like the Harrisons' driver, Martin,' she said as the car pulled up outside her home. She got out of the car and the man turned. 'Oh, it is Martin,' she said. 'Hello, is my mam not in?'

'Oh, hello, Bella,' Martin said. 'I've knocked a couple of times, but there's no reply.'

'She might be out doing her shopping, or at her mate Ethel's, a few streets away. What's up? You look a bit mithered.'

'Err, there's been an incident at the Harrisons' involving your sister Molly,' Martin said. 'Mrs Harrison sent me over to bring your mother to the house as a matter of urgency.'

Bella frowned as Basil, Fran and Edie climbed out of the car. 'An incident?'

'What's up?' Fran asked.

'I'm not sure,' Bella began. 'But I need to get to Bobby's house right away. Basil, can you run me over there now, and can we squeeze Martin in as well?'

Basil nodded. 'We'll just drop Edie and Fran off round the corner and then we'll go straight there. Get back in, all of you. Squeeze in the back, Bella, let Martin sit at the front next to me.'

They all piled back in the vehicle and Basil put his foot down.

'See you later,' Bella called out of the window when Edie was dropped off. 'I'll let you know what's happening as soon as I know myself.'

'Is Molly okay?' Bella asked anxiously. 'Has she had an accident, or something?'

'It's not really for me to say anything,' Martin said. 'Mrs Harrison will explain.'

Basil parked the car outside the Harrisons' house and they all hurried to the door. Martin knocked loudly and Bobby let them in. His eyes opened wide when he saw Bella.

'I didn't know you were coming home,' he began, inviting them all inside. He pulled her into his arms. 'Where's your mam?'

'She wasn't in. Basil had just brought me home and I'll explain why later. It's a long story. And Martin was knocking at our front door. What's up with our Molly? Oh my goodness, Bobby, what have you done to your head?' she exclaimed, seeing the dressing his mother had put over the cut. 'What's going on?'

'Never mind me; I'll explain that later too. Come through to the dining room. Mother is just upstairs seeing to Molly—' He broke off as Fenella came running downstairs.

'Please, do come through,' she said. 'What a lovely surprise, Bella, and Basil too. We weren't aware you were coming home this week.'

'We weren't,' Basil said. 'But I'm afraid we've had something bad happen today and until I get it sorted out, I've had to bring my girls back to Liverpool.'

'That doesn't sound good,' Bobby said. 'How was Molly just now, Mum?' he asked, turning to his mother.

'She's still sleeping, but not quite as deeply,' Fenella replied. 'Please take seats and I'll make some tea and explain the situation. Is your mother not at home, Bella?'

Bella shook her head. 'She may be at the shops. You're worrying me. What's wrong with our Molly? Has she been taken ill? Should we get the doctor?'

Bobby took hold of her hand and held it tight. 'Let Mum make the tea and then we'll explain what's happened.'

After running upstairs to take a look at her deeply sleeping sister, Bella stared open-mouthed as Fenella Harrison told of the events of the morning.

'And you let this man leave the house? But why?' Bella exclaimed. 'He sounds dangerous.'

Basil nodded. 'He does indeed. Do I understand this right? He's your older brother, you say, but you hadn't seen him for years?'

Fenella nodded. 'Not since I was sixteen years old,' she replied, tears in her eyes. 'George said he'd tracked me down from old newspaper reports of my husband's death and Robert's accident.

He came to let me know that our younger brother Tommy had died out in France, and then he asked for help as he was destitute. He deserted and then he lost his civilian job and had no money. I just felt I had no choice, even though deep down I knew it was wrong. He's just about all I've got left of my family. Not that we were ever very close, but as they say, blood's thicker than water.'

'I'm surprised he was able to get a job after deserting, never mind lose one,' Martin said. 'If he'd got no identity papers employers would frown on that. He could be anyone. A German on the run, even. Surely his name would be on a list of people who have gone AWOL and employers should be checking that?'

Fenella sighed. 'He wasn't a normal worker and he'd changed his name after he deserted, so he may have got his hands on some fraudulent identity papers. There's nothing left in his room to identity him, I checked. He'd changed his name to Freddie and oddly enough worked in the same business as you, Bella; he was an entertainer doing magic acts. But when I told him I might be able to help him get a new job through ENSA and you, Basil, he said he wasn't ready to go back to work yet.'

Basil and Bella stared at one another. Basil spoke first. 'Your brother did a magic act? What name did he work under?'

Fenella shook her head. 'He never told me if he had a stage name, but he'd changed his name to Freddie Cagney instead of George Carter.'

Bella clapped her hand to her mouth, shaking her head in disbelief. 'Oh my God!'

Basil gave a low whistle. 'I don't bloody believe it. So this is where he vanished to.'

'You know him?' Fenella asked, her eyes wide with shock.

'Oh, we know him all right,' Basil told her. 'He worked for me on my team. I had to let him go a few months back because he had been behaving inappropriately with the young girls from my dance troupe. He was also hitting the bottle a bit too often and we believe he'd tried to tamper with a round of drinks that would probably render my young ladies unconscious.'

Fenella gasped. 'Like he's done with Molly? Oh my lord, he's evil. And to think I let him into my home. What was I thinking?' She stopped as a voice called from upstairs. 'Molly's awake,' she said and got to her feet. 'Bella, you come with me.'

Molly was sitting up in the bed looking bewildered, the blanket wrapped around her body. She stared as Bella and Fenella walked into the room.

'Molly, dear, are you okay?' Fenella asked as the young girl stared blankly at her. Then she looked at Bella and started to cry. Bella sat down beside her on the bed and held Molly in her arms.

'Where am I?' she managed eventually. 'I feel really strange.' She looked around the room and shook her head. 'Where's Freddie? We were going to London today to work together. Why are you here, Bella?'

Bella stared at Fenella over the top of Molly's head. 'What do I tell her?' she whispered.

Fenella shrugged helplessly and shook her head. 'The truth.'

Bella nodded and chewed her lip. 'Molly, Freddie has gone without you, love. I'm sorry.'

Molly pulled away from her sister and stared at her, disbelief in her eyes. 'Why would he do that? He promised me we would be famous if I danced around him while he did all his magic acts. He bought me clothes to wear, taught me how to do the tricks with him and showed me how he liked me to dance. He promised we'd be famous.'

Then she clapped a hand to her mouth. 'I'm not supposed to tell you anything. He said I had to keep what we did a secret. Did you all make him go away and leave me behind? Freddie would never just go without taking me with him, I know he wouldn't.'

Fenella sat down next to Bella and took Molly's hand. She swallowed hard. 'Molly, listen to me. Freddie is a very dangerous and bad man. When we came back to the house you were here on this bed unconscious. He must have given you something that made you fall asleep very deeply. Can you remember what you did before you came up here?'

Molly shook her head slowly. 'I'm not sure. Not really. Ah, I made us mugs of coffee and we drank it in the kitchen.' She screwed up her face as though remembering. 'It was that funny stuff, real coffee, not Camp like Mam buys.'

Fenella nodded. 'Did you at any time leave Freddie alone with your coffee mugs, even for a second or two?'

Mollie chewed her lip.' I don't think so. Err, oh wait a minute though. Yes, I filled the sugar bowl with cubes in the big pantry and when I brought it to the table he'd put the milk in the mugs already and told me to add three sugar cubes. But it was a bit too sweet for me.'

Fenella snorted. 'No doubt that was to hide the taste of anything that he'd added, like sleeping pills or something.'

Molly frowned. 'But why would he do that? We came up here and he asked me to put my red sparkly outfit on and we danced and then I don't really remember anything else…' She trailed off and touched the blanket she was wrapped in. 'I haven't got any clothes on,' she said, her eyes wide with shocked realisation. 'Where are my clothes?'

'They were on the floor but they're over there now.' Fenella pointed to a chair under the window, where she'd folded and placed the clothes. As Molly sat fully upright Fenella noticed the finger-mark bruises on the girl's upper arms. 'Did Freddie give you those marks?' she asked.

Molly nodded and started to cry. 'He said if I told anyone that he'd hurt me, I would lose my job here and he wouldn't take me with him. But I never told a soul, honestly, and he's still gone without me.'

Bella hugged her sister tight, tears filling her eyes. 'Thank goodness you didn't go with him. He's a very bad man and not nice where young girls are concerned.' She bit her lip and carried on. 'Molly, he was just about to rape you when Martin and Mrs Harrison burst into the room. He had you stripped naked and unconscious. You were so lucky that they came back when they did. He pushed Bobby down several stairs and Bobby cut his head and then Freddie stole the car. So we are going to get the police involved. You may well be asked to tell them everything he's done to you and how long he's been doing it. Do you understand what I mean?'

Molly nodded, her eyes wide. 'I can't believe he would do that to me. He was always touching me in places he shouldn't, but he's never tried to rape me. I don't think so anyway. As far as I know I've always been awake and I've never felt sleepy or anything before.'

'We can ask a doctor to talk to you, Molly,' Fenella said. 'Just to reassure you and to be on the safe side.'

Molly nodded and then looked puzzled. 'Why are you here, Bella? Is Mam here too?'

'We've had a bit of a problem with the show,' Bella said, thinking there was no point in adding to Molly's worries until they had to. 'We've just got to sort a few things out. And no, Mam's not here but Basil will go and see if she's arrived back home yet. She wasn't in earlier.'

Molly yawned and lay back down. 'I still feel very sleepy,' she said, snuggling into the pillow, her eyes heavy. 'Can I stay here for a bit longer?'

Fenella got to her feet and tucked the blankets around Molly as the young girl closed her eyes once more. 'We'll leave her to sleep for a while until we decide what to do next.'

Basil drove Bella round to her home, both of them silent for the short journey. 'Are you thinking what I'm thinking?' Bella asked, pointing to the pile of newspapers in the footwell. 'It's just too much of a coincidence not to be Freddie that did this.'

Basil nodded. 'He no doubt stole that photo of Levi from Bobby without Bobby realising it was missing until it was too late. Like you say, too much of a coincidence not to be him. Well, at least we can get HQ to start an investigation and to get onto all the newspapers to have the story retracted.'

Bella sighed. 'Some of it is still true though. Levi, Earl, Bobby and me.'

'Yes,' Basil began. 'But we can use that and be truthful about it. Freddie made it sound all sordid when in fact it's not at all. Maybe a nice photo can be taken of you and Bobby with the little fella and show the world you are not ashamed or hiding him or indeed abandoning him with your mother. The three of you will show a united front and the promise of a happy-ever-after life. The readers will love that, especially the women, who love a bit of romance. Also it may help any other young girl in a similar situation to know that her baby will be accepted and loved.'

Bella smiled as they pulled up on Victory Street. 'It all sounds very nice. But we still need to tell Bobby's mother yet. And Freddie needs to be caught by the police. Oh God, I do hope Fenella doesn't get arrested for taking him in.'

Basil shook his head. 'I doubt she will be. Once I've had my say and told them of the damage this man has done, his abuse of Molly, and that Fenella was afraid of what he might do to her, they'll be lenient, I'm sure. Now go and see if your mam is in and we'll get back over there.'

Chapter Nineteen

Fenella took a cup of tea up to Mary, who was sitting by the bed, waiting for Molly to wake up. Mary looked up as she came into the room. Her face was drawn and her eyes looked worried. She'd been told everything that had happened and said she had a funny feeling something was going on, as Molly had become a bit withdrawn and secretive over the last few weeks.

'I thought maybe she'd met a lad I wouldn't approve of, but most lads her age are away fighting the war.' Mary took a deep shuddering breath, sipped her tea and continued as Fenella pulled a chair over to sit by the bed with her. 'She's had this bee in her bonnet about joining the ENSA troupe and making a bit of a name for herself like Bella's done. I wish I'd taken her more seriously and let her go off with Bella and then this fella wouldn't have been able to influence her so much.'

'I'm so sorry, Mary,' Fenella said. 'I feel guilty for allowing him to stay here and manipulate Molly like he did.'

'It's not your fault. I still can't believe he was your George, Fenella, going under a false name like that. He was always a bit of a handful. I liked your Tommy though and I'm so very sorry he's passed away.'

'Thank you. It was a shock to get that news. There was always a part of me that thought about our Tommy often. I would like to have met up with him again at some point.'

'So, have you reported all this to the police? Basil said it was going to be dealt with.'

Fenella looked down at her shaking hands, clasped together in her lap, and sighed. 'I'm going to go downstairs in a moment and make the phone call. I'm worried; there's a chance they might arrest me, with me knowing George was a deserter. But Basil said I've to tell them he was threatening me if I let on to anyone; which he was, but not in the way Basil means. His threats were to expose something that I've kept to myself for most of my life, a huge secret, Mary. One I've hidden for many years. I'm scared that once it becomes no longer a secret, everything I hold dear to my heart will unravel and I will lose the one person who means more to me than anything else in the world. It may ruin the rest of my life – and his.' Tears flooded Fenella's blue eyes and rolled down her cheeks.

Mary rooted in her cardigan pocket and produced a clean handkerchief. 'Here, chuck, use this. What on earth can be so bad that it's upset you so much?'

Fenella sighed. 'Mary, there are some things that were never meant to be told. But I feel that I can trust you. After all, you know where I originally come from and you've only ever mentioned it once. You've let sleeping dogs lie about my past life; even though you could have bad-mouthed me all over Wavertree, you chose not to.'

Mary nodded and patted Fenella's hand. 'It wasn't my business to. We didn't all have the happy family home that I was lucky enough to grow up in,' she said. 'We didn't have much, but we were loved. I know it wasn't like that for you and your brothers.'

'No, indeed it wasn't. My father was a bully, and I'm afraid that George takes after him. Dad used to beat my mother black and blue if he couldn't have his own way or money for a pint. We hardly ever had enough to eat and the house was always cold. No proper beds to sleep on and just the clothes we stood up in. One night, after Dad had punched me hard and made my nose bleed,

I swore that was enough. I had to get away. I stole some money from his pocket after he'd fallen into a drunken stupor by the fire. I tidied myself up the best I could, grabbed a few things in a bag, walked out of the house while my mother was ill in bed and took a train from Lime Street station to Chester. I slept in a shop doorway that night and the next day I walked around the town looking for work.' Fenella paused, a haunted, faraway look in her eyes.

'I saw a postcard in the window of a small hotel for a chamber-maid's position. I went inside and a nice man on the desk, who turned out to be the owner, asked me what experience I'd had. I told him I was a school leaver and that I'd looked after the house for my mother and knew how to keep a place clean as well as cook. That was a lie because we never had anything in to cook and the cleaning was non-existent in our house.'

'Oh Fenella, I had no idea.' Mary took her hand.

Fenella took another deep breath. 'I knew I must have looked a bit of a mess, but I think he took pity on me and he said he would give me a trial run and that the position was to be a live-in job with a nice room and meals while on duty. That was such a relief for me as it meant I had a roof over my head and I would get fed as well. Uniforms were provided, so that helped me out on the clothes front until I had a bit put by to get some new ones. I'd only got a change of underwear with me and one spare dress that I'd shoved into the bag as I walked out.

'I enjoyed the work and I loved feeling clean; it was good to have regular baths. I was well fed and felt appreciated. I worked my way up from lowly chambermaid to front-of-house receptionist within the first two years. It seemed I'd managed to escape very successfully from my family – they didn't come looking for me and I never heard a word from them. The hotel guests were all very nice and I got plenty of tips from them to put by for a rainy day. They were, in the main, businessmen who stayed with us regularly and I got to know them all, as individuals who treated me kindly and with respect. One man, James, asked me out a few times and he was really nice, very smartly dressed, tall, blond-haired and blue-eyed. But he was a good few years older than me.

'James was also a bit secretive about his background. He told me he was in banking, and he had lovely manners and a nice way with him for the better things in life, which seemed to rub off on me. I wanted to experience all that as well.'

'Well, you did really well for yourself. Look at this house,' said Mary, giving her a squeeze.

'Well, it wasn't quite that simple. Another of our guests was also a very nice man and we became good friends and confidantes – his name was Charles. Charles told me he'd been let down by a girl and that he was a trainee pilot with the Royal Air Force. He asked if I'd write to him when he was stationed away as he was expecting to be sent down south. I said yes but I didn't think anything would come of it, because I was already stepping out with James.'

Fenella paused again and looked at Mary, who was still listening intently, a concerned expression on her face, almost as though she had guessed what was to come next. 'When I discovered I was pregnant and I told James, he vanished into the night, never to be seen again. The manager told me he was a married man with adult children and a very demanding wife. He'd run scared and that was it. He left me to deal with matters on my own. I was terrified and I cried on Charles's shoulder that night and to my surprise he asked me to marry him. I was very fond of him and we'd grown close. I knew there was a chance that I might even fall in love with him given time, which of course I did.

'He told me that he'd been ill as a child with a case of severe mumps and was told he would probably never be able to father children. He said he would bring my child up as his own and we'd take the secret to the grave with us. Well *he* did just that, of course. But on a visit to Liverpool when Robert was two, I bumped into my mother, who told me she was dying. I foolishly told her my secret, thinking it would go no further, because a girl's mother is the one person she should be able to trust. I have no doubt it was she that told George – there is no other person in the world who could have done that. He could do no wrong in my mother's eyes.

'I never set eyes on them again, but I knew my parents had died as I kept an eye on local news and the obituaries. Charles and I went to live in Oxfordshire near Brize Norton air base, where he was stationed until Robert was due to start primary school. Charles's parents owned this house and he inherited it when they both passed away within weeks of each other. And that's how we came to be living back in Liverpool. George has threatened to tell Robert that Charles wasn't his real father. I'm terrified that he'll come back or lie in wait for him somewhere and do just that. Robert will hate me for lying and keeping the truth from him for so long.'

Mary shook her head as Fenella's long confession came to an end. 'Don't punish yourself any more. Robert won't hate you at all. Our kids are more forgiving and understanding than we give them credit for.' She gazed at Molly, still slumbering peacefully. She smoothed her hair from her face and shuddered inwardly at what could have happened to her daughter if Martin and Fenella hadn't walked in. It didn't bear thinking about. George might well have murdered Molly, never mind raped her. Her heart went out to Fenella and a sudden thought struck her. It was also confession time for both her and Bella. There would never be a better moment than this.

'Let's go downstairs for a while,' Mary suggested. 'I don't think Molly will wake up any time soon. Whatever he gave her has well and truly zonked her out. Martin's gone off to get ready for his ARP session and Bella and Bobby might be glad of a bit of respite from Levi for a while. He can be quite a handful when he wants to be and they're not used to that.'

Fenella nodded. 'I'll just go to the bathroom and wash my face. I don't want Bobby to see that I've been crying.'

'Listen, Fenella, oh bugger it, can I call you Fen, it's less of a mouthful!'

Fenella smiled. 'Of course you can, Mary. It's what my friends all call me.'

'Then I'll consider that a compliment and call myself your friend. Leave washing your face. Bobby won't mind and I think you really need to say something to him today. Don't put it off any longer. George could turn up here any time. He may lie in wait over on the park and then break in. At least once you've told Bobby you have no reason then not to call the police and they can track him down and get him arrested for all that he's done.'

'Okay.' Fenella nodded. 'Before I lose my nerve, let's get it over with.'

Downstairs all was quiet. Mary popped her head round the dining room door to find Levi, his thumb in his mouth, fast asleep on Bobby's knee, and Bobby with his arm round Bella's shoulders. The pair were snuggled together on the sofa, gazing into each other's eyes with Levi between them, totally oblivious to their mothers observing them from the doorway.

'Bless them, they look so good together, the perfect little family,' Fenella whispered.

Mary nodded her agreement. 'They do, and they are,' she replied. She pulled Fenella back into the hall and pointed to Bobby's bedroom door. 'It doesn't seem like the moment to interrupt them. Can we go and sit in there for a few minutes? I'm going to tell you something that's also been kept a big secret, but when I've finished, you must promise me that you will speak to Bobby.'

Looking puzzled, Fenella opened Bobby's bedroom door and then closed it behind her and Mary. They sat down on the sofa under the window. Mary took a deep breath. 'Right, what you saw back there, the perfect little family, is exactly what those three are. That baby is our Bella's child. The result of a very brief relationship she had with a married American pilot when she was trying to pick up the pieces after your lad got wed to that Alicia girl. She wasn't in love with the man; she loves your Bobby, as you can see.'

Mary rushed on before Fenella could interrupt. 'She was going to have the baby adopted but I offered to take care of him, and I'd thought about maybe even adopting him myself so that Bobby and Bella could get on with their own lives once they are married. But your Bobby is really taken with our Levi and seeing the little lad fast asleep on his knee, I think the feeling is quite mutual. Bobby has already told Bella he wants to bring him up as his own child. They knew they would need to tell you soon, but the time has never been right. I think you can see for yourself that Bobby will be as good a dad to Levi as Charles was to him.'

As Mary finished telling her tale, Fenella burst into tears and gave Mary a hug. 'Bella makes my boy happier than I've ever seen him. If he can be half the father Charles was then Levi will have the best daddy in the world – and I intend to seriously compete with you in the grandma stakes, Mary, make no mistake about that,' she finished with a watery smile.

Mary burst out laughing. 'Right, you're on. That kiddie deserves nothing but the best, no matter what the gossips will no doubt have to say. I'm going to go and bring our Bella in here now, and Levi too, if I can prise him away from your Bobby. While you've got some privacy before Molly wakes up and Basil gets back, just sit with Bobby and tell him the truth. It won't be as hard as you think it will. Bobby's a good lad and an understanding one at that. Come on. Do it before you lose your nerve. Then we'll let Bobby tell Bella in his own time. What we've got here now is a bit like history repeating itself in a roundabout sort of way.'

*

Bella fidgeted on the sofa next to her mother. Mam had beckoned her to leave Bobby's side and follow her. She'd indicated for her to bring Levi as well, but he was fast asleep and Bobby whispered to leave him be for now. His mother had joined him on the sofa; her face was a mask of worry and Bella knew without a doubt that she'd been told Levi was Bella's child. She was no doubt trying to talk Bobby out of marrying her and taking Levi on as his own.

Mam had confirmed she'd told Fenella the truth and said she had to let Bobby talk to his mother on his own. They'd been ages now but she didn't think for one moment Bobby would let her down; he would tell his mother that he'd already agreed to bring Levi up as his own son. But even so, after this morning's shock over the newspapers, anything was possible. Mam hadn't mentioned that yet, so Bella assumed she'd not seen that morning's *Echo*.

Bella had just opened her mouth to start telling Mam the tale of the scandalous news reports when the door opened and Fenella walked in carrying a smiling Levi, Bobby, leaning on a walking stick to help his balance as he was still a bit shaky from his fall, in her wake. Both wore serious expressions and Bella's heart sank.

Fenella spoke first, her voice shaky. 'Bella, you go with Bobby, he's got something to tell you. I'll stay here with Mary and this little man.'

Bella got up slowly, feeling puzzled. Levi shrieked 'Gan, Gan' and held his arms out to her mam. Bella smiled. It was the first time she'd heard him say a real word that made sense. She followed Bobby back to the dining room and sat down on the sofa.

'Please don't look so worried, Bella,' he said, sitting down beside her and taking her hand.

'I can't help it,' she said and burst into tears. 'Mam told me that she knows Levi is mine. Has she told you not to marry me?'

'No, of course she's not,' Bobby replied. 'And I wouldn't listen to her even if she did. But no, she's keen that we *do* get married and she's really looking forward to being Levi's grandma.'

'Really?' Bella smiled through her tears.

'Yes, really. She had something important to tell me that came as a huge shock, I've got to admit, but once I'd heard all her story

I understood why she had to do what she did.' Bella looked at him, his eyes moist with tears as he carried on. 'She's my mother, and I have to forgive her because I love her and I know she only ever tried to do her best for me, well apart from the Alicia saga, of course.' Bobby went on to tell Bella his mother's whole sorry tale. She shook her head from time to time and squeezed his hand reassuringly.

'So you see,' he concluded, 'I'm following in my father's footsteps by wanting to become a good father to Levi.' He pulled Bella into his arms and kissed her and hugged her tight.

Bella stroked his cheek. 'I love you so much, Bobby Harrison. I really do.'

'And I love you too, my darling. Shall we go and see the boy and his grannies now and then we can all start to relax a bit and my mum can get that phone call made to the police. She doubts George will have got very far in the car, but even so, he needs to be found.'

Bella hesitated. 'Well, seeing as today is for revelations, I'll tell you why Basil was here first and then you will be ready for when he comes back. We need to tell our mothers as well because it's a nasty business and they'll be part of it for a while.' She gave Bobby a brief outline of the newspaper reports and said that Basil would bring back the papers in the car so they could all read the malicious scandal that George was responsible for.

Bobby shook his head. 'I can't believe that evil man is related to me. Let's hope he's behind bars soon before he does any more damage.'

Chapter Twenty

With Molly safely back home and tucked up in her own bed, Levi asleep in his cot beside her, Bella made cocoa for herself and her mother. As they relaxed in the front sitting room with the blackout curtains pulled together to shut out the dark night, Bella had reflected on the latter half of the day. Fenella had called the police and Basil had got back to Wavertree at the same time as the police had arrived at the house. Statements had been taken from a still bewildered Molly and from Fenella.

The full details and description of George Carter had been radioed to the powers that be and a manhunt was now on. Basil had showed the news reports to the officers and told them he believed this was also linked to the wanted man. Ever thoughtful, Basil had also arranged for new locks to be fitted at the house as there was concern that George may come back in the dead of the night and try to gain entry with the keys he'd taken. ARP wardens would be given the information and told to keep a watch out for him as they made their nightly patrols in the area, and Martin was on local watch, so he would be sure to keep an extra eye open.

When the officers left Bobby's home, Basil had made calls to the base he'd just left and was informed the military police were now involved in the search too. 'I've spoken to our HQ in London,' he told Bella after everyone had been shown the papers he'd brought back. 'Within the next couple of days a further report will be published, telling the truth. A phone call will be made here to arrange for a photographer to come and take a nice photograph of Bella and Bobby and also one of the pair of you with Levi. I've also spoken to Earl, Bella, and he was upset of course by the reports, but more for you than himself. He said to wish you and Bobby well and if you need anything, like his signature on adoption papers for Levi, just to contact him at the base.'

Bella had breathed a sigh of relief and she and Bobby had agreed to do that. Both Mary and Fenella also said it would be a nice idea.

'I felt proper out of me depth this afternoon,' Mary admitted as Bella handed her a mug of cocoa and sat down on the armchair under the window, her hands wrapped round her mug. 'I've never heard anything like it in me life before, except in films at the picture house. But them policemen were really nice, weren't they, chuck? It's funny because whenever I see a policeman in the street I always feel guilty even though I've not done anything wrong.'

'Oh Mam, you worry too much,' said Bella.

'It's because me dad always used to threaten us with a policeman if we were naughty when we were kids. How things stay in your mind, eh? But them two were ever so nice and reassuring, they were good with our Molly and it must have felt so embarrassing for her having to tell them what that bugger did. And I know Fen felt sick with worry as well, but they treated her kind once they'd heard her tale in full. She's been through such a lot the last few months – but then, haven't we all.' She took a sip of her cocoa and smiled. 'Oh I'm so glad they're accepting our Levi into the family, you know. It means such a lot.'

Bella nodded. 'It does to me as well, Mam. He's going to be spoiled rotten by you two grannies. All he'll need to do is bat those long eyelashes or pout his lip and you'll both be putty in his hands.' Bella paused for a moment before continuing. 'Mam, you have no idea how very grateful I am to you for looking after Levi for me. He's such a good boy and that's all down to you. I know it's not always been easy for you and I also realise how hard it will be to hand him back to me.'

Mary smiled. 'I can see how much you love him, chuck, and that makes it easier. I was upset for you at first, love, being let down by Earl, but I can see that wouldn't have worked out. You'd never have settled in America. You're too much of a Liver bird to leave Liverpool. Being with Bobby is better for you both, and for us.'

'I agree. And I like that you and his mum are now the best of friends. That will make life so much easier for us all in the future.

*

Bella had tossed and turned for ages on the sofa, trying to get to sleep. Her bed had been dismantled to make space for Levi's cot and as she was hardly ever home anyway, the sofa would do her fine for the odd night's visit. She held her breath as she listened to footsteps on the pavement outside, but decided it must just be the ARP patrolling the street.

It was hard to switch off her mind from the events of the long and draining day. So much had happened since Basil had summonsed them all to the Nissen hut this morning. It felt like days ago now. She hadn't even had a minute to catch up with Fran and Edie yet. She would call and see them both tomorrow. Basil had called on them just to give them a quick briefing, as he'd put it.

The ENSA show tonight had been cancelled as advised by HQ and the troupe would be moving on in a couple of days. Bella hoped that the Bryant Sisters would be moving on with them. Otherwise her career was well and truly over. Ah well, there'd be nothing standing in the way of her and Bobby getting married this year then.

Her eyes had just started to shut when the wail of the air raid siren began. 'Oh, for God's sake,' she muttered. 'I don't bloody believe it. This is the last thing we need tonight.' She dragged herself off the sofa and called upstairs to rouse her mam and Molly, then remembered Levi and ran up to lift him out of the cot, his eyes wide with fear. Poor little soul. This is why Wales was better for them all. They'd never once had to go in the shelter Bertie had built in the yard, according to her mam.

She wrapped him in a blanket and carried him down to the cellar, followed by her mam and Molly. He was crying and reaching out for her mam and Bella reluctantly handed him over. She had to keep reminding herself that although she was his mother, he didn't really know her. They curled up on the camp beds to try to get some rest. The damp air of the cellar wasn't very pleasant and Bella sat up and wafted herself with a magazine.

Levi spotted her and giggled. She smiled at him and waved. Maybe not going back to work might be a good thing. She could be a proper mummy to him and a good wife to Bobby. But she loved her job and the buzzing feelings she felt onstage when she was entertaining. It was like a drug that she couldn't do without. But did that make her shallow? She sighed and lay back down again, listening to the drone of German bombers flying low overhead.

A loud piercing whistling and the sound of squealing overhead as a bomb was released close by had Molly shooting upright.

'It's them horrible screaming bombs again,' she cried, 'and it sounds right overhead. Oh God, I wanna go back to Wales. I hate it here. I don't wanna die yet.' She put her hands over her ears and screamed louder than the bomb as a dull thud and explosion sounded nearby.

Bella jumped up and grabbed Levi from her mam. 'Get your slippers and dressing gown on, Mam. We may need to get out. That sounded a bit too close for comfort.' She stopped at a loud hammering noise on the door.

Molly screamed again, shaking with fright. 'What if it's him come back to hurt me?'

'Who?' Bella and their mam asked together.

'Freddie,' she sobbed. 'He knows where I live because he walked me home one night when I worked late.'

'It won't be him, Molly, honestly,' Bella assured her. 'He's long gone. It'll be the ARP warden. I'm going to dash up and see what he wants us to do.' As she spoke, she heard glass shattering. 'Sounds like one of our windows. Mam, get our handbags and gas masks. Come on, Molly, hurry up.' Bella shot upstairs and opened the door, Levi in her arms. The ARP warden was standing on the pavement along with a few of their neighbours who were still in the area.

'The property three houses down got hit,' he told her. 'We need to get you somewhere safe in case there's a gas explosion. Just take what you need for now and you can get the rest tomorrow if we can allow you back in. Just follow that man over there, love. Church hall is open. The WI will be along shortly to look after you all. And we'll patch that window up, so don't worry.'

As they trooped up the road with their pyjama-clad neighbours, Bella shook her head in disbelief at the gaping hole in the nearby roof. Two fire engines pulled round the corner, their bells clanging, and stopped in front of the blazing house. 'Oh, God, I hope no one was in there,' she gasped, feeling sick. 'They would never get out if they are trapped in the cellar. My God, it could have been us.' She clutched Levi tightly and looked behind to see her mam with her arm round Molly, who was sobbing.

'As far as we know the house was empty – the owners are with family out of the city, according to the neighbours opposite,' said the ARP warden. 'But the front door was ajar when I went to call for them to get out, so someone will check inside when the fire is out and they say it's safe to go in and look.'

In the church hall Bella found a table and saw that her family were seated and comfortable and then went to the ladies'. As she came back through the porch, she saw Bobby and his mother making their way into the hall. Fenella was pushing him in the wheelchair.

'Bobby,' she called, dashing to his side.

'Bella, oh thank God,' he said, clasping her hand. 'When we heard it was Victory Street I insisted on coming here with Mum.

She's on care duties tonight in the event of a raid. You go, Mum, Bella will look after me.'

Fenella gave Bella a hug. 'I'm so glad you are all safe, dear. I'll see you later.' She dashed away to join her team of volunteers.

'We got a lift over from an ARP warden,' Bobby continued. 'Oh my goodness I am so glad to see you. I was hoping to see someone who at least knows your family and to find out if you are okay. I haven't got my new limb on so I can't even stand up and hug you right now.'

She smiled. 'Don't worry about that. And we're fine,' she said. 'Just a bit shaken up, needless to say. Mam, Molly and Levi are in there. Are you coming to join us? You might get in the way of the tea ladies.'

'Yes please,' he replied. 'What a day. I wouldn't like to repeat this one in a hurry.'

'Nor I,' she said, pushing open the doors and taking Bobby across to her mam and Molly.

Levi beamed at Bobby and held his arms out to sit on his knee. Bella lifted him across and he snuggled into the warm blanket tucked over Bobby's legs, stuffed his thumb in his mouth and closed his eyes.

Mam shook her head. 'Well would you look at that. He's certainly got a soft spot for you, son.'

Bobby smiled. 'And me for him.'

'I'll go and get us a tray of tea,' Bella said.

'See if there are any biscuits, Bella,' Molly said. 'I'm a bit hungry.'

'I'm not surprised,' Bobby said. 'You've slept nearly all day and hardly eaten a thing.'

When everyone had been given refreshments and settled on the wooden floor as comfortably as they could with the donated blankets, pillows and eiderdowns that the WI had been collecting over the weeks, Fenella made her way over to the table where her son and his soon-to-be family were seated. She dragged across a seat from another table and sat down next to Mary. 'Oh my, well we could have done without that shock tonight, of all nights,' she said. 'Phew. Wonder if they've managed to put the fire out yet?'

'I hope so,' Mary said. 'Before it spreads along the terrace. The roof had gone completely; it was a right mess and blazing like billy-o. Ah well, the last twenty-four hours will keep my Mass Observation diary-writing going for weeks.'

'And mine.' Fenella smiled. 'Mary,' she began. 'Bobby and I sat talking about the future after Basil took you all home. We have a suggestion to make. Please don't feel under any obligation, but it seemed like a good plan, didn't it, son?'

Bobby smiled. 'It did. It still does, in fact.'

'Well we're all ears,' Mary said. 'Isn't that right, girls?'

'Yes,' Bella and Molly chorused.

'When the sirens went off tonight and we had to go down to the cellar, I remembered you telling me how cold and damp yours always felt, Mary. How horrible it was to spend hours down there until the all-clear sounded. And I know that's one of the reasons your Bella made you join Molly in Wales.'

She paused and they all nodded. 'You know how big our house is and we're rattling around in it, just Bobby and me. There are also four cellars – two need clearing but the other two are fully furnished and heated and ideal for a night like tonight. We've had a ramp put in at the back so that we can get Bobby down there easily, and it's a good job we have as tonight he'd just settled down without his new limb.'

She paused for breath and then continued. 'Anyway, I digress. We have all that space in the house, spare bedrooms, sitting rooms and the two bathrooms. We wondered if you'd all like to move in and make the place your home? After all, we'll be family before you know it.' She sat back on her chair as they all stared at her, mouths open. She fully expected Mary to turn her down, but to her surprise the other woman smiled and looked at her girls, who were nodding their heads.

'I don't know what to say, Fen,' Mary began. 'It's very generous of you and I think it's a wonderful idea. I insist on paying you rent, of course, and our share of the bills like I have to do now.'

'I wouldn't expect you to pay rent,' Fenella said. 'I own the house outright, so there's no need. If you want to help with the bills then we can work something out and we can do the grocery shopping between us.'

'We can't live there for nothing,' Mary said. 'I'll help our Molly out with the cleaning and cooking if you and Bobby help look after his little lordship. I was going to get a job soon anyway, but having someone to mind Levi is my main problem.'

Fenella's face lit up with a big smile. 'Mary, if that's what you want, it would be our pleasure. The house needs bringing back to life. The soul has gone from it since Charles passed away. Molly, dear, I know you've had an awful experience in the house, but I hope you will be able to put that behind you in time and enjoy living there. I have a lovely bedroom for you. It's perfect for a girl and overlooks The Mystery Park. You can help to choose the paint for the walls, and new curtains. We'll make it exactly as you want it.'

Molly smiled shyly at her and Fenella turned to Mary. 'There's a small room at the back that will make a nice nursery for Levi. Mary, there's a lovely bedroom in between mine and the bathroom that you can make yours, and Bobby and Bella will have his downstairs converted room when they are married. Meantime there are three attic rooms for Bella to choose from for when she's home. Martin will do the painting and freshening up and all we ladies need to do is pick our favourite colours.'

She looked round at their smiling faces. 'I feel so excited, I don't know about you lot.' She laughed as they all nodded enthusiastically, then turned as a lady called her name and beckoned her to the porch. 'Won't be a moment,' she said and hurried across the room.

'Mrs Harrison, there's two police officers asking for you,' the lady said.

'Thank you, Clara. Wonder what they want?' She hurried into the porch and saw the two officers who had been to her house earlier in the day. 'Hello, officers. Can I help you?'

'Mrs Harrison,' the taller of the policemen said. 'We have some news for you. Your car was found abandoned on the Dock Road this evening. The keys were still inside. It's been taken to the station for examination and fingerprints. It appears to be in good order, but it was out of petrol, so it seems like our man didn't get very far. Now this is just to warn you that he's on the loose somewhere, possibly still in Liverpool.'

Fenella covered her mouth with her hands, her heart racing.

The policeman continued. 'We found an empty whisky bottle in the footwell so it's very likely he's in an intoxicated state. We believe he's a dangerous man and quite possibly out for revenge. His plans to drive wherever he was going to disappear appear to have been scuppered. In view of the fact he may be out for revenge, we feel you should have someone with you at the house tonight. We saw your driver out on ARP duties earlier, so we let him know and as soon as he comes off duty he will come straight to your house.'

'Thank you, officer. The locks on the house were changed earlier, so he won't be able to get back in, which makes me feel less nervous, but even so…'

The policeman nodded his head. 'Is there anyone who can give you a lift back to your house tonight?'

'I'll sort something out, don't worry. And thank you for letting me know.'

Fenella went back inside and rejoined the others. She related what the officers had told her and patted Molly on the arm as the girl's colour drained.

'What if he tries to come after me?' Molly said. 'I feel really scared now. I don't want to go back to our house. He knows which street we live on. He might break in and murder us all.' Molly's voice was getting higher and people were turning to look at her.

'Shhh, Mol,' Bella said, slipping her arm round her sister's shoulders. 'Don't worry, he won't. Shall we all come back to yours tonight, Bobby? It might be the safest thing to do.'

'I think that's a good idea, don't you Mum?' Bobby said and Fenella nodded.

'We'll have to make do with what's there for now,' she said, 'until we get it all nice, but at least there's safety in numbers.'

'I need to get some things from our house for Levi,' Mary said. 'Nappies and his dried milk powder and bottles.'

'Let me just see if any of my ladies has a car, so they can run us to your house,' Fenella suggested. She dashed to the kitchen area and was back in minutes with a tall lady who jangled a set of keys as she walked. 'Rose is going to take us,' she said. 'Shall Bella and I go?'

Mary nodded. 'Just be careful and don't go in unless the firemen say it's all right. I hope they do, but it's not worth taking chances for a couple of nappies. We'll manage somehow or other.'

*

Bella took her door key out of her handbag as the car approached Victory Street. 'One of the fire engines has gone now but there's an ambulance outside the house that got worst hit,' she said. 'That's really odd because the house was empty. The family are staying with relatives in a safer area.'

'Maybe one of the firemen has been injured,' Fenella said. 'Shall I get out and ask if it's safe for us to go inside yours?'

Bella nodded and watched as a stretcher was carried out and whoever was on it was covered head to toe. The stretcher was placed in the back of the waiting ambulance, which drove away with no bells clanging, a sure and certain sign that the person on the stretcher had lost their life. Rose made the sign of the cross as Fenella got out of the car. Bella watched as she approached one of the firemen, who was busy rewinding reels of hosepipe.

'Yes, madam, can I help you?'

'I hope so. My friend needs to get into her home for some things for her baby. She's staying with me tonight for safety's sake. Will it be okay to enter?'

'Which house is it? I'll come in with you.'

'Three doors down. The one where someone is boarding up the window. There where the car is parked.'

He nodded his head. 'Come on then.'

Fenella beckoned to Bella, who got out of the car and followed the fireman. She nodded at the man boarding up the window and thanked him. 'I won't be a minute,' she said. 'Everything I need is in the back sitting room.'

She dashed through and pulled several dry nappies off the clothes maiden, two pairs of rubber pants and a couple of bibs. Two romper suits were folded on the table ready to go upstairs, so she added those to the pile, and got a tin of National Dried Milk for babies from the cupboard in the kitchen. Levi's feeding bottles were on the draining board with a bowl of washed teats.

Bella sighed. All these things her mam did as a matter of course, that she herself hadn't got a clue about. She hadn't even made him a bottle since he was three months old and she'd gone back and rejoined the Bryant Sisters. It was time she learned.

She stashed everything away in Mam's big shopping bag and went back outside. Fenella was by the front door staring up the darkened street as a fireman came out of the bomb-damaged house carrying a suitcase. There wasn't much light because of the blackout, but in Rose's dimmed headlights Fenella was staring at the suitcase as though she recognised it.

'Are you okay?' Bella asked.

Fenella nodded. 'I won't be a minute.' She dashed up the street, leaving Bella staring after her.

*

'That case,' she began. 'May I look at it please?'

'It's a bit wet and mucky I'm afraid,' the fireman said. 'But feel free.'

She bent to look at the catch on the left-hand side. Scratched into the chrome, just as she suspected they would be, were the initials FH. This was the case she had used to travel to see Charles when he was first posted to Oxfordshire, just before she joined him for good when Bobby was born.

It was an unusual shade of blue and she'd chosen it because it was the same colour as the uniform he wore. She'd taken it on the train and had scratched her initials on in case she lost it. She'd had a label attached, but it was an extra precaution in her young eyes. *What was it doing in that house?*

'Do you recognise it?' the fireman asked.

She nodded. 'I'd like to know what it was doing in that house. The last time I saw it was in the attic room at…' She tailed off as realisation dawned, and clapped her hand to her mouth. George had rushed out with a case, the one he had knocked Bobby down the stairs with. She hadn't noticed it was hers. She supposed she'd just assumed it was one he'd bought from somewhere while he was living at the house.

'Are you okay, madam?' the fireman asked. 'Here, sit on the wall a minute.' He put the case down and helped her to the low brick wall that fronted the terraced house.

Bella came rushing towards them. 'What's wrong? You're white as a sheet.'

Fenella pointed to the case. 'That's mine. George must have taken it when he left the house. That person they took away on the stretcher, I think I might know who it is,' she told the fireman. 'You need to contact a policeman urgently.'

As she spoke Bella spotted Martin doing his ARP patrol on the opposite side of the street. She called him over and explained what had happened.

'Okay, just leave it with me. Get Mrs Harrison home and I'll see if I can locate the two police officers that were patrolling on the next road. I'll see you after my shift. Look after that case,' he said to the fireman. 'It's needed as evidence in a serious matter.'

Chapter Twenty-One

Liverpool, August 1944

On Monday afternoon during the last week of August, Bella, Fran and Edie sat back on the plush velvet chairs in the grand, half-empty lounge at the Adelphi Hotel, enjoying tea and biscuits while waiting for Basil to join them. They'd had a day off and a wander around what was left of their beautiful city. Fran said she felt like crying at the devastation. Newspaper reports told that much of Europe had now slipped from Hitler's grasp, but you'd never think it when you looked around Liverpool. Rumour had it that he'd now got new rocket weapons, so God help them.

'And all because some jumped-up little German idiot with a stupid moustache fancies himself in control of the world,' she said. 'Well he's not having any more of our city. Enough is enough. Look at all the problems he's given just us lot. Mine and Edie's lads are God knows where, your Bobby has lost half his leg, you've both lost your dads and we nearly lost our jobs – although that wasn't all down to Hitler; but they did reckon Freddie, or George, or whatever you want to call him, lost his mind when his brother was killed and then the drink turned him into a demon.'

Bella and Edie nodded. 'Good job he died in that fire, because who knows where his warped mind would have taken him next,'

.id. 'Your Molly is lucky to still be alive, when you think .it it, Bella.'

'She is,' Bella agreed. 'I dread to think what would have happened if Martin and Fenella hadn't run up those stairs.'

'Well at least you're all safe now and it must be lovely living at Bobby's house.'

'It is. Mam and Molly love it and there's so much space. Levi is being spoilt rotten by all four of them. Bobby's as bad as the women at spoiling him. Levi loves to play in the garden and toddle about on the lawn. And he's got a swing that he enjoys. He rules the roost in that house.'

Fran laughed. 'And to think how worried you were at telling Bobby about Levi.'

Bella nodded. 'I know. And he's such a natural with him, Levi just loves him. Molly is teaching him to say Dada now, and Bobby is so thrilled when he manages it.'

She let her thoughts wander back to the week of the move into Bobby's family home, which had taken place as soon after the bombing as could be organised. Mary had taken some of her nicer things with her and then given the rest to help people who had lost everything. The WI organised the collection and all went smoothly.

Molly loved her new lilac-and-white bedroom with a pretty brass double bed and a grown-up dressing table where she could sit and do her hair and practise putting on her make-up. She never ventured up to the attic rooms and nobody asked her to.

The body removed from the fire- and bomb-damaged house on Victory Street was eventually identified as George Carter, Fenella's brother. It horrified the Rogers family to think that he'd broken in there knowing full well it was only three doors away from Molly's family home. They could only surmise why and then try to put it out of their minds for good.

Basil and the ENSA headquarters had managed to sort everything out over the scandal stories and, just like Basil had said, those newspapers were now the wrappings for someone's fish and chips. The girls had been back at work for several weeks, travelling up and down the country, with Bobby joining them when they were close enough for him to be driven to the shows by Martin. Their popularity hadn't waned at all and Bella was also singing more solo songs than ever before. They were still loved by all the armed forces up and down the country.

Fran spotted Basil by the entrance doors to the lounge and waved him over. She poured him a cup of tea and he sat down and took a big sip.

'Just what the doctor ordered,' he said. 'Right, ladies, have I got a surprise for you three.'

They looked at one another and sat forward in their chairs as he finished his cup of tea. 'Well that was very nice, but I think we may need something a little bit sparkly to celebrate with when I tell you my news.' He waved to a waitress and when she came to the table he asked for four glasses of champagne or their best sparkling wine.

'We've got champagne, sir.' The waitress smiled.' It's in short supply but there was a wedding at the weekend and we've some left over.' She looked at the girls and gasped. 'Oh my God, you're the Bryant Sisters. Oh, my two soldier brothers love you girls. They've seen you sing a few times at their camp in Catterick before they got sent to Europe.'

Bella smiled. 'We love playing for the soldiers at Catterick camp. They're a lively lot. I hope your brothers are safe over there.'

'As much as they can be,' the girl said, tears filling her eyes.

Bella patted her hand. 'We know,' she said. 'Believe me, we know.'

The girl nodded and walked to the bar. She brought back a bottle and four tall champagne flutes. 'Compliments of the management,' she said, nodding over to the bar, where the manager raised his hand and smiled.

'Thank you kindly,' Basil said and raised his hand back. 'How very thoughtful of them. That's what comes when you begin to make a name for yourself, ladies.'

'Basil,' Fran said. 'Are you going to put us out of our misery, or shall I beat this special news out of you with my bare fists!'

He laughed. 'All in good time, my dear Fran.' He took an engraved silver case from his pocket and took his time choosing a cigar.

Bella smirked as Basil lit up and puffed contentedly. 'All good things come to those who wait,' he teased.

Bella thought Fran would burst a blood vessel as Basil flicked ash into a glass ashtray. 'Right, ladies,' he began finally. 'On Friday night we are doing a very important show right here in Liverpool at the Grand Central Hall. Which fortunately has not suffered much damage and is ready to use again after a clean-up. It's not one of our usual ENSA variety shows, no Tina's Tappers or Tommy, Tuppence and the Tumbling Terriers. This show is all about the best in swing music that there is.'

Fran frowned. 'Just the music, no singing?'

'Oh there'll be singing all right,' he said. 'That's courtesy of you ladies.'

'Okay, but what about the band who'll be backing us?' Edie asked. 'Are they any good and will we have time to rehearse with them before Friday?'

'They're *pretty* good actually.' Basil raised an eyebrow and flicked more ash into the ashtray. 'Probably the best band in the world right now, I'd say, and yes, you'll be rehearsing on Wednesday and Thursday afternoons this week.'

Bella frowned. 'Where are they from, this band?'

'America,' he said. 'Where most of the best bands are from. But this is *the* best. Many members are from the army and air force and the band is now known as the AAF band. And their leader specifically asked HQ for the Bryant Sisters.'

Bella's hand flew to her mouth as realisation dawned. 'Oh my God, Basil, are you teasing us, or do you honestly mean that Glenn Miller has really asked for us?'

'He most certainly has,' Basil finished, leaning back and grinning like a Cheshire cat. 'So what do you say to that?'

Fran was speechless for once in her life and Edie just shook her head in disbelief.

'I'll take it that's a yes.' Basil grinned. 'Right, let's get that champagne open then.'

*

Bella took several deep breaths to calm her frayed nerves, and pinned her khaki cap to her carefully set hair with shaking hands. They were seated in quite a posh dressing room with lights round the mirrors, a far cry from the poky storage rooms they usually used at the base camps. 'I really can't believe we are doing this,' she said. 'I mean us, of all people, about to go onstage and sing with Glenn Miller.'

'I know,' Edie said. 'My mam is so excited. All our mams are. Bet they never thought they'd see this happening, ever.'

'Bobby and his mother are out there too,' Bella said. 'But our Molly wouldn't come. She's staying at home looking after Levi. Said she'd had enough of show business for this year.'

'Oh bless her, poor Molly,' Fran said. 'But I can't really blame her.'

Bella went to answer a knock at the door and gasped with surprise. It was a young man in a US air force uniform, carrying three large bouquets of colourful flowers, who said, 'With compliments from the band.'

'Oh my, these are gorgeous,' Bella cried. 'Thank you so much.'

'Our pleasure,' the young man said, doing a little bow as he left.

As the girls admired their beautiful flowers there was another knock at the door. This time it was Basil.

'Five more minutes, ladies,' he announced. 'How are you all feeling?'

'Nervous,' they chorused.

'You'll be fine,' he assured them. 'The rehearsals have all gone well, Glenn is really happy with that. There's not an empty seat in the house and the band are in fine tune. Just go out there and give them your all. I'm very proud of you and you look great in those new uniforms. So very smart. I'll see you all later.'

*

Bobby's heart was filled with pride as he listened to Glenn Miller make the announcement, 'Please give a warm welcome to Liverpool's own, the Bryant Sisters.' Loud clapping, cheering and whistling filled the large auditorium as Bella, Fran and Edie ran onto the stage. Bobby smiled and took a glance at his mother, who was smiling broadly as Bella walked towards the microphone and thanked the audience for such a warm welcome.

'We are so proud to be singing for you in this beautiful theatre in our home city tonight.' She paused as the cheering started again. 'And the fact we are standing here onstage with this wonderful band and Major Glenn Miller is honestly beyond our wildest dreams. Please enjoy yourselves, and if you feel the urge, well there's plenty of room to dance in the aisles.' A ripple of laughter sounded and the band struck up with the opening bars of 'I've Got a Girl in Kalamazoo'. The girls swayed side by side until the instrumental section finished, and then cheers erupted as they began to sing.

'They're very good,' Fenella said, clapping as the song came to an end. 'That's my future daughter-in-law there,' she said proudly to the woman sitting next to her. 'The one in the middle, Bella.'

Bobby smiled as the woman gave her an envious look. His mum had changed so much over the last few months. She was more relaxed than he'd ever seen her, probably because she'd unburdened herself of all the guilty secrets she'd kept hidden for all of his life. She and Bella's mam got on so well. They went everywhere together and seemed to really enjoy each other's company. They competed in the granny stakes over Levi, who played one off against the other.

He wasn't daft, Bobby thought. It was good to have Molly around in the evenings as well. When Bella was away, they played board games and listened to programmes on the wireless. Molly had confided in him that she'd like to learn to be a schoolteacher to young children. He'd suggested she enrol at college and his mother was also paying for Molly to have extra tuition, as payment for all she did in helping out in the house and with Levi.

All in all, it was a happy and contented household to live in. All Bobby needed now was for his future wife to be by his side permanently. But while Bella was enjoying herself and doing fabulous shows like this, he knew he'd have to wait a while longer. There was talk the war would be over next year. All they could do was live in hope.

He turned his attention back to the show as the band started to play the opening chords to 'Chattanooga Choo Choo'. 'In the Mood' followed and several young couples took to the aisles. Bobby sighed, wondering if he'd ever be able to dance with Bella again. They could maybe manage a smooch, he supposed.

As the show came to a close Glenn Miller approached the microphone and asked the audience to give an extra-special round of applause for the Bryant Sisters. 'You just watch these girls,' he said. 'Mark my words, they are going far, and it's been a pleasure for me and the band to work with them tonight. Next time I'm back in the UK, I sure hope we get that opportunity again.'

Bella went to stand by his side. 'So do we,' she said. 'Thank you, Major Miller; we've had the time of our lives.'

The Bryant Sisters took a bow and trooped offstage to tumultuous applause.

Basil was standing in the wings and he enveloped them in a group hug. 'That was the height of your careers, ladies,' he said. 'So far, that is.'

*

1944 was drawing to a close and plans for Christmas and Levi's second birthday were being put in place at the house on Prince Alfred Road. Bella arrived home on the fifteenth of December for a short break. With the wireless playing Christmas songs in the background, she and Bobby, with Levi's help, dressed the tall pine tree in the warm and cosy dining room. Bella smiled as Bobby encouraged Levi to sing along to Glenn Miller's band playing 'Rudolph The Red-Nosed Reindeer'. It was lovely to spend time with her family again. The ENSA troupe was off to Yorkshire in three days' time but this year they would be home in Liverpool for Christmas.

Fenella had invited Basil and Martin to spend Christmas Day with them all. Everyone was looking forward to a real family celebration. Basil had promised to do his best and get some treats from the US air force base in Burtonwood, where they would be performing a few days before Christmas Eve.

Martin had a friend with a smallholding who had promised him a large goose for their dinner, and Mam and Fenella were making endless lists that changed daily depending on what they could get on the rations. Like Mam said, there were plenty of ration books in this house, so they'd fare better than most families, but so much was in short supply.

'Shh,' Bobby said to Levi, who was squealing, as the newsreader interrupted the Christmas music with an urgent news update. 'Oh, God, what's Hitler done now? He turned up the volume on the wireless.

Bella picked up Levi and gave him a shiny bauble to keep him quiet. The newsreader began:

> *We interrupt this programme to bring you a news bulletin just in. It has been confirmed that a small plane carrying the US Army bandleader, Major Glenn Miller, has crashed into the*

English Channel. Major Miller was on his way from RAF Bedford to France to perform for troops stationed there. We will bring you further updates when we receive more news.

Bella sat down heavily on the sofa, her mouth agape. Bobby stared at her horrified expression, shaking his head.

'No,' she stuttered. 'I don't believe it. Oh God, that lovely man. How can this happen? I bet the bloody Germans shot him down. Oh I hate that flaming Hitler and his cronies.'

Bobby sat down beside her and held her in his arms as tears poured down her cheeks. 'Well that's a shock,' he said after a few minutes. 'Not the sort of news you expect to hear.' He looked up as the dining room door opened and Bella's mam Mary came in carrying shopping bags, followed by his own mother, her arms full of holly and greenery.

'What's wrong?' Mary said. 'Why is our Bella crying?'

Bobby blew out his cheeks. 'Some very sad news has just been broadcast,' he said. 'Glenn Miller's plane has gone down in the English Channel this morning.'

'No,' Fenella said, her eyes wide with shock. 'Oh my goodness. Do they know what happened?'

Bobby shook his head. 'They'll give updates when they can.' He stopped as someone hammered on the front door.

'That'll be Fran and Edie,' Bella sobbed. 'They were coming over later but I bet they've heard the news too.'

Mary went to let them in. They were both crying and windswept from their sprint across The Mystery Park without hats or scarves over their hair. 'They're in the dining room,' Mary said as they both hurried down the hall, bringing a blast of very cold air in with them.

Fran flung herself on the sofa next to Bella and Edie dropped to the floor by her and Bobby's feet, both sobbing, which set Bella off again.

Fenella picked up a bewildered Levi and took him through to the kitchen. She sat him in his high-chair and gave him a drink and a biscuit. He smiled at her as Mary hurried in and filled the kettle. She put it on the gas hob and spooned tea leaves into the big earthenware teapot.

'Tea, with plenty of sugar for those four,' she said. 'Bless them, they're heartbroken. What a terrible thing to happen. He was such a very nice man. Made us feel so welcome after the show. Oh I really feel for his poor wife and their two little boys. I know just how she'll be feeling and so do you, Fen dear. What a tragedy and so close to Christmas as well.'

Fenella sat down at the table and looked at Levi chomping on his biscuit. She ran her fingers through his curls and smiled tearfully. 'You never know what's round the corner, do you? Thank goodness we've all got each other. We might be a bit of a mixed bag, but we're a family and we are so lucky.'

*

Fran took the tray of mugs from Mary and carried it to the coffee table. 'I just can't believe this has happened,' she said. 'Why is it always the nicest people that lose their lives? God, we were going to do another show with him next year and I was so looking forward to it.'

'Me too,' Edie sobbed. 'Such a lovely man and his band are a dream to work with. I've never known a band like them.'

'Tremendous brass section,' Bobby said. 'I hope they all carry on, it's what he would have wanted. But then again, will their hearts be in it now they've lost their leader? I'd like to hope they find him alive in the Channel but it's so cold this time of year that he'd surely have needed rescuing right away to stand any chance of survival.'

'Ever the optimist, Bobby,' Fran said. 'It would be nice, but...' She took a sip of tea. 'Edie has some news for us, Bella. She'd just told me when we heard the report on the wireless, so we ran straight over here.'

Bella smiled. 'What's that, Edie? Good news I hope, we need it.'

Edie gave a watery smile. 'Well I think it is,' she said. 'Mam saw our old foreman Mr Barratt from Bryant & May's last weekend and she told him we were coming home for a few days. He told her that they are having their Christmas party early this year and he has invited us as a surprise for the workers. It's tomorrow night and Bobby is also invited. It's to be in the canteen as usual. What do you think? It will do us good to go out and not mope about. And he'll be sure to want us to do a few songs for them.'

Bella smiled. 'Well I'm up for that. Are you Bobby?'

He nodded. 'Yes, definitely. We could do a few of our usual songs and a couple of Glenn Miller's as a tribute. I think that would go down well.'

'We'll have to just wear our normal dresses,' Bella said. 'Our stage stuff is packed away in the trunk on the bus.'

'That'll do me,' Fran said. 'Just wear your best dress, we'll curl our hair, a touch of make-up and then we'll look a bit glam. They'll expect that.'

*

Mr Barratt welcomed the girls and Bobby back to Bryant & May's match factory with open arms. 'I'm so thrilled you've managed to get here,' he said. 'I know you're really busy and you need a bit of a break before Christmas, but it will make their night when I tell them you are here. Now, I've managed to book a band to play for the dancing and I've had a quiet word with them that you may be here. They class themselves as a jazz band, but they can play all the stuff you sing; Andrews Sisters, Vera Lynn and what have you.'

'What about Glenn Miller?' Fran asked.

He nodded. 'Terrible news that, wasn't it? Very sad that they still haven't found his body. I saw the review of the show in the *Echo* when you played with him in the city. But yeah, the band will do some Glenn Miller songs as a bit of a tribute. Have a word with them. Work out the choices between you. I'll take you through now. I've put a table by the side of the stage so that hopefully we can keep the surprise for a bit longer, but you know how nosy some of the women can be and you might be spotted.'

The foursome followed George into the crowded, dimly lit, but festively decorated canteen and, keeping their heads down, hurried to the table George pointed out to them. 'There's a bottle of sherry and some glasses on a tray there for you as well as a jug of orange squash,' he said. 'The buffet will be announced after the lotto at nine. Just help yourselves.'

Bella looked around the room to see if there was anyone she recognised from when they had worked here. She recognised a couple of middle-aged women, Marge and Patti, over the far side of the room, but most people seemed to be new faces, which was good as they could sit quietly and listen to the band until it was their turn to get up and sing. Bobby poured them all a sherry and they raised their glasses to Glenn and took a sip.

'I've got an announcement to make,' Edie said, her eyes shining. 'I got a letter in a Christmas card from Stevie today. He still can't tell me where he is, but he wants us to get married when this war is over.'

Fran smiled. 'That's really funny, because my Frankie said exactly the same thing in his last letter. I was saving it to tell you all tonight. He wants to marry me as soon as he gets home.'

Bella and Bobby smiled. 'Oh, girls, congratulations!' Bella said, jumping up to hug them both. 'Let's hope it won't be too long. We're desperate to tie the knot as well, aren't we, Bobby?'

Bobby nodded. 'You can say that again. I can't wait but we've said we'll do it as soon as the war is over. We'll have to wait until you three have finished touring with ENSA.'

'You two are so lucky because you've already got somewhere to live,' Fran said. 'There'll be such a shortage of houses with so many being damaged by the bombings. We'll probably end up living with his mam or mine. But we'd never get any privacy at mine when Dad and the boys are all home.'

'Same with us,' Edie said. 'But Stevie lives down south so we might end up living out of Liverpool. I guess we'll have to wait and see.'

'You know what would be nice,' Fran said. 'We could have a triple wedding. Get this war over and done with and all get married on the same day.'

Edie and Bella smiled. 'How do you feel about that, Bobby?' Edie asked.

Bobby laughed. 'Well if it's what you all want, I think it's a great idea. What a way to celebrate the end of the war. A Bryant Sisters' triple wedding. That would be really special. Basil would love it.'

*

Bobby put down his drink as the band played 'Moonlight Serenade' and encouraged everyone to have a last smooch. The night had been lovely and they'd all enjoyed themselves. The girls' former colleagues had been overjoyed when the bandleader announced they were going to sing a few songs for them for old times' sake. Bella had finished with 'We'll Meet Again' and everyone had joined in, many teary-eyed, as the song came to an end. Bobby took a deep breath. There was one thing he was determined to try to do tonight. He took Bella by the hand and looked into her eyes.

'Come and dance with me,' he said as she smiled at him.

'Oh, Bobby, that would be lovely, are you sure you can manage it?' She stood up and helped him to his feet.

'Only one way to find out,' he said, leading her slowly onto the dance floor. 'Just be gentle with me,' he teased and took her in his arms, swaying slowly. Bella melted into him and closed her eyes. He laid his head down on top of hers. He was glad they'd come here tonight. Everyone had been welcoming and accepted the girls right back into the fold.

Since the newspaper scandal Bella had avoided mixing with anyone from near home. Most people had been accepting of their situation, and supportive. But when they'd recently taken Levi out in his trolley for a short stroll on The Mystery Park he'd felt eyes on them and seen people nudging each other and pointing. Mainly women enjoying a gossip, but it still hurt to feel that anyone might judge them when all they were doing was what was right for them and Levi.

Bella's mam had a go at a judgemental woman the other week. When Mary'd arrived home with his own mother in tow, they'd had a laugh about it, but he knew it had upset the pair. Time was a great healer though, and Bobby hoped that memories were short and that people would stop interfering and get on with their own lives.

Bella looked up into his eyes and smiled as the music came to an end. 'Well that was perfect, and it felt so good to have you hold me like that again.'

'I think I'll be able to manage the first dance on our wedding day now,' he said, dropping a kiss on her lips.

Chapter Twenty-Two

RAF Burtonwood, Warrington, May 1945

Basil crossed the NAAFI floor at the air base, a big smile on his face. The girls were seated at a table near the window, enjoying a late breakfast of scrambled eggs on toast and mugs of hot tea. They looked weary, like nearly everyone felt lately.

Up until today it had looked like the war would go on for ever. But most of Germany's cities had been destroyed and Hitler's various army groups were practically no more. The news he was about to give his girls would perk them up no end. They were due to move on to Catterick later today after two busy nights here. He pulled a chair from under the table and sat down.

'Good news, ladies,' he said, punching the air with his fists.

'You've booked Bing Crosby to join us in Yorkshire,' Fran said, grinning.

'Ha-ha, no, but that sounds like a good plan for the future. Better than that though, much, much better.'

Fran frowned. 'Basil, what can be better than us and Bing on the same stage?'

Basil smiled. 'Ah, well what about if I were to tell you that Hitler is dead!' He sat back and watched their shocked faces.

'Get away,' Edie said. 'You're having us on.'

'On my mother's life,' he said. 'Mind you, she's no longer with us so I'm not sure how that would work. Seriously, he's committed suicide along with that woman Eva Braun, who he only married a few days ago. Don't know her cause of death, but Hitler shot himself in the underground bunker he'd been hiding in.'

'Oh God,' Bella said, clapping a hand to her mouth. 'So does that mean the war is over?'

'Looks like it. The powers that be are expecting Mr Churchill to make an announcement later today.'

'So life could all be back to normal soon then? Will our boys be coming home?' Fran said.

'They will be; as soon as everything is sorted, they'll start to bring the troops back,' Basil said. 'You do realise that our ENSA shows will probably now be coming to an end.'

Bella nodded. 'I expect they will be. But that won't be for a few weeks, surely? Many of the troops are still here in their base camps defending our territory. They'll still need entertainment for a while.'

*

Hitler's death was confirmed by Winston Churchill later that day and an air of celebration met the team as they arrived at Catterick camp. A celebratory party was thrown that night and the ENSA troupe put on the performance of their lives. Even the little tumbling terrier dogs seemed to sense something was different and capered about all over the stage, making the soldiers in the audience laugh. As the girls lay in bed later that night, exhausted but unable to switch off, Fran spoke first.

'I know it's all got to be done officially, this end-of-war thing, but if it really is over and no one is rushing in to take Hitler's place, we can actually start planning our weddings. I mean, once the lads are home, there's nothing to stop us going ahead really, is there?'

'I guess not,' Bella agreed. 'You have to put banns in a month before, I believe. So as soon as we know when Stevie and Frankie are definitely coming home, we should do it, because you can bet your life we're not the only girls talking about this right now. There'll be hundreds of weddings being booked in Liverpool and we don't want to be at the back of a very long queue. Are we having church weddings or the registry office?'

'Oh it'll be nice to do it in church,' Edie said. 'I'd like a nice white dress as well.'

Bella and Fran nodded their agreements.

'I think Mam would expect a church wedding for me too,' Fran said. 'But how will you and Bobby go on, with him being divorced and you having Levi?'

'Oh, God, I never thought about that,' Bella said. 'That's me out of the white wedding dress stakes then, being the fallen woman that I am.'

'Bugger,' said Fran, laughing. 'Can't Bobby's mam have a word with the vicar, seeing as she's top dog with the WI and you both used to be in the choir?'

Bella laughed. 'I'm not sure it works like that, Fran, but I can ask her. She might be able to pull a few strings and I guess I can go for a cream or ivory dress at the end of the day. The one thing that really saddens me is that my dad isn't here to give me away.'

'Neither is mine,' Edie said. 'There's no one, not even an uncle that could do it; he's dead too.'

'You can share my dad,' Fran said generously. 'He'd be dead proud to walk us up the aisle.'

Edie and Bella burst into tears and climbed out of bed and bounced onto Fran's bunk. The three hugged, tears streaming down their faces.

'You have no idea how much that means to us,' Bella said as Edie nodded her agreement. 'Thank you so much.'

*

The girls were back in Wavertree by the time VE Day was celebrated on 8 May 1945. Victory in Europe was declared and communities all over Britain celebrated with street parties. The Mystery Park was crowded as friends and neighbours all joined in and provided buffet food on trestle tables. Bunting was sewn and hung by the ladies of the WI, who also made cakes and jellies for the children, and a local brass band made up of various ARP members provided the musical entertainment.

Molly helped to arrange the small children, who had been brought home for evacuation, into groups and organised games to keep them occupied while their mothers took a well-earned break. Fran and Edie were still anxiously awaiting news of their boys' return from the front. They'd been told any day now. Fenella had spoken discreetly to the vicar, who had agreed to marry Bobby and Bella, and the three girls had put their banns in. A triple wedding had been organised for June the ninth and 'wedding planning overdrive', as Bobby described it, had taken over their lives.

Fenella had reserved the church hall and the WI ladies were doing the decorating and buffet with whatever they could lay their hands on. 'We might not be able to get dried fruit, but we'll have the best wedding party and cake we can manage with what's available,' she said.

The three girls, Bobby and Levi were sitting on a blanket on the grass as Molly came running over to them. 'Shall I take him to join in with the other kiddies?' she offered.

Levi eyed his Aunty Molly up and down. He had a small plate of food in front of him and was savouring every bite of a sausage roll, rolling his eyes blissfully.

Bobby laughed as she held out her arms to him and he shook his head and carried on eating. 'Sorry, Moll,' Bobby said. 'There's no chance of prising him away from that plate. Maybe later.'

Bella shook her head. 'Food is Levi's first priority. Pleasure takes second place I'm afraid. Apart from singing and dancing of course, but he'll get up and have a waddle to the band in his own good time.'

'There are Basil and Martin.' Fran waved as they came into view. 'Oh I'm glad they've come to join us. Look at your mother, Bobby, rushing over to greet them looking all excited. I'm sure she's a bit sweet on Basil.'

Bella laughed and looked at Bobby. 'That's exactly what we both said.'

Bobby nodded. 'Be nice for them if they got it together. Basil has never been married and Mum's single now, of course, so there's nothing standing in their way.' He waved as his mother, Martin and Basil came over to join them. 'Afternoon, how's it going?' he greeted the threesome.

'Where's my mam got to?' Bella asked, shading her eyes and looking into the distance.

'She's over there with Ethel Hardy and some ladies she used to work with at Olive Mount,' Fenella said, pointing to a group of women. 'She'll come and join us in a few minutes, she just said.'

Bella looked around as someone called Fran's name. She looked up and tried to keep her face straight as Frankie came up behind Fran and put his hands over her eyes. Fran screamed and jumped to her feet.

'Oh my God, Frankie, you daft bugger, you frightened me to death. Why didn't you tell me you were coming home today?' She flung her arms round him and burst into tears.

Frankie grinned round at everyone. 'All these years apart and I get a telling-off and called a daft bugger,' he joked. 'I can't win.' He swung Fran round and round and kissed her. 'That's shut her up,' he said, laughing. 'And Edie, your Stevie is on his way as well. We couldn't get on the same train to Lime Street but he'll be here before nightfall, he said to tell you.' Frankie dug in his pocket and pulled out a letter. 'He scribbled this for me to give you to be going on with.'

Edie jumped up and gave Frankie a hug, and also burst into tears as he handed her the envelope.

He shook his head and looked at Bobby. 'Women eh, mate!'

Chapter Twenty-Three

Wedding Day, Wavertree, 9 June 1945

Basil had ordered the cars to take the three brides and their brides-maids to St Mary's Parish Church on North Drive. They were being picked up from their individual homes; Fran would travel with her father on her own and then he would walk the brides down the aisle one at a time.

Basil was trying his best to keep Bobby calm and out of the way. Bobby had asked him to be his best man and he'd been delighted to accept. Bella was upstairs with both mothers and Molly, helping the bride to get dressed. Bobby and he were also in charge of Levi, who was dressed in a royal-blue velvet pageboy outfit with a crisp white shirt and dark-blue satin dickey bow that he'd already pulled off three times in the last half-hour. He was also supposed to carry a matching velvet cushion holding the three rings.

They'd had several rehearsals but he just ended up kicking the cushion and shouting 'goal'. In Basil's opinion, a not-yet-three-year-old was a bit too young for that sort of responsibility, but Fenella's friend who had made his outfit and the cushion had attached the rings firmly so that they would be held in place until the vicar asked for them. *They could only do their best*, Basil thought. He wasn't used to kiddies but Levi captured everyone's heart, including his.

He felt sorry for Earl, in a way, in that he would miss his comical little son growing up, but he knew that Bella and Bobby had promised to keep in touch and send photographs from time to time. Earl had now flown back to the USA, along with many others from RAF Burtonwood.

Basil was going to miss his ENSA troupe and the soldiers and airmen who had been his life for the last six years. He wasn't sure where life would take him next, but planned to stay in the entertainment business if possible. He'd worked as an agent prior to the war, so that was a plan he had in mind.

But he didn't want to go back to London. He loved Liverpool and its warm and friendly people, and he'd spoken to Fenella about maybe setting up an agency in the city once it got back on its feet again. They'd have to see. She'd thought it a good idea and said she wouldn't mind helping him and getting involved if he needed help. He'd definitely like that.

The door to Bobby's room flew open as Fenella dashed in. Basil thought she looked very glamorous in her lilac suit and matching hat. She was an attractive woman and he had to admit he was quite taken with her.

'Now whatever you do, don't open this door or look through the window until the car has pulled away,' she directed at Bobby. 'Bella is just about to come downstairs with Molly and you can't see her because it will be bad luck and we don't want any of that today.'

She continued, 'You two should really have left by now and be waiting at the church. Typical that the bride's car should arrive first.' She picked up Levi, who tried to pull at the flowers on her hat, and glanced out of the window. 'Oh, here's your car now. Right go on, shoo. Have you got your buttonholes on? Oh you have. Go on, go on,' she finished, wafting her spare hand at them.

She dashed back out of the room and yelled up the stairs: 'Don't come down yet, the men are just leaving. Phew,' she added, closing the door behind them as Bobby and Basil left, laughing at her panic. 'That was close. And they might well laugh. It's so much easier for men.'

Mary ran down the stairs and stood by Fenella's side. She adjusted her navy hat that matched her dress and lightweight jacket, looking in the hall mirror to make sure it looked straight. 'You can say that again,' she agreed. 'Right, girls, it's safe.'

Both mothers gasped as Bella slowly walked down the stairs in her full-length, full-skirted, ivory satin gown trimmed with matching lace. The sweetheart neckline had a modesty panel of ivory lace with matching long sleeves. A short veil that came down over her face was held in place with a diamanté tiara.

'You look like a princess,' Mary said tearfully. 'Your dad would be so proud today. And look at our Molly, that pale green really suits you, my love,' she said, admiring Molly's full-length bridesmaid's dress and matching headdress. 'Right, let's get our flowers and go.'

'Is he still clean?' Bella asked, looking at her wriggling son in Fenella's arms.

'He'll do,' Fenella said. 'The sooner we get him there the better though.'

*

The road to the church was lined with people, who waved as the individual cars carrying the brides all arrived at the same time. They were helped out and each appointed bridesmaid arranged their dresses on the church path.

'Oh my God, don't we all look glam,' Fran said. 'We scrub up well, girls.'

Bella laughed. They were always dolled up onstage, but she knew what Fran meant. Their three dresses were identical in design and Fran and Edie had also chosen ivory so that Bella wouldn't feel awkward. As Fran had said, white made her look pasty anyway. The only difference was that they all carried different-colour bouquets of roses and greenery. Fran's was red, Edie's yellow and Bella's pink.

The other bridesmaids, cousins of Fran's, also wore the same pale green as Molly.

'Are we ready?' Fran said as her dad held out his arm for her to link it. 'Let's get ready to roll. He'll take me in and then come back for you two. See you on the other side,' she said with a grin as Bella and Edie laughed nervously.

*

Mary smiled proudly as her daughter walked down the aisle on Fran's dad's arm, smiling and nodding at the congregation in the crowded church. The girls looked lovely and Fenella's ladies in the WI had done the beautiful flowers in the church as well as the bouquets and buttonholes, and they'd also made all the dresses. Mary personally didn't think royalty could have done any better and she'd bet they weren't on such tight rations either.

The waiting grooms were all smart in their freshly dry-cleaned and pressed military uniforms. As Basil had said, this was definitely the wedding of the year. The community had pulled together with all sorts of contributions, from making dress patterns to sourcing reasonably priced bales of the ivory satin and lace. It was a wonderful feeling to share today with their friends and neighbours as well as members of the armed forces who were friends of Bobby, Frankie and Stevie.

Bella had been so pleased to spot Marie with others from Brize Norton in the congregation. Ruth from Wales was also here with one of her land girls, and they smiled and waved discreetly as Bella passed by them. She'd catch up properly with them later, as no doubt her mam would too. The church hall next door was ready for the buffet and evening's entertainment and Basil had got some of the soldiers together to form a band so that the Bryant Sisters and Bobby could sing a few songs.

As Edie took her place with the other two at the front, the vicar began his service by welcoming everyone to this very special one-off event at his church.

Mary kept her eyes on Levi as he played peek-a-boo with a lady sitting at the end of a pew two rows down. 'He's okay,' the lady mouthed as Mary rolled her eyes and smiled. Molly tried to pull him back in line to stand with the other bridesmaids, but he was having none of that and threw the cushion with the rings into the air, giggling. Fenella, sitting next to Mary, suppressed a grin as Molly went to retrieve the cushion. She signalled to her mam and Fenella that she would hold onto it for now.

'Oh dear,' Fenella said. 'He is a one, isn't he? But you have to laugh.'

Mary agreed, her mouth twitching. 'He's going to be such a handful for them.' She nodded towards Bella and Bobby, who were just starting to say their vows. 'Good job they've got us three to help out.'

*

As the service came to an end and all three couples walked back down the aisle and outside into the glorious sunshine, they were met by a barrage of newspaper photographers. Shouts of 'smile' met them as they posed on the church steps.

Bobby squeezed Bella's hand and whispered for her to look happy rather than dismayed. 'It was bound to happen,' he said. 'This is how life is going to be from now on while you are still singing.'

Bella squeezed his hand back. 'I think I'd rather have a break,' she whispered back, 'and concentrate on you and Levi for a while.'

'We'll see,' he said. 'I think Basil has got other plans, but we'll see.'

As the three sets of newlyweds led the way to the church hall they were surrounded by well-wishers and covered in rice and confetti.

'Are you gonna chuck yer bouquets, gels,' a woman from Bryant & May's that Bella recognised from the Christmas do yelled. 'Give us a bit of a chance of finding a handsome Mr Right like you three have.'

Bella looked at Fran and Edie and smiled. She turned to the woman and said, 'I'd love to, but I want to put it on my little sister's grave if you don't mind.'

'Oh, you go ahead, chuck,' the woman said. 'God bless yer.'

'Shall we?' Bobby said, leading her off the path and over to where Betty's grave was situated.

They held hands as Bella placed her pink roses on the ground next to the headstone that bore Betty's name. 'Her favourite colour, pink,' she said. 'I'm sure she will love them.'

Bobby nodded his head and took both of Bella's hands. 'It's chaos back there,' he said. 'And I know we won't get much peace for a few hours yet. So it's nice to have a couple of minutes to ourselves. I am so proud to have you for my wife, Bella. You look stunning. And I'm so very proud that you will allow me to become Levi's father. I know I'm not the man I was, half a leg and all that, but my heart is whole, and no one will ever love you more than I do.' He bent to kiss her gently on the lips.

'Nor I you, Bobby,' Bella said. 'I can't quite believe we've actually done it. That we're husband and wife at last. I wish we could go home and just spend the rest of the day together.'

'So do I. But we've got our honeymoon to look forward to. For now we've got to go back, enjoy our wedding party, and do a final performance for the guests. Well, a final one for now, anyway.'

'Fran and Edie are not sure they want to continue performing after today,' Bella said.

Bobby raised an eyebrow. 'What about you, Bella?'

'We could sing together instead,' she suggested.

He smiled and pulled her close. 'I'd love that.'

'Can we do "Over the Rainbow" for Betty tonight?' Bella suggested.

'Most definitely, Mrs Harrison,' he said and, smiling broadly, he led her back to the path.

A Letter from Pam Howes

I want to say a huge thank you for choosing to read *Wedding Bells on Victory Street*. If you did enjoy it, and want to keep up to date with all my latest releases, just sign up at the following link. Your email address will never be shared and you can unsubscribe at any time.

www.bookouture.com/pam-howes

To my loyal band of regular readers who bought and reviewed the Lark Lane stories, thank you for waiting patiently for my new series. I hope you'll enjoy meeting and getting to know my new characters, Bella, Fran and Edie, and their families. Your support is most welcome and very much appreciated.

As always, a big thank you to Beverley Ann Hopper and Sandra Blower and the members of their FB group Book Lovers, and Deryl Easton and the members of her FB group Gangland Governors/ NotRights. Love you all for the support you show me. I would also like to thank my friend Claire Lyons for having such a beautiful baby boy. Young Riley has been my inspiration in creating Levi. His daily update photos, big smiles, stunning eyes and that gorgeous mop of curls bring such a joy that I had to put him in a book somehow. Love you, Riley, my little inspiration. xxx

A huge thank you to Team Bookouture, especially my lovely editorial team, Maisie and Martina, for your support and guidance and always being there – you're the best – and thanks also to the rest of the fabulous staff. Thanks also to my wonderful copy-editor Jacqui and excellent proofreader Loma.

And last, but most definitely not least, thank you to our wonderful media girls, Kim Nash, Sarah Hardy and Noelle Holten, for everything you do for us. And thanks also to the gang in the Bookouture Authors' Lounge for always being there. As always, I'm so proud to be one of you.

I hope you loved *Wedding Bells on Victory Street* and if you did I would be very grateful if you could write a review. I'd love to hear what you think, and it makes such a difference helping new readers to discover one of my books for the first time. I love hearing from my readers – you can get in touch on my Facebook page, through Twitter, Goodreads or my website.

Thanks,
Pam Howes

 Pam Howes Books

@PamHowes1

Acknowledgements

For my lovely and supportive partner, my gorgeous girls and grandchildren and the rest of my family as always. Thanks for being there and for the support during this particularly horrible year. Thanks also to Brenda Thomasson and Sue Hulme for beta reading. Much appreciated. Love you all. xxx

Made in the USA
Coppell, TX
12 January 2021

48070308R00128